THE DARK WALL
Journey through the Underworlds
Duane T. Craig

ISBN-13: 979-8-9932157-3-0

To Cheryl, for inspiring fantasy and magic in my life. And to Allison and Andrea for teaching me the wonderful value of suspense, and surprise.

CHAPTER ONE

Flying From Darkness

Flung from nowhere, I clung bareback to a bay horse racing from darkness into a huge, glowing valley. Magnificent trees stood in the distance, their trunks straight, their canopies lush and cooling. To my right lay a shallow lake, and spread out before me as far as I could see was a carpet of green and golden grasses dancing in the breeze.

My horse was clearly under my control and I wondered if she had a knowing of where we had been, and of where we were going. Sensing her tiredness I got down at a spot where a shallow pool of water lay around short grass stems, their tops delicately breaking through the clear liquid. As Horse drank, the moment was all I knew. Behind us I saw an immense wall of blackness rising as far as I could see and stretching seemingly forever to each side. I had no memory of where we had been before piercing its surface. To my left was a range of low rolling hills, their grasses shimmering golden, brown and copper as waves of air fanned across them. I sensed a permanence to the place and that its history was somehow part of mine. Still, there were so many things I didn't know - things that lay before me, and things that lay behind me.

I heard an ear splitting crack and as I turned toward the dark wall, five steeds with their riders exploded into view. They were cloaked in silvery blackness, brandishing weapons of unimaginable torment. I immediately knew their prey, and Horse also sensed their awful calamity. As I leaped astride her, she was already bolting, her powerful flank muscles surging with energy. In just seconds her pounding gait carried us like the wind toward the canopy of trees. Each stride was perfectly placed, her rear hooves obliterating the impressions left by her front hooves, as her rippling shoulder muscles and deep, steady breaths offered us hope of escape.

The trees neared and I glanced behind. The horsemen were just five lengths back, their features exaggerated and blurry. I saw one raise a crossbow, hanging onto his mount with only his knees. The bolt left the cradle on its deadly journey. But then, with fluid, slow motion insight, I saw the trajectory from beginning to end. I shifted my weight hard to the right causing Horse to turn sharply. The bolt found its home in a tree just to our left as we broke into the darkness of the forest.

Now, everything changed. We raced through thickets of brush, dodging tree trunks and low-hanging branches. I leaned forward with my cheek next to Horse's neck, my arms stretched forward and fingers loose on the leather reins. It was up to her now for I had no idea where I was or where sanctuary might lie. Strange animals darted from the underbrush leaping to safety from the onslaught of hooves.

What was this madness, I thought? With no remembrance of where I'd just been, and no idea of where I was, my fate seemed far beyond my control. I fought to remember, but my mind was blank of anything before breaking through the dark wall. The riders behind must have knowledge of me, yet I had none of them. Was I dead? Was this just another step in my evolution, a new place to master, and one where starting as an infant was not part of the plan? Or, was I continuing a previous journey, but without memory? There was no time to ponder though.

We rounded a small clump of trees that hid the path ahead, and then we were airborne. The rush of wind took my breath away and Horse flailed her legs trying to stay upright. I could feel her start to drift away from me so I clamped my knees against her sides and locked my toes below her belly to keep us from being separated. We rushed downward, plummeting from a cliff toward a raging river. Fear drained away, replaced by knowing. I was focused on the water's surface, gauging its distance, imagining an outcome. Horse stopped flailing and gracefully extended her legs. With slow motion once again on our side, we broke the river's surface at barely the speed of a bird piercing the water tension to retrieve a fish. But then it was pandemonium again as Horse fought to get out of the current and dodge boulders and rocks both seen, and unseen. I glanced behind to see one of the riders plunge into the river while the others stood at the edge of the cliff watching the spectacle.

Horse struggled to avoid a boulder but a whirlpool made her stay the course bringing the rock squarely against my leg. I could feel the pants and skin tear together and felt the searing pain seconds after the blood appeared in the water. That was quickly forgotten though when I saw what was before us. A massive cave was swallowing up the river, and there was no light foretelling of an opening somewhere beyond. The water rushed faster and faster as it was sucked into the void. At the mercy of the current, Horse was wisely resting, merely paddling to stay upright as we were swept into the opening.

The blackness of the cave was a shock after the bright sunlight and I couldn't make out anything before us. Suddenly, weightlessness struck once again and we fell within a torrent of water, ensconced, as if a part of it. The drenching fall went on and on, and I felt my body tighten in anticipation of its end. But then, light appeared below, quickly followed by the surface of foaming water where the fall met its fate. Once again slow motion took over, this time without thought or effort, and we gently splashed into a deep pool while being assailed by the water falling from above. Horse sprang into action, her powerful legs jettisoning us from the calamity and releasing us to a huge, calm lake.

Water poured off me, my entire being drenched to the bone. My mind raced at the possibilities of the strange land I mysteriously found myself in, and I was startled by both my knowledge, and lack of knowledge. I knew about water. I knew about gravity, and I knew about being wet. I knew what a horse was and I knew about being pursued. At the same time though, I had no idea of who I was, or even if it mattered. And why didn't I remember any reason for the riders to be chasing me? More mysterious, was this ability to slow down motion. Did I just acquire it, or had I always been able? Regardless, slow motion had already saved me three times.

Horse swam toward the shore, now just meters away. As her feet met the lake bottom I was raised out of water with each step until we were on the beach, our drippings leaving small rivers in the sand. I jumped down and screamed out. The focus on survival had masked the mangling of my leg, but now it all came back very painfully. I hobbled to a nearby rock to check the damage. It was not good. A two-inch wide filet of skin almost a foot long was folded back from my calf revealing torn muscles and a chipped bone at the side of my knee. Being in the water had stanched the flow of blood and now the wound just oozed a light-colored liquid and burned relentlessly.

As I struggled to imagine how I'd repair the damage I was struck by a movement just a few meters away. I turned slightly to my left and peered into tall swamp grass where I saw a pitiful creature, trembling, rolled in a ball so that I couldn't tell what it was. My heart was taken by its fear and seeming inability to confront whatever it was facing. Ignoring the pain in my leg I stood up, stepping closer to it.

Suddenly it rose slightly and I saw it was a man, unkempt at first, but then seemingly in front of my eyes changing to be clothed in fine linen and leather. He wrapped his arms around my waist as he kneeled before me and with the side of his head resting against my stomach he spoke clearly and intelligently.

"Is there some way I can help you?"

I was taken aback because I had expected to be assailed with pleas for help, or worse assailed with a sharp weapon. He clung tightly with his arms wrapped around my thighs as if he was reconnecting with me.

Finally, I managed to come back to the moment, and when I spoke it was as if someone else was speaking.

"Well. I have this problem with my leg..." but before I could finish I felt a new sensation and I knew it had been healed already. I jumped back and as he released his arms he curled back into a ball and returned to the state he had been in.

A distant sound caught my attention and I quickly looked away toward the water and back to the falls that had birthed me into this place, watching for signs of the horsemen. Seeing nothing, I turned back but the balled up creature was gone, replaced with a stone obelisk. Carved on its face were the words: "In illusion we arrive, and in illusion we leave." I traced the words with my fingers trying to connect their meaning to my current state of affairs. Was I simply in an imaginary place, living through imaginary experiences? And if so, was there a way to escape? Or, was escape itself an illusion? So many questions with no answers made my mind numb, and tired.

A cool breeze came across the water and the tall grass danced, shimmering golden in the sunlight. I sat on the moist ground, leaning against a comfortable rock. The ripped remnant of my pant leg draped across the grass so I tore it from the garment and folded it, placing it in my pocket. I knew surviving might depend on only the things I had arrived with. The glint of something on the water sent me to my feet, scanning the way I had come. I knew one of the riders had plunged off the cliff and I was apprehensive about the prospect that the others had followed. I cautiously surveyed the lake shore all the way to the tree line, waiting, watching for some sign of movement. After a long time of watching and waiting and of seeing nothing, I sat back down.

The scene around me was serene, and it seemed so long since I had plunged through the dark wall that I was overcome with a wave of tiredness. I watched Horse grazing contentedly on the tender, short grasses along the bank until she faded to a blur and I drifted to sleep.

CHAPTER TWO

Welcome to the Underworld

My dreams were immediately peaceful and I saw familiar faces in them. Not so familiar that I knew who they were, but familiar nonetheless, with a sort of knowing or sixth sense of their deepest essences instead of just their finely crafted egos. There was no sadness or longing to be with them, only a knowing that in some way I already was, and that my journey was different, yet on the same path. Deeper I sank, wandering through stranger and stranger landscapes. My confidence in meeting each new experience was impeccable as I navigated peaceful and then progressively treacherous terrains and events.

At the darkest levels of my dream state I entered a space of complete blackness. I couldn't discern any length, or width or volume, and there was a clear lack of matter. It was as if substance did not exist except for my own being. But then as I tried feeling for one of my arms with the opposite hand, neither was there, only what seemed to be a memory of them. I had no feet to move, no head to turn and the immense and thick darkness seemed to not just be all around me, but within me as well. My being hung there, suspended with no sense of time or place, yet I was infinitely present and whole. I was nothing more than nothingness and everything more than everything. Suddenly, a profound fear rose inside my being that this was the end. That I was no more. Yet I was aware of that fact, and even knew that if I never left that state, I would still be forever aware.

Summoning all the consciousness I could muster I gave in to acceptance of what was, and what wasn't. At that very second, any fear disappeared and I was propelled through scenes that felt familiar, physical places separated by long expanses of emptiness, and even passing through other beings I had a knowing of, and others I didn't. Yet to everything there was a connectedness, a sense that I was speeding through a universe of oneness, until suddenly I could feel my body again. Something cool and moist pressed against my face and I awoke, startled. It was Horse, nuzzling me to my more familiar consciousness.

In the fog following the dream I felt no particular hurry to rise, and I lay my head back on the rock, studying the sky with its three moons, two suns and several quickly orbiting asteroids. There had been daylight since I arrived and there was no sign of dusk approaching. The question now was, what to do next?

I rolled to one side, examining the lake and the way I had come. So far the horsemen were nowhere in sight. Across the small waves with sunlight dancing on their caps there was no sign of any reasoning life. The air carried the scents of water, sweet grasses and sunlight. So I arose, having decided to explore along the edge of the lake. I figured if I stayed between the shore and the tree line I'd have a good chance of spotting danger while leaving enough time to take cover.

Exploration however, was not going to be serene. Within three steps the soil shifted, opened, and we plunged downward, landing on a ledge jutting into a massive cavern. We had fallen four meters, and had the ledge been any smaller we would have missed it, no doubt plunging to a much deeper bottom. Apparently my slow motion skill only worked when I had time to focus.

I peered below trying to make out shapes and features and concluded we were a long way up the wall of an immense cavern. I looked toward the sky trying to see a way to get back up, but the walls were smooth rock with just a thin layer of soil. The hole we fell through seemed to be exactly configured for the two of us, no bigger or smaller than necessary. The rock on the walls was glassy and slick, no doubt another machination designed to force us to go in any other direction but the one we preferred.

As I pondered the predicament, Horse grew uneasy, and seconds later I knew why. The riders were back! Their horses pounded to within a few feet of the hole. As I peered upward I saw their gaunt faces, almost skeleton like, with matted manes and mouths dripping foam. They reared as the riders dismounted, grabbing their crossbows and fixing razor-tipped bolts for an all out assault. These were hideous creatures and I could now see their terrible features and proportions. They had human shapes but that's where the similarity ended. Their heads were fly-like with huge, bulging eyes having multi-facets. The noses resembled proboscis and just below them two sets of mandibles framed tooth-filled mouths. Their long black hooded dusters were open down the front revealing rippling muscles covered in coarse hair.

I leapt onto Horse convinced our only chance was to once again trust slow motion. We plummeted off the ledge, free falling away from the volley of bolts, but directly into a black hole with no visible bottom. The air rushing over us carried a dank and putrid smell. Once again I clung to Horse's neck and locked my legs and feet to her sides expecting at any second to slam into a protruding ledge, or worse, smash into the bottom of the void.

The air changed, becoming drier and carrying less stench. Then, far below, a glint of light appeared, growing larger by the second. As I saw what appeared to be bottom, our speed dropped and it seemed as if we were barely moving. The light grew, illuminating what lay below, and suddenly we emerged from the tube of darkness and into an underground world of huge proportions.

Stretching in all directions I saw canyons of intricate stone, as if carved by master stone masons. The canyons went deep and some housed rivers of molten lava at their bottoms, while others at higher planes flowed with a water-like substance. The illumination of the scene seemed to originate within certain stones that glowed bright yellow and orange, sometimes banded together in long vertical strands within the cliff faces, and other times as large globes randomly laying on the plateaus and mesas supported by the cliffs. Fortunately, Horse and I were dropping directly to one of the plateaus and when we touched down we were between two rock outcroppings that vaulted, spire-like upward. My sense of elation at having escaped the creatures and then landing safely lasted only as long as taking a quick breath. Horse took one step and collapsed, sending me flying forward, over her head and onto the rocky surface.

As I struggled to my feet, bruised, but not broken this time, I quickly studied her. She had not been as fortunate as me for I saw one of the bolts lodged in her hindquarter, a pool of blood already forming on the stony surface where she lay. I went to the injury and knelt down, examining the damage. I was heartened to see the blood was not gushing and that some was beginning to coagulate. Still, the bolt was a good six inches into her hip and I suspected it had lodged into bone. This was not a good situation, yet Horse seemed unconnected from it. I watched as she continuously licked the stones below her mouth, first running her coarse tongue across them in one direction, and then the other.

I moved up to her head and saw she had discovered a crack in the stone and was licking some kind of fluid from it. Putting my finger into the crack the liquid felt slippery and slightly warm. I tried to follow its flow in one direction but after a few feet it disappeared below the surface. By tracing it in the other direction I discovered it originated on the backside of one of the spires we landed near, flowing down inside a natural stone channel, and at a perfect speed so as to not splash outward.

I put my finger into the liquid and tasted it. Slightly sweet and salty. It also had a lubricating quality to it that made my thirsty mouth feel immediately hydrated. I figured if Horse was drinking it, then I might as well give it a try. A small pool of the liquid collected at the base of the spire, just large enough for me to get my cupped hand into, so I drank a few handfuls of the substance. The hydrating properties were spectacular and I began to feel rejuvenated from my recent stresses. I fashioned the torn remnant from my pants into a makeshift bowl, filled it with the liquid and raced back to Horse where I poured it on her wound. I repeated the process several times until I was satisfied the area was clean. I knew the arrow had to come out, but I was very concerned about the possibility of the razor-like tip staying behind. Still, there didn't appear to be any other options, other than waiting, which I suspected would simply mean death for Horse from either infection, or being on her stomach too long.

I comforted her, gently rubbing her flank and once I felt my resolve reach its peak I quickly grabbed the bolt with both hands and pulled it upward. Horse flailed and sprang to her feet sending me tripping backward. I looked down at the bolt's shaft and was relieved to see the tip, still in place. Horse at first tried to run, but quickly stopped, no doubt from the pain in her hindquarter. Blood ran from the wound quickly at first, but then slowed just as quickly. Several more times I grabbed my makeshift bowl and ran to get more liquid from the pool to pour and blot on the wound. Horse seemed to like the process and I spent a long time tending to the wound. Once I was satisfied I had been able to get plenty of the liquid deep into the wound, I applied pressure with the fabric until the remaining flow of blood stopped. Horse continued licking the fluid from the crack in the rocks and I hoped it would hold her attention for awhile so she'd stay still until the blood coagulated more.

Meanwhile, I continued exploring around the spire, stopping just beyond the pool. I was marveling at the intricate designs in the rock, trying to understand how they could have possibly developed from natural processes, when I saw a tiny, worm-like creature inching along on the surface. What I saw next made me step back in surprise. The stone in front of the worm's path was smooth and unworn, but behind it, the rock was channeled out. The worm was carving the patterns, and when I adjusted my focus I saw there were more than one of them. Many more. At each place where a smooth patch of stone existed, there was at least one worm carving shapes into it. I studied the patterns each was carving trying to find a commonality, but it looked like each one was marching to its own beat. Everything about this place seemed both new and ancient all at the same time and I wondered if I'd ever solve any of its mysteries.

As I followed the walls of the spire I discovered a very large arch in its side that appeared to be too precise to have been created by natural processes. When I stepped up to it and looked closer inside I saw a flat floor and smooth, curving sides except for one place, the back wall, where there appeared to be a panel of carved stones. I stepped carefully onto the floor, staying ready to leap backward in case of danger. When nothing happened, I continued to the back wall and examined the panel. The long, skinny carved stones, no more than a finger's width wide, were slightly depressed in four vertical columns into the smooth, tan-colored wall. Each column was only a few inches long, had a background of emerald fossils and was carved with its own intricate design. I studied them closely, but once again couldn't make any meaning of them. Then, I had a strange sensation, like I was inside a device that would move up and down, and what I saw next convinced me of that. At the place where the floor met the wall there was a slight gap that suggested the two were not one solid mass and I could easily imagine the floor moving independently of the walls. The discovery, if it was true, would take care of a big concern I had - how to move through the surface of this place with all the canyons cutting through it. But, I didn't want to try out this potential new mode of transport, without Horse, so I walked back out and headed her way.

By now, Horse had seemingly drunk her fill of the liquid and stood quietly. She turned her head to watch my approach, no doubt wondering what other painful episode I might have in store for her. I rubbed her long face and jowls hoping to reassure her and she grunted a sort of approval, perhaps letting me know all was forgiven. I walked to the wound and inspected it. To my amazement it was already healed with only a large scar marking its place on her hide. I found myself wishing I had a container of some kind, a canteen, or even a bottle to carry away some of the magical liquid with me. But, realizing it just wasn't possible, I drew some hope there would be more of it readily available in the ever-surprising land.

I went back and rubbed Horse's neck and put my hand under her mouth, giving a gentle tug. She fell in line behind me as I headed toward the arch and entered. At the back wall I studied the panel of carved stones hoping to discern their functionality, but to no avail. Finally, I threw caution to the wind and touched the one on the right. Nothing happened. After touching each one individually, and nothing happening, I began to despair, thinking I might have to navigate the treacherous canyons after all.

I turned and looked out beyond Horse to the stoney landscape. Something seemed different. I was sure I had seen four distinct spires in the landscape nearby before we had entered the arch, but now I was seeing seven. I turned back to the panel and gazed at it in shock. It now had seven columns of stone. Was this part of the illusion the obelisk had been referring to? Or was it just an unexpected result?

I touched the right most column again and then turned to look out. Now, instead of seven spires there were five, and when I turned back to the panel there were also five columns, but this time with a horizontal bar of carved stone at the bottom. My mind froze at the possibilities. This was either some kind of illusion, or a very sophisticated method of travel that only those with maps could make sense of.

Going outside I tried to return to the spire with the pool of liquid, only to discover it wasn't there. Looking around I immediately could tell we were in a different place on the landscape and I was sure I could see in the distance the grouping of two spires where we had entered. This was definitely a form of travel much removed from anything I had any knowledge of, but I wondered how I could ever harness it to travel with purpose.

Back inside I studied the panel some more to see if there were repeating symbols, or something that would clue me in to how to operate the device more effectively. Then, the lower, horizontal bar caught my attention once again. What if vertical columns caused horizontal travel, and horizontal bars caused vertical travel? I touched the horizontal bar but wasn't prepared for what happened next.

CHAPTER THREE

A hint at Memory

With seemingly no movement at all, Horse and I found ourselves standing in an alcove nestled into the side of a canyon in the middle of what appeared to be a busy marketplace. I had no idea how, or why, that term and the associated meaning came to me, but I was beginning to understand that while I had no knowledge of myself, I had great knowledge about many other topics.

Looking up I saw a stone ceiling soaring fifty meters or more with no horizontal beginning or ending in sight. The canyon walls were themselves twenty meters tall. The strange lights in the canyon walls illuminated everything with a bright glow. I saw beings with highly variable features and of all shapes, sizes and colors. I was immediately thankful though that despite their variety they all had one thing in common - they had human forms. There were also horses, sheep, goats, cows and chickens, either roaming freely or caged at various shops carved into the stone along the walls of the canyon. Everyone seemed to be relaxed and almost carefree as they strode, talking in strange languages and interacting with each other.

Suddenly, I was jolted out of my observations by three beings who rushed up the long series of steps and crowded in with me and Horse. Almost in unison they inquired something of me that I couldn't understand. I was taken aback by their finely chiseled features and lithe forms, but I couldn't tell if they were male or female, or something else. They caught on that I couldn't understand them so they began assailing me with words until I suddenly recognized one - sun.

"Yes!" I exclaimed, "I know that word."

"Oh, so you must be from the Star Helios system," one replied in very proper English. "What's your planet name?"

"Sorry, I don't know," I replied, deciding not to go into detail about my strange arrival there and the fact I didn't remember anything.

"You know," said the tall one with a very long face, "You should see a local scholar to get some help with that."

I was taken aback, feeling almost like the being had read my thoughts.

"A scholar?" I asked. "How do I find one?"

"Just go down that way," the third one said, pointing, "And enter through the door with the...," it stopped short, looking at the others questioningly.

A volley of words flew among them as if they were testing each one for relevance. Then, the eloquent one said very precisely:

"It's shaped like this," gesturing to the alcove we stood within, "and has a door with a star above it."

I thanked them and took the steps to the busy canyon with Horse dutifully following. The alcoves carved into the canyon walls were more or less evenly spaced, and some went so deeply into the rock that I couldn't tell what was inside. Others were very shallow. Above many alcoves were carved pictures of what I assumed were the offerings of each particular shop. I stopped in front of a shop that had multiple baskets filled with what appeared to be stones of all imaginable colors and textures.

As I watched, a very short being approached the baskets and sifted through the contents, seemingly searching for something. Some of the baskets were too high for it to see inside so it started hopping, peering over the basket rims each time it went airborne. I was struck by its rather exaggerated features. A very long nose seemed perched almost on top of the upper lip and large ears, almost transparent, flapped a little each time it struck ground before heading upward again. Then too, its feet were springlike, making it easy for it to hop without expending much energy.

Finally, it stopped hopping and went back to rummaging in one of the lower baskets until it found a stone disk that it quickly pocketed before striding away. Further on I came to two fountains, one above the other, both being fed by the liquid that comes from the rocks. A few animals drank at the lower fountain while an almost normal being - one that looked like myself -- stood by.

The man eyed me briefly and then spoke in my language.

"Every being has an innate right to sustenance," he spoke smoothly and very eloquently. "There are many kinds of sustenance, but this one provides everything you need. Help yourself and your horse, if you need some."

Before he even spoke, Horse was at the lower fountain, drinking thirstily. I stepped to the upper fountain, took a stone cup, filled it and drank. It was very similar in texture and taste to the liquid Horse and I had drunk when we arrived. After two more cups I had the strange sensation of being full, and decidedly not thirsty.

"New here?" the man asked.

"Yes," I replied. Then, suddenly surprised that he knew my language, "There seem to be many languages here. How did you know my language?"

"Unfortunately, there are some things you can know here, and some things you cannot."

I reflected on the statement and thought about my experience with the balled-up creature earlier, and the writing on the obelisk. Perhaps there was much that couldn't be known. Still, I thought I'd try to get at least a little more information from the man.

"Is this what I think it is? A marketplace of some type?" I asked.

"There are no marketplaces in this land. If you are referring to places where beings exchange some form of currency for goods," he explained.

"Yes," I said, "I guess that is what I understand marketplaces to be -- places where beings pay something to get goods. So this is not that?"

"That's right. If you look closely you'll see that there are no exchanges. Beings simply help themselves to the items that are available."

"But what are the incentives of those who own the alcoves?"

"Look again closely and you will see the alcoves have no owners, or masters looking over them," he said. "You will also note many beings simply leave items they've carried here with them, at the various *alcoves*," he pronounced the word with a questioning tone, as he stared condescendingly at me, "what we call *foundens*. In this way, whatever is available, is available to all."

Something inside of me immediately recognized the wisdom, but I also wondered where and when I had formed my understanding of such places, and why. It was no doubt another example of my newly acquired selective memory which provided me with understandings having no contexts. I was however, intrigued by the possibility of finding some more durable, and less worn-out clothing. I turned and looked up the canyon, having to squint from the blazing intensity of the glowing stones, and I was taken by the uncanny resemblance to the surface, as if there was actually sunlight there, underground. I turned back to bade farewell to the man, but he was gone. So I lightly took hold of Horse's reins and continued toward my objective, but at a much slower pace, studying the various foundens more closely.

When I came upon a carved image of what appeared to be a shirt, I climbed the steps to enter. This was a deep one, and when I moved beyond an outer wall with stone doors, I saw tables piled with fabric and hides of all kinds. As I wandered the rows, a large piece of well-tanned leather caught my eye and I was drawn to it for its suppleness and rich color. A color that I thought was strikingly similar to Horse's color. I could see the value in a pair of pants and shirt made from the material, but it would need a lot of work before it would be suitable. Continuing through the rows I noticed there were no clothing items at all, just the raw materials for clothing, including zippers and buttons.

At the back of the founden I saw a woman. While I had seen many beings so far who were close to having the same features as me, she was by far the closest. She was loading some fabric into a machine that had emblems on its front. Then she stepped to one side and stood very erect in front of a clear, glasslike device. A light came on and seemed to trace her outline. Following a few touches on the emblems, and a short time, a wad of cloth dropped out of a chute further on. She went to the cloth and when she unfolded it I could see it was a garment, a sort of long tunic. Without any warning, and without even looking around to see if anyone might be looking, she removed her old, terribly dirty and worn clothes. I felt an urge to turn away, but my curiosity about her got the better of me.

She was indeed a perfect match to what I knew a woman to be, even though I had no idea from where that knowledge came. She lifted her new garment, and slipped lithely into it. Then, she placed her old clothes into an opening in the wall and started heading for the entrance.

I hurried to get in front of her and when I did, I tried to talk to her, but she made gestures that made me think she could not speak. She seemed to be in a hurry and clutched a small leather pouch, holding it down and to her side like she was trying to keep me from seeing it. She just stood there with a curious look on her face which all of a sudden turned to what I could only describe as recognition. Did she know me? Or was she just realizing that I was a lot like her?

For the first time I was able to see her face clearly and what I saw intrigued me. Just above her left eyebrow there were two tattooed dots and flowing from them were two lines that curved in an S-shape, up toward her temple and then down across her cheekbone, ending up stopping just below her ear lobe. I looked back to her eyes and saw she seemed to have immediately understood something.

She used her finger to trace one of the tattooed lines beginning at her ear lobe and stopping above her eye. Then, she did the same thing to me, looking at me questioningly. I shook my head, tilting up my eyebrows to signal I didn't understand. The next thing I knew, she took me by the hand and led me to the back of the space where some tall mirrors stood. I looked in the mirror at my image. Having no memory of what I was supposed to look like I had nothing to compare my appearance to, other than those I had seen since my arrival. But what immediately struck me was that I had the very same tattoo that she wore.

Standing there, side-by-side, with both of our images in the mirror staring back at us, I saw that we were remarkably similar when compared to many of the other beings I had seen. I looked at her reflection and smiled but once again she seemed apprehensive and in a hurry. She started to leave and then stopped, looking back at me pensively, a pained look in her eyes, only to turn and go toward the entrance. In that moment I sensed she was afraid. But of what? I knew I hadn't done anything threatening and she seemed, at least momentarily to be interested in me. My thoughts raced trying to understand about the tattoos we both wore and something else deep inside stirred, like a memory. The next moment when I looked up, she was gone.

That chance meeting left me feeling disoriented and little did I know but it was a meeting that would haunt me for almost as long as I was in that strange land.

But, I needed to put that out of my mind for the task at hand was to somehow get a machine to make some clothes for me. I went back to where I had seen the leather pieces with a similar color as Horse, retrieved them and went to the machine. There, I loaded the leather at the place I had seen her do it. Then, I stepped in front of the glasslike device and stood erect. The light came on and traced my form. To my relief each emblem on the machine resembled an article of clothing. So, I touched the one that looked like a shirt and the one that looked like a pair of pants. When I went to retrieve the result from the chute further on, I found nicely stitched pants and a shirt with stone buttons. I delighted in their fit and feel. They were much more substantial than the worn torn pants and shirt I had arrived in, and it was strange but they also made me feel a little bit more like I belonged there.

My next thought though went to her. Her seeming fear, and the last way she had looked at me, made me concerned about her. Was she running from something, like I was? Or was she lost and just too fearful to trust? There was also something about her that seemed linked to me. It was a feeling like we shared something, as if we were somehow connected. Right then, the only being I felt connected to was Horse, and even though that connection was so strong that I could barely imagine not having her with me, it was still a bit nebulous because of my memory problem. So the idea there was a chance of a connection with the woman I had just met, made me feel like I needed to find her. But how? And where?

A sad and empty feeling hung over me as I reached the exit. But then, a small spark of hope as I headed outside, thinking I might see her there. Horse stood patiently waiting, and all the typical activity of the canyon was there, but she wasn't. My heart sank once again as I studied the faces in the crowds and passers by. How would I ever find her?

The reality of that thought made me realize I was missing something I knew nothing about, in a place where I had nothing. For awhile though I couldn't just give up, so I stood there, waiting and watching, searching the faces for hers. Eventually, I felt Horse nuzzle my back as if urging me to move on. Stubbornly, though, I resolved to keep watching for her as I took Horse's reins and stepped into the canyon in search of a star.

CHAPTER FOUR

The Little Man with the Big Answers

The stones, smooth from the passage of feet and hooves, felt slightly slick below my steps, and a breeze blew through the canyon mingling the scents of the rock walls with the voluptuousness of life. It seemed as if the the scene went on forever in front of me, but I held to my quest, glancing at each symbol over each founden until at last I spotted it. The alcove this founden was within was very large, and instead of an open-doored passageway leading to the interior, there was a single, tall, smoothstone door. The symbol of a star hung on a stone placard directly over the door.

I stepped up and touched the strip of carved stones at the door's center. Immediately, a slot opened about at waist level and I saw the top of someone's head appear.

"What do you want?" a male voice asked my knees.

"I was told to seek you out to get help with my problem," I replied.

"What problem is that?"

"Wait a minute. How did you know my language?"

"I'm a languagician, among other things," the voice replied snappishly, "so I always know what language any being needs to be addressed in."

"I see. Okay. Anyway, I'm trying to find out things about my past, like what planet I'm from, and I was told you might be able to help with that."

"Very well then, touch the stone at the top three times, and the one at the bottom once," he instructed, his head disappearing back inside.

I studied the strip of carved stones because I wanted to see if any of the symbols would provide clues to me that I could use when I encountered others. After all, these stone buttons seemed to be a fixture in that place.

At the very top was a hexagon having a sickle-shaped carving with two vertical bars inside it, one slightly higher than the other. Below that was a circle with a tortoise shell oval carved in its center. Next, another circle but with a circle inside that was offset slightly to the right, and with the same tortoise shell texture. Inside the interior circle were three vertical bars of marble. At the bottom, another sickle, only this one was open to the left and only had one vertical bar which was offset to the left of the sickle. I wondered if the offsets were important, or if they were just anomalies from the carving process. That would certainly make remembering them easier so I decided to simply focus on the major aspects and hope for the best. I touched the top stone three times and then the bottom one, once.

The door slid briskly to the side and I entered a very large room with high ceilings that stretched as far back into the rock as I could see. The walls on either side were divided into tall rectangles and inside those were vertical strips of carved stone bearing unimaginable variations from one to the next. There were familiar symbols but there were also combinations of familiar symbols as well as symbols that were totally unfamiliar to me. The door closed and suddenly the little man was before me, the top of his head barely at waist level. He peered up at me through squinty eyes, the hair from his nose spilling out over the top of his upper lip.

"Your language is what we refer to as an English dialect," he said, turning and gesturing for me to follow. "That is not a very old language and is not unique as languages go." He stopped abruptly, turned to me and paused, as if considering his words. "Is that the only language you know?"

"Well, yes, I guess so," I said uncertainly. "I mean it's sort of what just spilled out of my mouth when I finally found the need to talk in this land."

"In this land?" he said quizzically. "Do you mean you've only recently arrived here?"

"Yes."

"This is a bit troubling since there are few ways to get here, at least in your current state" he sounded mysterious and slightly puzzled. "Tell me, *how* did you get here?"

"Well," I began, apprehensively. "I seemed to have ridden my horse through a very immense dark wall."

"Oh dear," the little man winced.

"That doesn't sound good."

"Well, I guess that all depends upon your perspective. Let me show you," he motioned with his index finger to follow as he turned and walked further into the long room.

After many steps we reached a place where he suddenly levitated and sped through the air a bit too fast, bumping heavily into one of the vertical strips on the wall.

"Yikes!" he exclaimed, spinning around and looking down at me as he cupped a hand around his nose. I held back a chuckle as he floated there, sniffing with his eyes tearing. "Can't believe I did that."

He spun back around and touched some carved stones on the face of a panel that had a carving of a circle with nine smaller circles arranged at various distances and places around it. Now, a drawer slid out and he removed a thin, glass disc and placed it into a slot beside the door. Immediately an image of an orb with blue and green masses covering its surface was projected into thin air.

"Okay," he began in a professorial way. "You're looking at planet three of an eight planet system. Well, actually there are fifteen planets but the activity of that system hasn't been updated on this record. There was a space ripple in that sector that moved some planets and the whole thing isn't sorted out yet but we're not concerned with that. What's important is that this is the planet where your language is generally accepted as having been developed. It's called Earth and it is the third planet circling the sun known as Helios. Which, coincidentally comes from a different language also from that planet. Now, if we zoom in..."

The floating image expanded toward a particular point on the orb until a green mass with jagged edges surrounded by blue, filled the image.

"This is what we know as England and it is where the language you speak, originated," he said confidently. "That language went on to be used quite widely across that planet and the universe, though, so it doesn't necessarily follow that you learned it there. That's just where it began. But, based on your knowledge of that language, and unfamiliarity with any other language, we can comfortably state that you are probably from the planet called Earth, in the solar system warmed by Helios."

With that, he extracted the glass disc, replaced it, closed the drawer, and dropped down to the floor.

"So, can you tell me how I got from there, to here?"

"Well, as you said, it was through a dark wall, a phenomena that randomly occurs throughout the universe. Dark walls are folds in space where worlds of different densities are briefly drawn together. On the heavier-density world there is no evidence it exists, but on the other side, the lighter-density world, it shows clearly as an immense dark wall of nothingness. For this reason people on the heavier density worlds often unwittingly pass through. And, that's probably what happened to you. You see, Earth, is a very dense world, and here, Octa, we have a lighter density, even with all the rock, which is largely metamorphic, so it's lighter."

"So, how do I get back?"

The little man looked amused and concerned at the same time. "Get back?" as if he was asking the question of himself. "That's probably not possible because even though dark walls are only visible on lighter-density worlds, that is determined by the two worlds in question. So, in some instances a lighter density world might actually be the heavier density world in a fold, ergo the wall would not be visible. Plus accidentally finding one would be quite impossible since they can happen anywhere at anytime, but then too, they rarely happen. The odds are about 358.77893 million to one that you'd happen to be in the right place, at the right time, and know that you were."

"So, what you're telling me is that I'm stuck here?"

"Well, I wouldn't call it stuck. After all, you probably won't want for anything, and there are plenty of things here to amuse you," he said with a glimmer in his eye.

I was startled by the idea. Since I had arrived it seemed all I had done was extricate myself from one calamity after another and so I must have looked at leaving the place as a way to escape, especially from my pursuers. The idea that this would be someplace I would stay hadn't occurred to me. The little man stared up at me quizzically, as if following my mental processes.

"I guess, staying here might be okay, but I have this problem that arrived with me," I started, unsure of how much I should say.

"You were followed here, weren't you," the little man said knowingly. Then, without waiting for my response, he turned and signaled for me to follow him once again, talking over his shoulder on his way. "I have some pictures that will help you to identify what you're up against."

I cringed at the phrase, 'up against,' and I wondered why he said it.

After another long walk the little man stepped this time to the left and reached up as far as he could. Out popped the drawer of his choice and he inserted this glass disk into the slot at the side. Images of planets appeared in thin air.

"Now," he began. "This is the group of planets where these super beings originate."

"Super beings?" I repeated, questioningly.

"That's right, and don't kid yourself, they are pretty fantastic," he explained as he manipulated the view of the planets, zooming in on cluster ofter cluster, each one orbiting its own star, or stars. "These beings are thought to have arisen at the point where a filament of dark matter is channeling its payload into forming the galaxy you see here," he zoomed out to a view of an immense region of space filled with stars. "You can't see dark matter but the false color overlaid on this image magnifies the gravitational lensing from distant galaxies to reveal it, and you can clearly see huge arcs of it, much like a web. This is all quite normal and is in fact the process that explains how the universe is constantly being created. But, things are different at this galaxy because of the extreme denseness of the dark matter.

So, the worlds that developed here, did so with incredible speed and with even more incredible anomalies of life. Over the eons the inhabitants developed into super beings with adaptable bodies that could resist many of the forces in the universe, including those found in dark walls. These beings take many shapes and forms and can appear as combinations of beings as well. Because of their special abilities, they started traveling the universe through dark walls and even black holes. They can be respectful of other life, and even helpful, but they can also be from one of many legions that seek to use other beings for their personal and collective pleasure. There are also legions of them that are well organized and that have objectives to conquer and enslave. Can you give me a general description of the ones that followed you here?"

"Well, the best way to describe them was fly-like, but with human bodies."

The little man just stared at me for what seemed like too long before exhaling a, slow breath.

"I see," he said seriously now, the usual professorial tone lapsing to apprehension. "Oh, boy, that's ah... that's pretty bad," he said removing the disc, placing it in the drawer and closing it. He turned back toward the entrance, motioning once more for me to follow. After a short stroll he darted to the left and levitated, touching a drawer slightly higher than the top of my head. He removed the disc from the drawer and popped it into the slot causing an image to appear once again. At first I saw more stars and planets, but as he fingered a carved stone next to the slot where he inserted the disk, the planet images moved away from each other until one planet filled the viewing space.

"This planet is Augus 576 which is the fifth planet between this one and our second sun. It used to be inhabited by beings with human forms, although they were different from you or I. They had physical and genetic adaptations that allowed them to breathe the much denser air on that planet, and to withstand the higher heat. They also had incredible mental abilities, including being able to levitate items of immense proportions and weights. It was an advanced civilization that was also resource-based much like ours."

"Was?" I repeated, questioningly.

"Yes, unfortunately they are all gone, pretty much eliminated by the type of being you describe. The resources were plundered to extinction also, so that now, the world is largely devoid of any kind of life. There have been an increasing number of sightings of these fly-type super beings in recent times on other planets, planets where we know they have not existed before. They are called Tachina, as in the Tachina Gigantus species, and are one of the more troubling species that has evolved, we think, on one of the planets near the dark filament. Many of the run-of-the-mill super beings are really not organized at all, lacking many of the cognitive processes necessary to form advanced civilizations. They sort of appear individually on planets and so if they are up to no good, so to speak, they are easily overpowered and contained, or terminated. But the Tachina are quite a different story. They quickly form groups, populate rapidly, and they are very smart. They are without a doubt the last of these kinds of super beings you'd want to have on your trail. How many were there?""

"I saw five."

"And you have no idea why they are after you?"

"Sorry, no memories."

"Yes, and that's expected, if you are not a super being. The rest of us lose and sometimes gain things when we go through dark walls, but we all lose one thing in the process - our lives."

"You mean I'm dead?"

"Well, you were. You see, when you go through a dark wall you die and then resurrect immediately. Unfortunately you most often leave behind memory. Not all memory of course or you wouldn't be able to speak a language, for example, or know about interacting in a physical world. But you do lose the memory of events and experiences unique to yourself."

His explanation put everything immediately into perspective. I was essentially a partially blank slate, endowed with just enough memory and acquired skills to interact on a physical plane with other beings along with an innate aspiration to survive, but nothing more.

"But what about feelings?" I asked him. "Since I've been here I've felt compassion, fear, and I think even attraction, like romantic attraction. Do those normally stay in tact?"

"Ahh, well fear, if it is fear for your life, it is simply a survival mechanism, but compassion and attraction are of the spirit. Your spirit has to pass through since it is what animates you, and provides the framework for your destiny. If your spirit doesn't make it through, then neither does your body."

I got lost in thought, perplexed by my situation and wondering what next. But the little man was growing impatient.

"I really have to get about my work, so if there isn't anything else," he said, leaving the word trailing.

"Well, yes, there's so much more, like what to do about these Tachina?" I inquired, hoping to detain him as long as I could for his wellspring of knowledge.

"I suspect there are no easy answers to that, but then, that's not my specialty. I can tell you that although the Tachina speak just about any language, their own language is very distinct and you will know it by its very guttural series of clicks, squeaks and clucks. And, if you ever hear a high-pitched whine that vibrates rapidly you need to take cover because you've been triangulated by their innate tracking systems. Once locked on to you, they can paralyze you by alternating the wavelength they use. And believe me, you don't want to be their prisoner."

"Is there any chance they will have stopped searching for me and I can just forget the whole thing?"

"There is no chance of that. They are driven by the hunt, and once they know their prey, they continue to the death. There may also be other reasons they are tracking you. Perhaps they are under orders from some in their cohort, or, you are just one part of a much larger scheme. If you had memory, perhaps you would know how you got entangled with them in the first place. But without that, you will be locked in this drama until something is resolved. You could say, in a very fatal way, that your destiny is now linked to theirs."

"Is there a way to defeat them, or at least throw them off my trail, permanently?"

"It's not possible to lose them, but there are definitely ways to defeat them. For that information you will need to journey to the lower levels."

"Lower levels? How much lower can you go here?"

"Well, the planet's circumference is 52,896 kilometers -- I know some using your language use another measurement basis, but we're metric here with seven base units. So that's 16,837 kilometers in diameter. We're currently a little over five kilometers from the surface, so you see, there's quite a ways to go before you'd come out the other side. Not that that's possible. Well, at least it hasn't been done that I know of."

"So what am I looking for at the lower levels?"

"Well, first of all you need to gather a StarStone Scepter so you can find your way through the underworld. Without it, you're as good as lost because the openings to each successive underworld are constantly changing. Although sometimes you can find a messenger and travel with them, but it's highly unlikely unless you happen to be in the right place at the right time."

"Then, you must make your way to the Land of the Misanthrope. Not at all a pleasant place for humans, but necessary nonetheless. There, you will find an ancient sect of peacekeepers known as the Arbitans that keeps the knowledge of super beings. They will know all there is to know about the Tachina."

My mind was swimming with even more questions and I could see he was getting more impatient. Still, if I could get just one more question answered...

"Do you have any hints about where to find a StarStone Scepter?" I ventured hopefully.

"You must travel east until you see the Spires of Micknok. In those canyons you'll find everstone growing in thin, vertical columns. Once you retrieve one you'll need to find a being of the Superterrestrial Order to enchant it for you. Once enchanted, it becomes the scepter you require. Now if there isn't anything else..."

I sensed his patience was at its end so I thanked him sincerely, bade farewell and started the long walk back to the entrance door. But before I could go more than a few steps, the little man was suddenly in front of me again, staring up through his telescope glasses and acting anxious, as if he was about to ask a favor that only I could grant.

"I just remembered something very important," he began apprehensively. "My name is Brukin, by the way, and I was put in charge of a boy many years ago and now he is beyond my care. It's not that he's a problem or anything," he added quickly and reassuringly, "but he is in need of seeing more of this world than just this canyon. He has been begging me to take him further into the underworld because in all his time here he believes he has uncovered evidence that the path to his destiny lies in the Mists, the third underworld. I just haven't been able to undertake such a journey, and to be honest, I am not really inclined toward adventure. He's a strong young man now and would be an excellent traveling companion who could be a great help to you in navigating the Canyonlands and the lower depths. You see, even though he's never been far, he does know how to get around."

I was a amused at the little man's request coming so unexpectedly and on the heels of his earlier impatience, but I could definitely see the value in having some help. And, it seemed there was probably much the young man could teach me.

"Certainly," I said. "I'd be happy to bring him along."

"Wonderful! But I have to ask him about it, and then, well, if he accepts, give him some last minute instructions. Can you come back when the glowstones are fully illuminated?"

"Sorry, glowstones?"

"Oh yes, you see," he brightened, "that's exactly like something he can help you with. We don't have the benefit of solar indications down here to help us track time's passage, but we do have the glowstones -- those spires of light in the canyons and the orbs of light on flatlands -- and because of their connections to the surface they approximate the passage of time. They brighten gradually and then dim gradually, to mimic the changes in light on the surface. They are dimming down right now and so when you next see them as very bright, come back and Bril, his name as told to me when he was left here, will be ready, right out front."

"Okay, I'll be back then."

Once again I thanked him and I suddenly got the feeling he was going to give me a hug, but he stopped short, and instead, shook my hand energetically. His hand was very warm, almost hot, and I had an instinctual urge to pull away, but caught myself so as not to offend him, remembering his kindness and willingness to share. In a way, I wished I could take him with me. After we parted I watched him walk deeper into the stone, until he disappeared. Then, I turned and headed for the door.

CHAPTER FIVE

Loss and Friendship

On my way to the exit I felt a strong desire to just sit quietly somewhere and assess all that I had learned. Being a blank slate was simple in some ways because I could choose my steps without a lot of mental noise. But on the other hand, it also meant I would be making important decisions without input from memory, other than my recent and very limited memory.

I wondered what I was missing by not having a history or remembrance of self. But my next thought startled me with the realization that I was now in the process of creating me, building a whole new being from the ground up. And, it was frightening to know I would be ultimately responsible for the being that emerged.

My memories included the understanding of how beings of all kinds began life, and so I knew that at one time I was an infant, had had caregivers and had been experienced with all kinds of other beings and their acquired experiences. What had they taught me? What had they done to me? What had we known of each other? And, how had they shaped the person I was before I crashed through the dark wall? For better or worse I could have always blamed some or all of them for the person I had became. But now, I would ultimately own it all.

Outside, Horse stood patiently, sparking another round of mental questions. How were we connected and where had our journey begun? I wondered if maybe she could have retained memory? Or, was she just responding to the moment, a tamed beast used to having a human master, and willing to accept me simply because I happened to be astride her when we crashed through the dark wall. On deeper reflection though it seemed like we were more than that. That somehow maybe there was a shared destiny.

Activity in the canyon had slowed and sure enough the glowstones were much dimmer. They glowed differently from when they were bright, giving off a luminosity that seemed to eliminate shadow. And now, there was a red glow to them. Everything was evenly lit and it was easy to see into the many crevices and recesses in the canyon walls. The absence of shadow made things appear flat though, making it harder for me to detect the alcoves harboring the various foundens.

I put my hand under Horse's mouth and gave a little tug as I stepped off to explore. I wanted to go back the way I had come and see if the tattooed woman was still there. Maybe she had returned to the fabric founden and was waiting there for me. I wondered why I felt like I did. Was it was some inborn tendency to want to be with someone, or, maybe it was just biology. I could imagine that in a universe as large and diverse as the one the little man had shown me, there would be an endless variety of beings, with an endless variety of likes, wants and desires. And an endless number of ways to satisfy them. I did wonder though if other beings had similar tendencies as mine. Did they feel? Or were they simply responding to want and desire?

My mental wanderings were tiring me and although I had no idea how long night lasted in Canyonlands, I knew I should get some rest. But where? It was then that I noticed the canyon was suddenly, very empty. The earlier robust activity was all gone, and in its place a sort of breathless tension hung in the air. I scanned the canyon behind me and saw beings ducking into foundens and turning quickly up smaller connecting canyons. When I turned back to face forward I saw a final trickle of others scurrying to shelter until within seconds it was just me and Horse. Everywhere up and down the canyon there was no one, not even a chicken. As the eerie feeling intensified, I felt a cool wind, driven with increasing force from up the canyon. This was followed almost immediately by an immense roaring and then way up the canyon I spotted white foam riding on what appeared to be a wall of water!

I leapt on Horse as she was spinning to face down the canyon, and then we gone. Once again she stretched in a long, flowing pattern, her hooves throwing off sparks as they skidded against tiny flint particles in the canyon floor. I leaned forward, wrapping my arms alongside her neck, focusing on matching her movements. Seconds later a white froth slide below her hooves followed by the full force of a wave slamming us forward.

In that moment I don't know how she managed, but instead of diving forward and skidding along the canyon floor she launched herself upward to catch the crest of the wave, and we slipped behind it, now riding in nothing more than a very fast moving river. Ah, this was something we were very used to, I thought.

The water had risen almost to the tops of the highest steps in front of the foundens but we were moving much too fast to get out of the current in the short distance from one side of a founden alcove to the other. Horse had wisely swum to the side of the canyon where she could have more control of her movement. I cringed though at the thought of getting knocked against the stone wall and urged her to move just a little further away by gentling tugging to the right on her mane.

Far down the canyon I saw what could have been a major drop off, which now would be a raging waterfall. It was then I noticed what I was sure Horse was going for -- a side canyon. If she could break out of the current soon enough, the water would gently push us to safety. She seemed to be resting, just doing what was necessary and reserving her strength. I marveled at her intelligence and oneness with the moment.

Finally, the edge of the opening to the side canyon came and went but not before Horse mustered all her strength to lunge to the left and break out of the current. I felt a force push us diagonally sending us right for the far wall of the side canyon. Horse struggled to get her footing on slippery stone so I knew the water was shallow. I dove off her to the left, hoping the lack of my weight would help her recover. I was submerged for seconds and when my head breached the water surface I instinctively started swimming. But after only a few strokes my hands and knees were slamming against rock so I reached out to grab at anything I could and found a crevice between two stones in the canyon wall.

I clung there feeling the pull of the water leave me and the weight of my body return. The sound of the roaring water diminished almost as suddenly as it had started. I struggled to regain my composure and slowly managed to stand up. I turned, expecting to see horse standing nearer to the canyon opening, but she wasn't there. I raced to the confluence of the two canyons, the larger one now running less than a meter deep in water. I studied my footing carefully and reached a point where I could peer around the corner. But, nothing. I looked back up the side canyon thinking Horse had ridden the water further into the canyon than me, but she wasn't there.

By now there was just a thin sheet of water sliding down the floor of the large canyon so I stepped out into it, studying the walls, the niches and crannies, and the alcoves, hoping to spot some sign of her. But, she wasn't there. Into thin air. She was just gone.

I cringed remembering the drop off I had seen and knew I had to go there. I took off jogging, racing by the reopening foundens and beings stepping back out into the canyon. Why hadn't anyone told me about these floods? The little man, the strangers in the elevator, the guy at the nourishment founden? I was sure, based on the way everyone had gotten out of the way that this was a regular occurrence. But no one warned me!

It seemed like forever reaching the drop off, all the time running and wagging my head side to side, scrutinizing the canyon walls and the alcoves, hoping to spot her. Finally as I was nearing exhaustion and slowing to a stumbling walk, I was there. It was indeed a drop off and one of immense proportions. I crept to the edge and peered into the abyss. Vertical glowstones continued down the walls a short distance, but then ran out, and beyond them there was only darkness. I sunk to the ground from the weight of an immense grief. She had been such a noble, trustworthy friend and had taken care of me almost without thought of self. Now, before I even had the chance to understand our connection, to know our beginnings together -- she was gone. I screamed at the top of my lungs across the abyss and collapsed in tears on its edge.

I don't know how long I laid there, watching my tears drop from my cheeks onto the stone beneath my face, but it didn't seem like there would ever be enough time to recover from this loss. My heart raced and my mind swam in a sort of sickening dizziness, incredulous at how quickly and easily she'd been taken. I cried in disbelief for what seemed like a very long time. Eventually, there were no more tears, just a soreness in my throat and a hammering headache.

Just then, there was a light touch on my shoulder that startled me, and I turned. Squatting there before me was a large man. Just one of his hands was the size of two of mine, and his shoulders obscured anything behind him. But when I looked into his eyes, it took my breath away. Somewhere in there, far behind pupils of glossy black I saw hope. And then he spoke, in my language.

"May I help you.?"

That strange question I had heard at the end of an earlier harrowing experience rekindled memories of one who had treated me kindly. I wondered if there was some connection between the two, but dismissed the idea when considering their obvious physical differences.

"I don't think there is anything you can do. I've just lost my horse to the flood and she was a very true," I stopped, shuddering at the truth behind my next words, "and only friend."

The huge man stood up and it was then that I noticed he wasn't huge in all directions. He was only huge in width. He was shorter than me, probably only up to my shoulders. But even with his contorted shape I couldn't get over the sense of hope he stirred in me and the quiet confidence he exuded.

"I lost a horse too when I first came to Canyonlands," he said with understanding. "It was not as noble as yours because it was always bucking me off, and it was not very pleasant to be with." A tear came to his left eye and dribbled down his huge face. "But, I really loved that horse."

He offered me a hand and I grabbed what I could, coming up with just his index and middle fingers. And then I was on my feet again. Now, looking over his head I could see the activity in the canyon was back, but much quieter than when the glowstones were bright. It was a peaceful scene with subdued conversations while beings mostly stood and sat. All up the canyon there was a sense of permanence, of some kind of ancient knowledge manifesting itself through the life within its walls. But even in the face of such comforting serenity, I felt no comfort. This loss was one that wanted to hang on, and right then all I wanted was to find a place where I could sleep, for a long time. But then, I was suddenly curious how he knew my language.

The hugely wide man said his name was Togn and that he was one of only a few hundred of his kind still in existence. He explained that his kind knew my language well because they traded heavily with others who used it. He added that he had met someone else recently who used my language. When he asked me my name, I was stumped. I didn't have one. Actually, I told him, I couldn't remember.

"Can I call you Keln?"

Why not, I thought. Names so far hadn't seemed to be important but having one might have advantages.

"Sure," I said tiredly. "But tell me more about this person you met who spoke my language. How did you meet them?"

He told me that a woman had just stayed with him and some

friends of his. He said she could only speak a few words at a time but then had to stop because there was something bothering her throat. He also said that since she wasn't familiar with the area he had helped her understand how things worked in the underworld. But what he told me next, startled me. He said she had the same tattoo that curved over her eye as me.

I was shocked. It seemed very strange that the very woman I had recently met had also met him.

"Did she say where she had come from?" I asked.

He said that was one of the mysteries about her. Of course she couldn't talk much, but when she did she only talked about places on Octa and the underworlds. I was very intrigued by the news. The possibilities raced through my mind and once again it seemed like I was looking for a connection. What was this tendency to want to see myself in a larger context and somehow connected to other beings? As I considered the chance of it all -- Togn being there when Horse had been swept away, and then him having recently met a woman bearing the same tattoo as me -- it seemed like there had to be more to it than just random coincidence.

But again, I caught myself running too far ahead, playing a mental game I couldn't win, and so I switched my focus to the moment. And right then I realized, I was very tired and I wanted to escape from sad feelings about Horse. But I was also angry. Why hadn't anyone told me about the floods? And why did they happen?

Once Togn understood I was a traveler he explained that water from the surface was always flowing into the underworlds and that in Canyonlands the water flowing through populated canyons was treacherous because it made the stone floors so slick. It was also a problem for many other reasons, so master masons had built dams at the heads of key canyons to hold back the water. Of course, eventually the water would reach the tops of the dams and have to be released, emptying the reservoir and starting the process all over again. He said that beings were warned of releases when the glowstones glowed red and that he suspected because it was such common knowledge that no one would probably think to tell me. As much sense as that made, it didn't make me feel any better, and my tiredness was really starting to show.

Togn suggested I go to a rest founden and said he would show me one, so we set off back up the canyon. On our way I continued searching for Horse, thinking anything was possible and that maybe she had escaped the terrible fate I assumed had befallen her. Togn moved knowledgeably through the canyon as if he had been there a long time. We came to a narrow side canyon and turned up it, climbing the first set of stone steps on the right.

CHAPTER SIX

Revelations of a Strange Land

Inside was a huge open room with several massive stone fireplaces all lit with roaring, blue flamed fires. Over the fires there were long rods with pots of all sizes hanging at different heights gathering heat. Long stone tables with benches filled the center of the room while wide walking spaces encircled them. Some beings were at the pots, ladling their contents into wide-mouth stone cups, while others sat at the tables, talking and eating.

Togn told me the fires were fueled with firestone from the Firston underworld and that just a few sticks created long-burning, very hot fires. He explained that while most beings in Canyonlands drew most of their daily sustenance from the tonc, or stonewater, many of the pots around the room hanging on the fires contained a special delicacy called rynd. Rynd, he said was an abomination made from helpless domesticated animals that are brought to Canyonlands from The Mists. As we walked in front of one of the fireplaces he pointed out the pots that contained the rynd, his face contorted with disgust. Inside the rynd pots I saw something that was familiar to me and without even searching my memory I knew it was stew. The aroma was very enticing and Togn could see I wasn't revolted at all. He pulled me aside.

"You know about rynd?" he asked.

"I guess so," I replied, not fully understanding my attraction to it. I didn't feel like telling him my very short life story though, and so I asked him why he was disgusted by it.

"In this land," he explained, "there is sustenance for all and it happens naturally as the carver worms go through their life processes. When they can no longer carve they mass in large numbers to die.

Their decomposition creates the tonc that you see flowing all across Canyonlands. So with such an abundance of a life sustaining substance available to all, taking the lives of those beings who offer no harm, yet provide treats like milk and eggs, is an abomination. The beings who consume it become fearful and warlike, and they crave the rynd."

"What about the other pots?" I asked gesturing to the ones hanging higher from the fires.

"Those have tonc stew, tonc and a mixture made with solestone and clelstone. It is very good," he said approaching a high-hanging pot and ladling a portion into a stone cup he retrieved from the hearth. "Here," he offered me the cup.

When he had filled one for himself we sat down across from each other at an empty table and sipped the mixture. It immediately sent warmth to my stomach and I could feel its aroma working on me, making me almost euphoric, and very relaxed.

Togn was a very likable character and his reassuring ways helped me feel safe. We sat there for a long time with the glow of the fires all around and the muted conversations echoing like whispers around the huge room. I felt at peace for the first time since I had arrived on the planet. I wasn't looking over my shoulder and I wasn't running, and I wasn't thinking. At the bottom of the cup there were three small, potato-like things which Togn said to eat. So, I did. In short order I was very sleepy. I remember following Togn down a long hallway and past many curtain-covered cubicles until we reached one with the curtain drawn open. Inside were two stone platforms topped with a moss-like material. I laid down on one, sinking into its softness and feeling like I was ensconced in a warm pile of leaves. That was all I remembered.

When I awoke I stretched and yawned, and for many heartbeats savored the feeling of being rested. Remembering Horse, I felt a wave of loss and lay there for too long, letting sadness wash over me. Eventually, I looked to the other bed, and saw Togn wasn't there. I thought maybe he had gone out to the dining area to eat so I jumped out of the moss and headed down the long hallway. There were many more open curtains now and along the way I saw the moss mattresses being collected by beings with small heads and very large, rounded ears.

In the large room I scanned the crowd but didn't see Togn. Disappointment set in. I wanted desperately to have some company for the upcoming travels and I wanted desperately for beings to stop coming and going in my life. And, yes, maybe I wanted a little help too. That's when I remembered my appointment for when the glowstones were bright. I ran through the large room and outside. Things were definitely very bright. In fact, brighter than I had seen them since my arrival. As I was about to bound down the steps I heard a familiar voice from behind.

"Where are you off to?"

I turned and was over joyed to see Togn, and I guess it showed.

"Well, you sure look better than you did when the stones were dim," he said, smiling broadly.

I went back to him and shook his two fingers. "I'm glad to see you, Togn," I started. "But I have to go up the canyon to pick up someone who is going to accompany me to a place called The Mists. And I think I'm late."

Togn's face turned serious. "Why to The Mists?"

"Well, it's not actually the last stop. I'll tell you what, why don't you come with me to pick him up and I'll tell you about it?"

On the way I told Togn about my arrival, the Tachina, the little man, and why Bril wanted to go with me to The Mists. But even as I spoke I kept scouring the canyon for signs of Horse, unable, or perhaps unwilling to accept what seemed to be her fate. Togn could sense my purpose and also seemed to be watching for a lone horse, perhaps injured. In the back of my mind I hoped I could convince him to travel with us, not just because I was sure his strength would come in handy, but also because he was highly intuitive.

When I finished my story, Togn seemed compelled to tell some of his. He told me of his early years with his people called the Kech and how they lived in Firston and were the ones who mined the firestone, usually trading it throughout the planet for commodities they lacked. Their short, strong stature made them perfectly suited to chip the firestone from the walls of deep, horizontal shafts. He told me the work was not hard because the firestone chipped out easily, and was not heavy, so entire families would work in the shafts. In little time each glowcycle they could chip and gather enough firestone to live very comfortably and many families had long stretches of free time to pursue learning and art.

Gradually though, it became more and more dangerous to mine the firestone because of cave-ins. The concentrations of firestone were laid down below a layer of sandstone, so as the Kech removed more and more firestone from the walls of the shafts it weakened the sandstone overhead. Even though the Kech employed advanced engineering techniques to shore up the shafts their efforts met with failure when tremors struck, as they often did in Firston, the most susceptible of all the planet to minor quakes. In one catastrophe thousands of Kech died. Gradually the people restricted women and children from mining the firestone, fearing their population would not recover its continual losses. Togn told me that once his people reached the point where they could not meet the demand for firestone, others from all parts of the planet descended to do the mining. They were not as well suited in stature for the work and many died, but they still continued to pour in and pick up where his people had left off.

But what he told me next explained why he had said earlier that he was one of only a few hundred of his kind left in existence. The strangers entering the Kech's part of Firston brought with them many other life forms including domesticated animals that had never existed there before. In the dense, hot atmosphere of Firston, bacteria that arrived with the new life forms mutated rapidly and while the new strains of bacteria took their toll on all the beings there, the Kech were decimated. Togn said everyone in his nuclear and extended families died except for him. I was silent for a long time, and I was amazed when I remembered him responding to my loss of Horse by talking about a horse he had lost, while he kept his greatest loss, one that mine could not even come close to, to himself. Who was this being who had faced such extreme hardship, but yet was capable of so much compassion? I stopped and grabbed his arm to bring him facing me.

"I am sorry to hear of all that has happened to you, my friend, Togn," I said. "I would be proud to be a part of a new family for you, if that pleases you."

Togn smiled his widest smile yet, which was very wide, and then he threw his arms around me and squeezed just a little bit too tight. But, I didn't say anything. When he released me I patted him on the back and we continued up the canyon each harboring his own deep understanding of our new relationship.

I hadn't realized just how far the flood had carried me and Horse for it seemed like a long time getting back to the founden with the star. Along the way we stopped momentarily so I could check inside the clothing founden for her, but she wasn't there. I studied the faces outside too and I could tell Togn was curious so I told him about my chance encounter with her and how it had affected me. He said he'd watch for her too as we continued.

Nearing the founden with the star I saw the little man pacing and fuming on the steps, and mumbling something to a very young man who didn't seem to pay him much attention at all. Then, the little man saw me and bounded down the steps.

"Ahhh," he said beaming excitedly. "You made it! We were beginning to think we got the time wrong!"

"Sorry," I said sheepishly. "I had a few problems."

"Well, no mind now, you're here," then turning and gesturing for the young man to approach he made the introduction. "This is Bril," he said, pulling the young man forward, "and Bril, this is…," he let the announcement hang in the air like a question.

I looked at Togn and we smiled between ourselves as if we had a humorous secret and then I finished the little man's sentence, "Keln."

"Wonderful!" the little man could barely contain himself, or at least he was putting on a pretty good act. "And, you are…" he left the dangling question while gesturing at Togn, to which the wide man supplied the answer.

"Wonderful," the little man quipped again. "So, Bril," he said turning to him, "Do you have any questions before heading out?"

Until now, Bril had seemed to be quite distant, or maybe just really shy, but when he spoke I realized it was neither, but rather that he was much older in mind and spirit than he was in body.

"Thank you, Brukin," he said to the little man, "but I see you have chosen wisely with these two and any questions remaining will have to be answered in their own time."

"Excellent! Well then, no more delays," he spoke quickly, turning to Bril. "Remember all you have learned my boy, and trust you will discover your destiny."

I could see Brukin was getting emotional but perhaps because of his intellect, was uncomfortable showing it. Instead of a hug, he reached for Bril's hand, and the two smiled at one another, each with his own resolve to assume only the best was about to happen. Then, Brukin turned and walked back up the steps turning once to wave, before slipping inside. I imagined him peering out from the darkened interior to see his protege for just a few seconds longer before the huge panel of stone closed the opening to the founden with the star.

At that point I was assuming that Togn would be accompanying us, but I wasn't really sure, so I asked him. He beamed his characteristic smile and confirmed. He told us he had never been to the lower depths. He said he had been drifting, not really settling on anything. When I had told him about the journey he said he was immediately drawn to it and had hoped he'd be asked to go along. That was good news to my ears but it was Bril who put our next moves into focus.

"We should be going very soon," he said urgently. "Brukin and I heard from an outpost this morning that Tachina had been spotted in the outlands and it sounds like they might be the very ones tracking you. There were five, right?"

"Yes. But what about all the beings here, won't they be in danger?"

"Fortunately not. Tachina have one-track minds and if they're tracking you they won't stray from their goal of catching up to you. While they are still largely a mystery to us we have gathered information on certain aspects about them, and their single-minded devotion to their task at hand has been borne out consistently."

"Fine then, lead the way," I motioned to Bril.

As we stepped off on what was no doubt our last walk in the canyon for some time, I had a nagging sense of doom. Maybe it was knowing the beasts were already on my trail again and that I'd sooner or later have to face them. But I was also still despondent from loosing Horse. At least I knew I could depend on her, especially after all we had been through. With Bril and Togn though, there was no history, just a new camaraderie that was untested. Would they stick with me in the tough times? After all, the Tachina were after me, not them. But in the end I knew I would simply have to accept their help for as long as they wanted to offer it. After that, it would be up to me.

CHAPTER SEVEN

Lost to the Canyons

As we made our way through the busy canyon I stopped momentarily in front of the fabric founden and wondered where she had gone. I didn't know if Togn had seen her before or after me, making it difficult to trace her movements against mine. And with the absence of clocks and just the glowing and dimming of the glow stones as the only seeming measurement of time, it was difficult to narrow down a series of events. I imagined a conversation between two residents:

"I need to fix an event to a certain time. Do you remember when the glowstones were bright, I mean really bright?" Asks one of the other.

"You mean at their brightest, or just kind of bright," answers the other.

"Well you know, it was when they were brightest but a couple of times ago."

"Oh, okay, I think so. Was that right before a red cycle?"

And on and on. There was no reliable way to fix a certain event in time. But then on second thought it seemed as if time was not really very important. As I surveyed the street scene there was no one running to get somewhere and no one frantically waiting on something to happen. It was all just peaceful and predictable. I knew the fact that there was sustenance for all was a big part of why beings seemed unhurried. But it also seemed like there was more at work. At any rate I had tarried long enough wandering around in my mind. As I turned to catch up with Bril and Togn I felt like I needed to relinquish my penchant for questioning and just be in the moment. There was much too much to see and take in, and spending my time analyzing it was just trading the real experience for a mental one.

When we reached one of those devices that made travel easy, Bril called it a placejumper, which made a lot of sense to me since you could travel vertically and horizontally. We stepped inside where Bril deftly touched the carved stones and instantly we were on the mesa above the canyon looking out from an alcove in a spire. It was then that I saw the landscape for the first time -- really saw it.

Before, under the stress of the chase and then Horse's injury, I had only been focused on a very small part of it, but now, it opened before me in a vista of unimaginable proportions with mesas, spires and canyons all glowing brightly in the luminescence of thousands of glowstones. Bril touched the stone panel again and the scene changed dramatically. Now, we looked out on a darkened landscape with only a fraction of the glowstones. Off in the distance great spires rose up, illuminated with a reddish light that seemed to be originating within the spires themselves. Bril pointed.

"The Spires of Micknok," he announced in a matter-of-fact way. "From here on out, there are no placejumpers so we have to walk."

His words were disappointing. I had gotten used to the easy travel afforded by the placejumpers and the thought of picking our way through the maze of canyons meant we'd be slowing down considerably. I looked at Togn to see his broad smile, as if he was pleased at the prospect.

"Do you look forward to the journey, Togn?" I asked quizzically.

"I prefer walking," he said confidently. "The placejumpers are strange to me."

"Okay then," I said boldly. "Let's get on with it." And we stepped out of the placejumper and into the subdued light of the new landscape. The stone beneath my feet had a coarser texture. All around us were clumps of rock that exuded an ambrosial vapor. Tonc flowed out of the rock mounds, from spires and through the cracks in the rock floor, traveling in all directions like tributaries in a massive network.

Bril stepped out confidently in front, striking a measured and precise pace. As I fell in line behind him, and Togn behind me, I was thankful for the two of them. Just getting this far might have taken me a lifetime on my own.

We moved without talking, while all around us we heard gurgling sounds, and hissing sounds and a few sounds that were indescribable. Through it all, neither Bril nor Togn seemed to be in the least bit apprehensive as we wound our way through the maze of spires, and drop offs.

At each new canyon that cut between us and our goal, Bril quickly changed course to eventually bring us to the point where the canyon originated so we could simply walk around and continue along its opposite side. All the while he seemed to be keeping us more or less heading toward the spires. At each successive canyon I peered inside, in many cases seeing their predictable bottoms of flat stone and rock. Others though, dropped off precipitously, some with narrowing sides disappearing into a contorted abyss, while others had sides that expanded outwardly into the darkness. In some canyons the water or tonc flowed like a river, while others only had a trickle. I saw a full range of glowstones in the canyon walls. Some emitted the common yellow light. Others glowed pink, or red or violet. Their intensities were also different with some almost too bright to look at, and others barely giving off light at all, as if they were simply colored stone.

The spires grew more numerous until we had to strain to keep our goal in sight, and there were subtle changes in the landscape and the light. The walking surface became more jagged with rectangular crystal-like formations jutting upward to slow us down and make it difficult to walk. My boot soles were torn causing me to walk gingerly on the side of my foot to keep from getting cut. At the same time the light dimmed to an almost intolerably low level adding to the difficulty of walking and picking our way around canyons. As we crossed over the head of yet another drop off, Bril stopped suddenly, craning his neck to get a glimpse of the horizon. But, there was no horizon. Instead we faced an immense wall of spires with no clear path through.

It was at that moment when Bril was lost in thought ahead of me, and Togn stood looking to the right beside me, that I caught a movement to my left. I peered intently into the shadows trying to make out a shape when suddenly I was struck with knowing. I turned to the movement and walked several steps to investigate. Then it was clear, and I recognized the creature, in a ball, trembling. One more step and a woman unfolded, reached out and wrapped her arms around my thighs, laying her head against my hip.

"Is there something I can help you with," she said clearly, and intelligently.

I found myself weighing a conflict between my damaged footwear, and the problem of our path being blocked. But, I was either too unclear in my thoughts, or the creature took it upon itself to decide my most urgent need, because in the next moment a supple pair of leather footings closed around my feet, adding a much needed layer of protection. With that, the creature rolled back into a ball and then transformed into an obelisk. The inscription read: We have but moments to become as momentous.

My mind pondered its gravity and I tried to make a connection between it and the message I had received from the first such creature. What was it? A code? A puzzle specially matched to me? Or, was it just a random display, meant for anyone? Feeling the raised letters with my fingers, as if reading them by touch, I wanted to believe they were for me, and that there were powers greater than me that were willing to help out on this journey. But then, there were the experiences of random events, like Horse washing away over the cliff, that challenged the possibility that I mattered at all. In the next instant I realized I would not think my way to the truth, and that, right then, there were more pressing things to deal with. I turned back toward Bril and Togn, crossing the few meters, and then seeing confusion in their eyes.

"What?" I asked, confused by their demeanor.

"Are you okay?" Togn asked me.

"Yes. Didn't you see that?" I questioned back, wondering why they seemed to be in the dark.

"See what?" Bril asked

It was then that I had my answer, and I felt a rush of comfort and elation.

"Oh, nothing," I quipped. "Just lost in thought." I wondered if they would notice my new footwear when the light got better, but decided that if they did, I would just make up a story. For now, I wanted to keep my little secret, a secret.

Bril motioned to the wall of spires that stretched before us, spreading across flatlands and canyons for as far as we could see in the dim light. The barrier was not straight but rather meandered, making it seem more formidable because of all the crevices and recesses, some of which might offer passages through. It was also impossible to tell from our viewpoint just how deep it was.

"Our best option is to just travel along its face and try to find passage through, around, under or over," Bril said matter-of-factly. "If we already had a StarStone Scepter the task would be much easier. But, we don't, so it's best to get at it."

When we reached the base of the spires I was amazed at their height and complicated structures. They were crystal-like with tall vertical, rectangularly-shaped forms rising 100 meters and more. Moving along the base of the wall made me see the enormity of the challenge ahead of us. The face was punctuated with hundreds of indentations, some extending just a meter or two deep before reaching dead ends. Finding a passage through was going to be a painstaking process of trial and error.

We struggled along, taking turns dodging in and out of crevices in a sort of insane dance with no accompaniment. Glowstones illuminated some of the openings, while others were practically pitch dark, leaving us to grope our way until we found their predictable ends. Carver worms were busy on many of the vertical surfaces making it difficult to feel our way without dislodging them, and the walking surfaces were treacherously uneven. Time and time again, one of us would find a promising opening where the others would follow only to be stopped by a vertical wall. Eventually we stopped, tired of the tedium and convinced there had to be a better way. Sitting near a tonc spout, we drank the refreshing liquid from cupped hands and talked of our options.

It was then, in between sentences, that I heard a humming noise coming from directly behind my head. Bril and Togn, caught off guard by what they saw behind me, looked at first concerned, but that gave way quickly to humor. I slowly turned my head and body just enough to see behind me and came face to face with a huge, segmented creature having six wings. It hovered just a meter away from me, it's nose moving as if sniffing.

"She likes your smell," laughed Togn.

"She?" I questioned, not taking my eyes off it.

"It's a uenthy moth," said Bril. "It lays the eggs that hatch into carver worms. It's totally harmless and Togn is probably right. They have a very acute sense of smell and often follow their noses more than they do their flight paths."

I relaxed, going from hunched to upright.

"How did you know it was a she?" I asked, half turning back to the two of them.

"The females have three segments and six wings," replied Togn.

"So, I guess the males are different?" I asked.

"Yes," said Bril. "The males only have two segments and they're not as friendly as the females. In fact, we'd have all been locked in battle with it right now if it had been a male. They are nasty and attack you from both ends -- mandibles in the front and a spike in the rear."

In the next instant the moth turned and lumbered off, flying slowly along the spires. There was a sort of quiet confidence to it, as if it harbored some wisdom innate only to itself, and to its kind. I felt a strange connection to it and wondered where it was bound, and if I'd see it again. But that thought was soon lost as I could sense something in the air, a change in flow, a difference in density. And there was this sound, a sort of deep drone. Slowly, other moths drifted into view, at first sporadic and few, but then gaining rapidly in numbers. The deep drone kept increasing until the sound reverberated off the stone, vibrating me to the core. And then suddenly, they were upon us. A huge swarm of moths, filling the air at all levels until it was difficult to make out any details on the horizon. They flew around us, some coming dangerously close before rapidly gaining altitude to clear the spires. Instinctively we dove to the ground and lay as flat as we could. It seemed like an eternity before the buzzing of the wings and the whoosh of moth bodies subsided. As we sat up there was just a wide stream of them at the highest elevation pouring over the spires.

"Does that happen often?" I asked, incredulous.

"It does," replied Bril. "The moths mass together when they're ready to lay their eggs and that's pretty frequent."

As I surveyed the last of the moths passing over the spires and then brought my view back to the ground, I caught my breath at the scene. There were hundreds of moths walking on the ground, working their way along the spires. Sensing my next question, Togn explained.

"Those are the frail ones," he explained. "For any number of reasons they can't make it over the spires so they have to walk. Some may be missing wings, others might have been injured and some no doubt won't make it just because they're ill."

"Have to walk?" I asked, a realization dawning.

Almost at the same time the others also made the connection.

"Maybe, we should follow them," I suggested, feeling sure they'd show us the way through the wall of spires.

"Exactly," quipped Bril.

CHAPTER EIGHT

Wrestling with Stone

We fell in line behind a moth that was moving at a strong pace and followed her along the wall. Eventually she fell in line with others and soon we were in a sea of moths marching blindly to wherever they were going. I only hoped that somehow they knew the way through the wall and that we weren't on an even longer journey of simply working our way around it. As the time passed it became clear that many were not going to make it. Almost every few meters I noticed one nearby would falter, stop, and then just quit moving, only to be passed by and summarily moved out of the way by those pushing forward from behind. It seemed like a cruel and unceremonious end at a time when they were on the doorstep to their final mystery. Fortunately, the strong one we had chosen to follow showed no signs of weakening and even seemed to be picking up speed.

Finally, after skirting along the face of the wall for an interminable time our moth dodged to the left and made its way through a wide opening with tens of others. Now we found ourselves in a zig zagging canyon that appeared to be blocked at every turn. But each time we thought our progress would be stopped, multiple holes became visible in the stone. Each hole would only accommodate one moth, or one of us at a time, so we took our turns with the moths, crawling through dense tunnels until we emerged once again in the next canyon. Then, it was uphill once more until the next set of tunnels. The tunnel sizes were especially troubling for Togn with his wide frame. Bril and I often found ourselves waiting for him when we exited our tunnels as it took him longer to find tunnels wide enough to pass through.

I lost track of how many tunnels we crawled through and even lost track of the lead moth we had started following. Now, they all kind of looked the same and it seemed these were probably the strongest ones, and the ones that would make it all the way, to wherever we were going. I was growing weary of the canyon's ascent and when we had to crawl that was also uphill, taking a toll on our knees and elbows. Fortunately my new leather pants kept my knees from being rubbed raw, but my elbows were not so lucky.

As each of us climbed out of yet another tunnel I could see a highpoint in front of us with what appeared to be a drop off on the other side. After helping Togn squeeze out from an extra tight tunnel, we staggered upward. At the top we breathed a collective sigh of relief. There, stretched before us was a downhill landscape, with the Spires of Micknok in the distance. Moths swarmed around us continuing their relentless trek and we gladly fell in line once again.

On this side, and from our elevated view, the landscape was more rugged and had denser canyons laid out in mind boggling maze patterns. I knew that when we were once again inside them, finding our way would become problematic. I stepped to the side, tugging at Bril and Togn to follow me so we could get out of the moths' path. On the sidelines I asked Bril what he thought about our chances of making it through the mazes. He was not optimistic and told me that when he first saw them, he felt great despair.

"Once we're down there, inside those canyons, we'll loose the view of the Spires of Micknok again. Then what?" he asked, forlornly. It was then that I saw Bril at his true age and experience level, and realized that I might have to adjust my understanding of his abilities. Togn, on the other hand, was largely undaunted, and quick to offer a suggestion.

"The moths like to place their eggs in secluded canyons that don't have outlets," he explained. "Those canyons are very still and have little air movement. If we follow the path where we can still feel the air, we should make it through."

Bril considered the suggestion deeply and finally brightened a little. "Yes. That might work," he said. "Plus we can watch how the moths enter the canyons. By now, many will be filled to capacity, so new entrants will have to wait, or turn and move on to another canyon. It might work."

With that, we fell back into the crush of moths and descended into the canyon maze. Time after time we stopped, watching the moth movements and sensing where the air was coming from. Sometimes we ended up hitting dead ends, but most of the time we made forward progress. The Spires of Micknok would stray into view at various intervals, helping us to stay on track with them. Within a short time the numbers of moths began to diminish as more and more turned up canyons in search of places to deposit their eggs and finish out their lives.

We rounded a corner and could see that finally the Spires of Micknok were getting closer so we picked up the pace. By now, just a few hundred moths accompanied us and I began to wonder why they weren't moving into the canyons we were passing. As we walked I studied their features and noticed their wings were much shorter than those we had first encountered, and they were shinier and seemingly more vibrant.

"Togn," I said. "These moths are different somehow."

"Yes," he said matter-of-factly, "they're nymphs. Young ones that have recently come out of their cocoons."

"So, where are they going?"

"Once their wings get dry enough to unfurl, they'll fly away, looking for mates."

The word mates slammed into our collective consciousness and at that moment we all looked at each other in horror, and then to the air, scanning it for any signs of male moths.

"We better get away from these" yelled Bril, and we broke into a run, dodging our way through nymphs. But, it was too late. A male strafed Bril, raking its tail spike down his back as he ducked to get away. I saw blood ooze through his clothes and raced to his side, grabbing his arm to help him get to cover. Cover was a small rock overhang just big enough for him, but not for me. As I let go of his arm he dropped to his knees and then crouched down low. I spun around and saw Togn deftly dodging mandible and stinger strikes from two males. In a panic I looked for some kind of weapon, anything that would be more effective than just our hands.

"Take this," Bril yelled, handing me a long, swordlike shard of stone he had pulled from the spire beside him.

I raced to Togn, wildly swinging the sword stone, hoping I'd be menacing enough to scare them off. Instead, they turned on me, swooping and diving, and maneuvering into striking or biting positions. Just when I was ready to break away and make a run for it thinking any hope of driving them off was futile, slow motion took over. An instant stretched into the future and I clearly saw each attack coming with incredible clarity. I was able to deal a blow to the one coming at my front and still spin around quickly enough to deal a blow to the one attacking from behind. In the meantime, Togn found a suitable stone shard and joined in the fray, jabbing and slashing with lightening-like strikes, taking on first one and then the next. as they grew more confused about where to focus their attacks. In one instance I spotted an opening. The soft underbelly was exposed as it threw back its stinger to gain altitude and at that second I thrust the shard upward as hard as I could. The surface gave way and the shard drove deep into the belly causing a torrent of yellow, fizzy liquid to cascade down onto me. At first I was sure it was my end, that the substance was acid. Instead I only felt its warmth and a slight stickiness as the creature collapsed on the ground, gyrating and convulsing. Almost at the same moment, Togn struck a solid blow on the second one's tail spike, sending it spinning uncontrollably. It glanced off a spire, regained its flight controls and shot straight upward before jetting off down the path ahead of us.

We ran to Bril unsure of how badly he'd been hit, and hoping against all odds it wasn't anything too serious. We found him sitting up, a slight smile on his lips.

"Are you okay?" Togn asked.

"Never better," replied Bril, standing up and stretching. "Thanks to a ball creature."

"Ahhh, good," said Togn.

"Are you two talking about that creature that asks what it can do for you?"

"That's the one," Bril said. "You've encountered them?"

"Twice now," I replied. "But where do they come from?"

Bril explained that no one really knew, but that they often show up when those with human forms are in distress, but only a limited number of times. He thought there was a finite limit to how often they'd assist one being, but Togn chimed in and claimed they were not limited in how many times they could assist, but rather in how often over a given period of time. He said they could only assist once every two glow cycles in the underworld, but that he didn't know the frequency in the upper world.

"What did yours appear as?" I asked Bril.

"It was a traveler, complete with grey skin and big round eyes," jokingly widening his eyes as far as he could. Togn chuckled from his belly, making a hilarious sound that we all cracked up to. Then as the laughter subsided he pointed to me and the yellow bug fluid sticking to me, and the laughter started all over again.

There, with my two new friends, sharing a laugh, I realized that if I had ever been creating memories before I arrived in Octa, they might have been very much like that one. We had already been put to some tests and had made it through, and that gave me a little more confidence that we might be able to survive whatever lay ahead of us. Now, I was glad there could even be some laughs along the way. But before leaving I looked around for a familiar obelisk like those the ball creatures had left behind for me. Bril and Togn looked at me questioning.

"Where is the obelisk?" I asked.

"Obelisk?" Bril questioned.

"Yes, when I've seen them they've ended up as obelisks with messages carved on their faces."

"That's unusual," said Togn. "The ones I've encountered just turned into part of the landscape -- a rock, a pool of lava..." his voice trailed off.

"Look," said Bril, resting his hand on a boulder. "This is the one I saw."

I studied the boulder to see if there was anything resembling carving, but it was just another boulder with nothing to indicate its previous existence. Apparently, my experiences were going to be different than theirs, and I briefly wondered how else that might be before turning to follow them.

As we stepped out into the canyon, setting our sights on the Spires of Micknok, we were relieved to see there were just a few nymphs straggling along. Still, all three of us carried long stone shards in case any male moths showed up. I wanted desperately to get the dried bug fluid off me as it coated my hair and clothes and was starting to reek. But nowhere was there even a tonc bubbler or stream, and other than the flood Horse and I had been caught in, I hadn't seen any other water.

The canyons began thinning out, the nymphs' wings dried so they could fly off, and our choices in following air movement became easier and easier until we emerged into a wide expanse of flat land with random outcroppings of spires scattered across the horizon. Beyond, lay the Spires of Micknok, glowing lavender with a blue-green mist along their bases. Togn said that it was in the mists that we would find the small lengths of everstone that we needed for a StarStone Scepter. As we walked, Bril pulled out a length of braided goat hair given to him by Brukin. He told me we should get a column of everstone at exactly that length and that its diameter should be no longer than the length of his thumb. He also said the piece we select would have to be a six-sided piece, and not the more common eight-sided.

Glowstones were low when we entered the canyon at the base of the spires. Their enormity made me catch my breath, for standing within a hundred meters of their bottoms, I couldn't see the tops. Scattered across their faces were vertical strips of glowstones giving them their characteristic lavender appearance, and the texture of the stone was like glass. Tens of meters up their sides started a layer of younger stone that cascaded downward, gradually becoming columns of smaller and smaller diameters. We walked to the base and began searching for clusters of six-sided columns. It was a daunting task as the ones that matched the length of Bril's goat-hair measure were not along the edges, but rather a few meters in. We had to climb on the outer, short columns and peer deeper in to spot the configurations of those with the right lengths. Not surprisingly the six-sided ones were difficult to find. But finally, Togn who was between Bril and I called out that he thought he had one. We moved over to him and sure enough, he pointed to a column that had six outer sides and that was made up of 12 smaller columns with six sides each. Bril laid his thumb on one of the outermost columns to confirm the diameter was correct. It was, but then we had to figure out how to remove it. It was completely encircled by other columns and as we studied the situation we realized we'd have to remove layer after layer of outer stones to finally get to it.

That prospect was definitely not one we wanted to face. After a while of studying the situation, it was Togn who said he had an idea. He reached in, placing his very large thumb on the top of the column and slowly began to rock it back and forth, trying to loosen the hold the surrounding stone had on it. At first it looked futile as time and time again he stopped to inspect, and then continued. Then, about the tenth time he paused we looked in, and we could see that a space had opened up between the column's sides and the surrounding stone.

While Togn continued loosening the column, Bril and I scouted around for some shards we could use to leverage the column from its place. We squatted at the edge of the spires and focused on the new growth. Those columns peeled apart easily because they weren't bound in by new growth. Bril loosened a couple of them and then pulled them from their sockets, leaving behind just the shards that filled the spaces between columns. We selected a variety of sizes and shapes, and went back to join Togn who had stopped loosening the column and stood there studying it intently.

"We found these shards," Bril announced, laying them out on the top of the column. "Do you think they will work?"

"We'll see," replied Togn, "but I wish I had my father's stone working tools instead. He had a stone drill he would use for loosening especially stubborn firestone shards and he even let me use it a few times," he stopped, seemingly reliving the experience. "He was the best," he said forlornly. Then, coming back to the task at hand, "Well, let's see if some of these will work."

Togn sorted through the shards and finally selected two long, thin ones. Each one had barbs on its pointed end. Togn leaned over the column, resting his elbows on the stones on each side to steady his arms, and lowered the pointed ends of the shards into the spaces on two sides of the column. Then, he rubbed the barbs on the sides of the column to create notches, and then applied pressure to trap the column between the shards, and lifted. To our surprise the column began rising. I could feel Togn's concentration as he tried to balance the pressure of the shards against the possibility of breaking them. Slowly the column rose and when it was far enough above the surrounding stone, Bril reached in deftly and grabbed it with his fingers. Togn breathed a sigh of relief and released the shards. Once Bril had the column farther up, Togn grabbed on and pulled it from its resting place.

At that point it was the most beautiful column of everstone I had ever seen, even though it was the only one I had ever seen. Bril used the goat hair measure to check the length, and announced it was long enough, but a little too long. Togn selected a flat, wide shard and using its sharp edge, carefully scored the column on each face around its circumference. Then he laid it on a solid piece of stone with the scored mark extending just over its edge, clamped it firmly with one forearm while swiftly bringing the edge of his huge hand down on the column just outside the scored line. It was a clean break, with the extra length dropping off leaving behind the one that would hopefully become our StarStone Scepter. Togn grabbed the column and together we bounded off the stone to the canyon floor, heading off in search of someone at the Superterrestrial Order.

As we traveled deeper into the canyon the air started to become more humid and for the first time we saw pools of water. I was relieved because even though the stench of the bug fluid that coated me from head to toe had subsided, it was stubbornly caked in my clothes and hair. We stopped at a large pool where I peeled off my leather and climbed into the refreshing liquid. Bril and Togn followed suit and before long we were basking in the simple pleasure of washing. I saved washing my clothes for last because I knew I'd have to put them on right away or face the wrath of dry, stiff leather chaffing my skin. We spent a long time resting on the glass-like stone surrounding the pool, watching the glowstones gradually grow dim. Togn was full of stories, partly because unlike me, he had memories, and unlike Bril, he had been around. When he started telling the third story about the time he had gotten lost in a shaft in Firston I drifted off into a deep, dreamless sleep.

CHAPTER NINE

A City and Answers

I awoke startled by hot air cascading down my left side and when I turned in that direction I faced a gaping mouth, filled with teeth and dripping saliva. For what seemed like an eternity I lay motionless afraid to even move my eyes. The creature attached to the mouth was a five-meter -long lizard with a three-veined fin on its head, a horn sitting at the end of its nose, and great spikes running the length of its back. I rolled my eyes toward Togn and Bril who were both still sound asleep and snoring almost in unison. The glowstones were very dim so I couldn't make out anything beyond the creature to see if it was alone. At that moment it turned its head to stare at me with one of its creepy eyeballs. My hand moved ever so slowly toward my stone shard weapon as I watched for any sign of movement from the creature. It was so close that not only was its breath enveloping me, but I could see its nostrils flare open and closed as it inhaled and exhaled. With the shard in my grip I was about to leap toward Bril and Togn when the creature lunged at me, just missing my left leg with its horn as I jumped back.

Bril and Togn were suddenly awake, wide-eyed and struggling to their feet. I swung my shard delivering a glancing blow to its cheek, but I might as well have saved my strength for running because its armored scales deflected the attack and sent my shard flying on a short trip to the ground by its feet. By now, Bril and Togn had sprung into action trying to draw it away from me as I backed away, closer and closer to a spire behind me hoping to find some type of cover. Bril and Togn shouted and lunged toward it finally capturing its attention. I yelled at them to be careful since the shards wouldn't pierce the scales.

The creature lunged toward them, bucking its horned head and gnashing its teeth. Bril dodged to his right as the animal came at him. It was then that Togn saw his opening. He deftly slipped in beside the attacker, wrapped his huge, strong arms around its neck and toppled on his back, twisting the creature's frame and throwing it off its feet. With the soft underbelly exposed, Bril raced in and sank his shard deeply into the beast, striking its heart. Togn maintained his grip while the life ran from the animal, and then slowly extricated himself from beneath its neck. I felt an overwhelming sense of relief as I dropped to my knees to stop the trembling in my legs. Bril and Togn now stood at the creature's head, talking admiringly about its complexity and strength. Togn said there were a few moments when he wasn't sure he could hold on any longer, and Bril told him laughingly that he had seen those moments in his face.

Now, recomposed, I joined them where we recounted the battle and tried to make light of the whole event. But I could see in their faces an apprehension born now from experience, and in myself I felt a creeping anxiety of things to come. We were after all, in perhaps the most peaceful of the underworlds, yet together, we had experienced two life threatening events, and neither was the kind that could be described as trivial, or of the nature that we could easily avoid dire consequences. I had an awareness that these tests were necessary so we could see if we really had the resolve to travel deeper into Octa's underworlds. From my own perspective there was really no choice. The Tachina were no doubt gaining on us and standing and fighting them without the critical knowledge we were seeking would mean certain death. My new friends however, didn't really have the same pressure as me, and could conceivably choose to part company with me at any point. I only hoped they would be able to find enough purpose in our journey to stay the course, because without them it appeared I would stand little chance of staying alive.

We gathered our few items and continued toward the Canyon of Micknok, hopeful that we could get our everstone enchanted and find a passage into Firston. The air moved past us with increasing force turning eventually into a wind as we neared a narrowing portion of the canyon in our downward trek.

When we rounded a corner and passed through the narrows, the canyon suddenly opened up to more than 10 times its previous width. The familiar foundens lined the canyon walls but because they were constructed into columns of stone, rather than solid stone, they had a highly refined appearance and were very stylish with rooftops made of short columns stepping back to ever taller and taller columns. The glowstones were bright and they illuminated the busy scene in the canyon where reasoning, and non-reasoning beings of all kinds intermingled. Here, in yet another community in Canyonlands, I was impressed with the tranquility and the conviviality that passed for everyday life. Perhaps it was something in the tonc, or maybe the lack of ownership that allowed the peacefulness to prevail. But I was perplexed that I even noticed. Did I have experiences to the contrary? Were there events in my hidden past where beings did not get along? Where they conflicted with each other? Fought with each other, even when life or death were not at issue?

We strode through the crowds taking in the sights, sounds and smells. Everything was so fresh. It was as if the place had just now arisen from the stone, and the air had a delicious feeling to it as it entered my nose and coursed through my lungs. We were so involved in the moment that we didn't notice the startled looks we were generating among the residents until four very large and officially-dressed men approached us, brandishing some sort of finely-crafted, glassy shards.

They surrounded us, shouting something I couldn't understand. It was Bril who interceded by raising his arm and speaking something back very apologetically. Next he turned his shard and handed it to one of the men, dull end first. Togn and I immediately understood and turned ours over to them as well. The men were immediately satisfied with our actions, each of them touching our shoulders lightly as they went on their way.

"Sorry," said Bril. "I should have thought of that. They don't allow any kind of weapon in any Canyonlands community. They're okay in the outlands, but we're supposed to check them in when we enter communities."

"What kind of weapons were those?" I asked, wondering about the glassy shards the four carried.

"They're Enchanted Greatshards," replied Togn. "All the rangers in Canyonlands have them. Those were glowing red so they have the stun and paralyze enchantment. Nasty things and nothing you want to mess around with."

"Sure glad you knew what they were talking about, Bril," I said. "How many languages do you know anyway?"

"I guess all of them," he replied.

"But how can that be? Is it just a natural ability or something?"

"Suppose it is," he replied. "When I was very young I started seeing connections between sounds and before I knew it I could understand anything, anyone said."

I smiled a broad smile, "Well, I'm sure glad Brukin suggested you come along because that skill is really going to come in handy." Then, to refocus our efforts, "You know, I guess we should figure out how to find that Superterrestrial Order. Do you think most here would know about them?"

"Most definitely," said Bril, "It's not like they're a secret or anything, and I've been kind of listening for someone speaking your language since you're the one who has to ask so you can get to the right Superterrestrial." He saw the confusion on my face so he explained further. "There are Superterrestrials for all languages and the only way to get to one using your language is to make your first inquiry to someone who speaks your language. I know, kind of complicated, but it's just the way it works. And I see what you're thinking, but no, I cannot do it for you because it is not my need"

We continued our walk, training our ears on the languages being spoken. On the way I also focused on the different kinds of foundens and noticed a much wider variety of them. Unlike in the first community I had entered, this one had foundens where crafts people used their specialized or artistic skills in creating unique or more highly useful items than those that could be created by machines in the standard foundens. Togn told me that many craft masters created what you wanted using the resources you supplied, and did it only for the simple joy they got from the task. Other times they might require you to supply something extra, or a resource that was particularly difficult for them to find. Sometimes too, they might want to trade something you had, in return for creating the item you wanted.

It was as we were passing a craft founden with packs, saddlebags and other containers made of a silky material that we heard my language being spoken by the craftmaster and a child. We all stopped in unison and bounded up the steps.

The craft master was actually a craft mistress who was going back to welding the silky fabric with a long wand. Sensing our presence she turned and greeted us. Her short hair was feathered across her brow with wisps dropping in front of her very large eyes. She was not of as refined an appearance as other females I had encountered in Canyonlands with her exaggerated lip and nose sizes, but she was pleasant and had an otherwise eye-pleasing and petite female form.

"Dear, dear, you are all in need of satchels or packs, or something," she said with a lilting tone. "Just help yourselves to whatever you need and if you ever get near a carver worm hatchling area remember me and bring back some egg cases for thread."

"Thank you for the offer," I replied, "but I was wondering if you might be able to recommend one of the Micknok Superterrestrial Order who speaks our language? We have an item we'd like to have enchanted."

"You will need to see Oshya," she replied, matter-of-factly. "And if I'm not mistaken he is probably teaching the fine art of discernment over at the Rune Summit. If you leave soon you can probably catch him as he's returning to the Order's grounds. You get there by continuing down the canyon until you see the huge statue of Micknok, and right behind that you'll find the entrance to the Order. Just wait outside and Oshya will approach you."

"But how will he know we're there to see him?" I questioned.

"That's a silly question," she teased. "After all, I just told you he was teaching discernment, and one must have a high degree of that to teach it. So he'll probably not only know you're there to see him, but will also know what you want," she smiled even more teasingly.

"Of course," I chuckled. "Makes sense."

"If you have a piece of everstone for a scepter, I have a pack somewhere here," her voice trailed off as she sorted through a stack of satchels and packs. "Ah, here it is," she hoisted a pack with shoulder straps from the pile. "See, here? That's a special slotted pouch for your scepter, and it seals up so you can't lose it, even when you're running from Drac Lizards," she smiled broadly.

"You mean like that thing that attacked us just outside of town?" asked Bril.

"Really long, with a horn and spikes on its back?" She inquired matter-of-factly, and then seeing us nod in unison, "Yes, that's a Drac. They love to feast on carver worm nests but if you're carrying everstone they are attracted to you. Something to do with the way it interacts with your skin and the odor it produces that apparently only they can smell. Anyway, putting your scepter into a pouch when you're not using it helps a lot. There are also several pockets that will hold other useful items you might need to carry."

As I took the pack and slipped the everstone into the pouch I was amazed at the strength of the fabric and the multitude of various sized pockets on its interior. The outside had intricate designs she had embellished on its surface. There were four, elaborate concentric circles, each open on one side and linked like a chain at their openings. Elongated spirals connected the lower openings of each circle to the upper openings of the next, and the whole colorful design stood in 3D effect on the pack's stunning pale green, shimmering finish.

"You do really beautiful work," I said. "Is there a meaning to the designs?"

"That one's what I call an interworld traveler's pack," she explained. "The designs in this case symbolize Octa's four underworlds with their spiral connectors -- the places you'll be able to locate with a StarStone Scepter. Can I ask where you're traveling to?"

"Eventually we need to reach the Land of the Misanthrope," I said.

"Well, you'll be going into the other two underworlds then because you can't just skip the ones in between here and there. While you are here be sure to get up to eight enchantments on the pack, which is its limit. Also, I would love to have some brood foot plant for making the dye like the color used on your pack. You can find it in The Mists near rock outcroppings with springs. Just send it back with a messenger," she stopped, suddenly looking concerned and sad. "The Mists are bad enough, but the Land of the Misanthrope is really dangerous. You should learn all you can as fast as you can before getting there. Ask a lot of questions of everyone you encounter, but once you reach the Land of the Misanthrope be very careful who, and what you spend time with. I only wish I had more I could give to help you," her voice trailed off.

I offered my hand, but instead she threw her arms around my neck and hugged me very tightly, and then did the same to Bril and Togn.

"I'm Ataia," she announced, "and the three of you are now in my heart."

None of us knew what to say, until Bril broke the silence.

"Ataia, I am Bril," and he gestured at Togn and me, "and they are Togn and Keln. We are honored to be in your heart and will always strive to stay true to our spirit essences."

Immediately she seemed relieved and comforted, and she smiled a big, wide smile and said, "Then go, get out of here before you miss Oshya," shooing us with her hands.

Outside I asked Bril what it was all about and he said he was sure she was a Spirit Familiar, a being that identified with the spirit essences of others. He said it was good to be in her heart because we would each get a certain level of protection from beings that might try to bend our spirits to do things in their service. But what he told us next made me even more anxious about our journey.

"Spirit Familiars also have a clairvoyant ability to see spirit challenges in your near future," he explained. "Her apprehension about our travels into the underworld showed that she has foreseen troubling events affecting one or possibly all of our spirits. We will need to watch closely for changes in each other."

CHAPTER TEN

Magical Things

And so it was, with increasing trepidation we set out down the canyon to find Oshya. I could tell that Togn was perhaps as troubled as I was, but Bril on the other hand seemed to be optimistic and very much into the moment. I took that as a lesson for myself, realizing once again that I had been too transfixed on the future, and that paying more attention to the moment might serve me better. I resolved to practice being more aware, and that began with focusing on the life and events all around me as we made our way to the Superterrestrial Order.

In that new found awareness I began to notice so many subtle differences in the beings we passed, and in my immediate surroundings, that I drifted into a consciousness other than my mind. It was as if a deeper level of my being came to the surface making the ordinary become extraordinary. What I had originally seen as just a long, winding canyon lined with foundens of all the same construction, actually turned out to be a community as architecturally diverse as it was population diverse. The stepped-back roofs of the foundens used a wide variety of spires and columns and many of them were ornately decorated with carvings. Even the entrances displayed an amazing wealth of separate details setting each one off from the next. The beings we encountered came in all colors, sizes and shapes, and even though all the reasoning ones had the familiar human form, the differences in facial and body features were immense. I also saw subtle differences in their interactions with each other where some would touch and caress freely and openly, while others maintained distances between themselves that were not breached. The variety of language was also immense and I wondered what it was like for Bril to be picking up bits and pieces of all the different conversations.

Eventually we came to a narrowing of the canyon and a sharp bend. As we rounded the corner a huge statue appeared, rising almost as tall as the surrounding spires. The image was of a male human form standing in a knowing pose with one hand on his hip and the other at his side. The stone head bore thick hair cascading downward on each side of his face. The eyes were narrow set, framing a large nose against his wide face. His ears were unnaturally large, extending to his jawline and his lips were pursed. The expression was one of resolve with a sort of knowing that made me feel a sense of security. A flowing tunic extended to his knees barely obscuring the folded-down tops of form-fitting boots. Around his waist he wore a sword-like instrument and on his shoulder was a long-slender pouch hung by a strap. Standing there, against the backdrop of the Micknok Spires he seemed to be exactly where he should be, a sort of beacon to the history of the place.

We strolled beneath the statue and around to the back where an immense alcove, previously obscured by the statue, rose 50 meters or more with nothing more on its face than an inscription meticulously carved into the smooth, glass-like stone. Bril read the inscription out loud.

"Order of the Superterrestrials."

Extending outward from the center of the alcove was a stepped-down water fall leading to a circular fountain. Beings congregated around the fountain and on benches scattered across and around the scene. I had never yet seen so many strange and wonderful creatures in this land that felt so strange to me. The variety was at once startling and breathtaking so that my senses were overtaken. The sights and smells and light transported me to serenity, and I could see Bril and Togn were affected the same way.

We found an empty bench nestled between small spires, and sat down.

"Have you ever seen this before?" I asked Togn.

"It is my first visit," he replied. "I have heard stories about it, but they didn't really prepare me for this."

In the next moment we were swept away by surprise for appearing before us, as if dropped onto the stone floor from nowhere, came a short being with features similar to the ones of the statue. He had silvery-white hair thick on the top and falling to thin, cropped strands surrounding his face. His eyes were intensely green, narrow set and his ears stuck out on each side of his head, poking through the hair. His tunic was cropped at the knees and the attached hood was fastened with a finely carved green stone clasp resembling what I immediately recognized as plant leaves. Before any of us could speak, he did.

"I believe you have need of a StarStone Scepter," he said with an all-knowing lilt.

I slipped the piece of everstone from its pouch in the backpack and presented it to him, surprising even myself at the ceremoniousness of it all.

"Yes," he said admiringly. "This will," he paused handling and studying it, "almost do."

My heart sank remembering the difficulty we had in acquiring it while wondering at the same time if it would work at all, or if we would need to repeat our efforts.

"You see," he began slowly. "The everstone you have here is near perfect in dimension and is a fine specimen. But it will need some polishing before it will be ready for enchantment."

"Polishing?" Togn questioned, seeming to immediately understand his implications.

"Yes," Oshya replied lightly. "It needs a reflective luster. Not one hastily done on a simple whetstone, but rather done with tonc water and the very fine fibers of carver worm egg cases. It should be a simple matter once you have the egg case fibers," he paused, adding cautiously, "if one of you has some knowledge of polishing stone."

We looked to Togn, hoping, from his experience in Firston and working with stone all his life, that he might just have that skill. Catching our gaze he smiled knowingly.

"My father was a master at smoothing and polishing stone and fortunately for us I learned from him."

"Excellent!" quipped Oshya. "I thought so. The nearest place where you can acquire egg case fibers that aren't already spoken for is in Wind Silk Canyon. You continue out here to the left until you come to a fork in the road. Take the left fork and you will find it on your right. It has a narrow entrance, but that denotes it from all the other canyons nearby. This time of the seasons it should be empty of moths laying eggs but you should beware of flesh ripper serpents. They are particularly troublesome in there and greatly covet the egg cases. Your best defense is stealth."

With that, he held out his hand, gesturing for the back pack, while simultaneously pulling out a cylindrical crystal from a multi-compartmentalized leather pouch he wore hanging from his shoulder.

I handed the pack to him and he immediately appeared thoughtful, as if he was carefully considering his options. Then he turned his gaze to us, focusing on and studying each of us in turn. His eyes took on a luminescent quality with a blankness behind his pupils. Suddenly, the crystal seemed to come to life as a light grey light at first gathered in its core and then shot from its bottom, spreading instantly over the entire back pack. Oshya placed his thumb on the top of the crystal and the light went out.

Instantly he was back from the trancelike state.

"I have entrained the enchantment to respond to an individual memory of each of you. That way, only the three of you can use it, and, no one else will want it since it will be useless to them. You will find in the lower levels of Octa that there are many beings who want to acquire and own things. It's very different from Canyonlands in that respect," he paused, "Well in all respects actually, but that's one of the biggies. The activation sequence is the same for each of you, but it calls for each of you to use a memory unique to you and to be touching the pack in different places. That way, it is possible for all three of you to use it at one time."

With that he handed the pack to me and instructed me to think about my fall into Canyonlands while holding onto the left strap of the pack. I was at first taken aback, wondering how he had such deep knowledge of my existence on Octa. I could see he understood my concern.

"You," he said to me, "Are pretty much a blank slate, no doubt because you have lost your memories. I see these aspects of beings when I focus on them. It's not something I do unconsciously...I must have a need and the need must always be in their interest, not mine. Your fall into Canyonlands when you were astride your faithful companion you called Horse, was a defining moment for you. The Tachina on one side and a seemingly bottomless pit on the other. Diving into the abyss is indelibly carved in your memory and will be something that won't easily be erased. For that reason it is an ideal memory for entraining enchantments. Now, try it out."

I grabbed onto the left strap, but Oshya corrected me, saying the left is determined by it's position when being worn. I grabbed the other strap and then remembered being astride horse on the ledge, and then plunging into the darkness below. Immediately I felt very light, as if I could almost float upward without any effort. When I looked at Togn I could see pure amazement on his very large face. Bril was more animated in his ability to understand and he reached toward me, feeling in the air until his hand found my shoulder.

"I can feel him," he said with amazement, "But he's totally gone from view."

"Yes," said Oshya, "and that's important to remember. You may be invisible, but you're not invincible. Things can still harm you if they make contact."

Oshya then told me to change the place I was holding the pack, and immediately, the feeling of lightness went away and I could see that Togn and Bril were once again able to look into my eyes. Oshya then asked me to pass the pack to Togn. Togn followed his instructions and instantly disappeared before our eyes. In turn, Bril learned his activation, coming back into view only after he had "taken a little walk," he said.

"That is so amazing," Bril said coming back into view. "I can think of many interesting uses."

"And you should make sure that each use is really needed," counseled Oshya, "because they are not unlimited. You will know the enchantment is weakening when parts of you remain visible. So, always use your own stealthy abilities first, and then resort to the enchantment when those no longer work" he paused a long pause, looking off into the distance. When his attention returned to the trio his face was grave.

"You are going the the Land of the Misanthrope and of course must pass through Firston and The Mists, first. In Firston you will no doubt encounter Ash Rain for which none of you are prepared because you have skin, which Ash Rain burns."

With that he pulled a black crystal from his pouch and went trancelike again. This time, a black cloud formed around the backpack before sinking into the fabric and disappearing. He told us that when the rain begins that we should gather closely together and make sure that each of us is touching the pack in some way. The result is a large invisible umbrella that is impervious to the Ash Rain. He called the enchantment, Cover, and said it would also work for other types of damaging materials that might come at us from any direction.

Next, Oshya said that on such an arduous journey through three underworlds we would be in places where tonc would not be readily available. He removed a silver crystal from his pouch, and went trancelike causing a golden brown mist to form and drop heavily into one of the interior backpack pockets. He told us the pocket was programmed to produce Amber whenever the wearer's energy dropped to dangerous levels. The Amber was a solid version of Tonc that could be chewed and swallowed to boost energy. Everybody could share the Amber as it was not solely for the wearer. He suggested being fluid with who wore the pack and try to keep it on the person who was most tired. He said the enchantment was called Nourish.

"Now," Oshya began, "I am placing two more enchantments on this pack called Multiply," as he drew a golden crystal from his pouch. He went trancelike and yellow mist settled on the pack. But this time the color did not disappear, instead attaching to the finely embroidered threads Ataia had woven. The whole pack took on a silky, glowing appearance. He told us the Multiply enchantments readied the pack for an additional eight enchantments. Then he struck a very serious tone and facial appearance.

"This pack could be the only thing standing between you and certain death," he said. "If it gets damaged too greatly, the enchantments will lose power, and some might simply fade away. You must do regular repairs by using the golden threads of the embroidery. It is quite beautiful, but its real purpose is to provide a strong thread for stitching repairs. Keep this pack in top shape and it will serve you well. If you lose it, I feel sorry for your spirits for you will be surely lost."

"Now," he said brightening, looking at each of us in turn. "Your weapons were confiscated, but, they really weren't very good. You should see Ialeo in the founden right next to the weapons check point as you leave Micknok on your way to Wind Silk Canyon," he was very precise. "He will get you outfitted properly for at least the early part of your journey, and, while there ask him for the contact shard of a weapon maker in The Mists."

"A contact shard?" I inquired of him.

"Yes," he replied, "It's a small, flat piece of memory stone bearing the name of the being. You follow the auto-updating direction lines to find them. I have placed mine in the pack along with a journal shard. Because much on Octa depends upon the easy and free exchange of items you will need to keep track of what items are due to whom."

"Like the dye and thread Ataia asked us for?" I asked.

"Yes, and the cloud crystals you will hopefully bring back to me," he said grinning broadly. "The journal shard records all these transactions, and transactions-to-be. As you near an item you need to gather, or a being whom you need to trade with, the shard glows with direction lines so you can find them easily. It's all very automatic, although it can be challenging to get in the vicinity of an item or being so that the journal shard glows. Now, if you venture a little further beyond Wind Silk Canyon you will enter Crystal Cove and that's where you can find the cloud crystals. They are not easy to find because they form the bases of Sky Crystals. Just be careful of the dark pools in there because as far as we know they are bottomless and have a tremendous amount of downward pressure. Few have ever escaped them. So, stick to the stone bridges and don't be tempted by images in the pools."

"Wow," I said. "It all seems so difficult?"

Oshya smiled quickly and then turned serious and said, "When you leave Canyonlands you will be on a perilous journey so learn all you can while you are here. Firston is another learning opportunity too, although a bit more challenging. But when you reach The Mists you will be entering a land with many new perils, especially those that attack the spirit. Use this time wisely."

Once again, the dread pushed down on my shoulders like giant weights. I wondered if it might not be easier to just stay in Canyonlands, and wait for the Tachina to catch up and take my chances. Well, our chances, although I wouldn't expect Bril and Togn to stick with me. And that was another factor. Bril was in search of his destiny, or at least a clue about it. And Togn was a bit of a lost soul perhaps in need of simple companionship, although I sensed a deeper aspect to him. Something venerable, like a craftsman who had lost his craft, or maybe, hadn't found it yet. It was at that moment that I sensed a stirring inside, like a recognition of something unique to myself that lay in the journey ahead. From that stirring in my consciousness came a new resolve to continue the journey, regardless of the perils. After all, what else did I have to do?

We bade farewell to Oshya and left the serenity of the Order. Back in the canyon the press of life continued at its leisurely pace and as the glowstones began to dim we reached the outskirts and found Ialeo's founden. Inside, a tall, dark-haired human-like being with a very square face and an eyepatch over its left eye stood up from a work bench and approached.

"Quark untoh nek etch?" he inquired in a mechanical-like manner.

"He wants to know who sent us," Bril translated. But as he was about to respond back, the being spoke in English to Bril.

"So it must have been Oshya," he half-inquired, half-stated.

"Yes," Bril answered. "Are you Ialeo?"

"You have found me," he replied. "What is your mission?"

"We are going to the Land of the Misanthrope to discover the secrets of defeating the Tachina," injecting myself into the conversation. "Oshya said you would know what kinds of weapons we'd need and that you could provide us with a contact shard for a weapon maker in The Mists."

"Certainly," Ialeo responded, reaching into a stone half-barrel and pulling out a long, slender stone weapon that very closely resembled a sword. "This is a crafted piece of steel stone that will serve you well in these upper regions. It is incredibly light, so you can swing it swiftly, yet is sturdy enough to deal damage to even the scales on a Drac Lizard. With the Sweet Water enchantment it will also serve you well in Firston when you get downwind from Smoke Striders or even Cinder Shell Titans."

He handed the stone sword to Togn, who immediately took to swinging and flailing with it in a sort of mock fight. Bril and I laughed at his antics causing him to stop and do a deep bow.

"It is amazingly light," Togn said, handing it to me.

"You're right," I said, feeling its weight as nothing more than the back pack I wore.

Ialeo pulled out two more steel stone swords and handed them toTogn and Bril in turn. Then he turned to a second barrel and removed a short stone cylinder a little bit longer than my forearm. It was white stone with orange and magenta swirls. At the end in his hand there were three notches. He demonstrated its use by placing one finger in each notch, aiming at a well-worn stone target and squeezing where he gripped it. Instantly, a hole the diameter of the weapon and half its length appeared in the thick target. We all let out a collective gasp.

"If not for the thickness of the stone that target is made from, the hole would go all the way through," explained Ialeo. "Aim for critical parts of beings -- heads and upper bodies to get the quickest results. It's called a Shot Stone. There are other types that punch numerous holes all at once that are better suited to the lower levels of Octa."

He handed the weapon to Togn and then passed by us going to a small, stone box. He withdrew a contact shard which he handed to Bril. The face of the stone was blank except for some carved letters.

"It says Warr," Bril told us.

"Yes," confirmed Ialeo. "You know your Gurji well," speaking first to Bril and then turning to all of us, "Warr is of the neut gender and so has the necessary temperament for making weapons fit for the lower levels. Down there, the challenges become more about emotion and spirit and less about brute force and strength. Warr will equip you well once you are beyond Firston."

Ialeo then strode to a compartmentalized stone face, reached inside one of the cubicles and withdrew a small, crystal orb. He held it out, resting it on his flattened palm where it turned deep blue. Immediately, we all felt a sense of dread, with great fear rising inside of us. Ialeo lifted the orb from his palm and instantly the feelings of dread and fear left us.

"You have experienced the power of a Dread Orb" Ialeo explained. "As long as you are behind it you will not be affected by it, so use it carefully. Otherwise it will affect many different types of beings on this planet, both on the surface and in the depths. Now, I believe you are well equipped for the early part of your journey, and don't forget, when you come back to Micknok you can securely check your weapons here with me instead of using the public founden next door. That way I will have time to inspect them and make any repairs or upgrades."

In turn we each thanked him, and then Bril asked the question that was fast becoming the one hanging on all of our lips whenever someone assisted us.

"Is there anything you need that we might be able to acquire for you?"

"Now that you ask," Ialeo said quickly, "I could use a length of Edge Stone for weapons maintenance. I go through quite a bit of it so whatever you can get would be most helpful. You can find it along the edges of dark pools. It will be the glossy black columnar stone that separates easily."

"Consider it done," I said.

Ialeo had three more items for us -- scabbards and belts to house our steel stone swords. We put them on, sheathed the swords and placed the Dread Orb into a perfectly-fitting pocket in the pack. The journal shard fit nicely into another pocket. Bril placed the contact shard for Warr in one of his button-down shirt pockets, and then we said goodbye once again and headed out into the canyon.

We turned left, basking in the now amber light of the glowstones and feeling more confident with our new weapons, and new knowledge. In a short distance, the canyon turned downward and began to narrow while its spires and cliff faces grew in stature and numbers. Spires were often topped with orb-like glowstones, casting their light great distances, while vertical, column-like glowstones illuminated the canyon from their embedded places in the canyon walls. Boulders of all imaginable colors lay fallen along the edges of our path. I wondered about the immense nature of Canyonlands and the seemingly infinite variety of stone. What amazed me more was how so many types of stone occurred naturally together, in a sort of hodgepodge arrangement that was not really arranged at all. The glowstones seemed extremely peculiar to me for their ability to mimic the passage of time on Octa's surface. Because many of them were at my level I strayed closer to them and noticed a very thin filament of light at their centers. So thin in fact that I couldn't understand how they emitted so much light. Their lengths and diameters were all different from each other so it seemed there weren't even two that were alike.

Bril and Togn had moved a distance ahead of me so I hurried to catch up, ever conscious of the unknown dangers and the comfort and safety in numbers. I was greatly appreciative of their companionship. After enduring my early time on Octa disconnected from reasoning beings it was now enjoyable and comforting to be able to converse and share life experience. It was especially encouraging to have help available for what I now understood would be a challenging journey.

CHAPTER ELEVEN

Challenge of the Serpents

We rounded a bend and there was a draft of warm air filled with the smell of stone and something I couldn't name. Bril was first to comment saying he thought we were close to Wind Silk Canyon because of the decomposing egg case smell. He explained the odor as one similar to burnt grass and I knew immediately that it accurately described what I was smelling. We stopped at a pool of tonc and drank our fill. I was amazed at how long I could go between tonc feedings. The substance had significant staying power so that I felt full and energized for extremely long periods. It seemed to have the same effect on Bril and Togn, although Togn seemed to need more of it, and more often than Bril and I. I thought perhaps that was simply due to his stature.

We had only traveled a brief time after leaving the tonc pool when the canyon split. Following Ialeo's instructions we took the left fork and within another very short time we reached an opening to a canyon on the right. The entrance was strewn with boulders forcing us to pick our way through, following no particular path. Togn was in the lead, guaranteeing easy passage for Bril and I. Suddenly, Togn stopped short and let out a gasp. Bril and I moved up behind him peering over his shoulders, one on each side. There, in front of him was a huge serpent skin, no doubt shed very recently. We studied its enormity of easily seven meters long with the largest section being at least a meter around. Opposite the long seam where it split from the beast there were two rows of razor sharp crystals.

"That must be where it gets its name from," said Togn, seeing the crystals as very effective flesh rippers.

Bril was struck by the potential use of the crystals and wondered out loud if we should take some in case they might come in handy. We all thought they would be hard to transport because their sharpness would cut through whatever we placed them in. But then Togn had an idea. He wielded his Steel Stone Sword and carefully cut the serpent skin so it could be safely folded over a length of the crystals. It seemed to work. The skin immediately around them was seemingly immune to the abrasive and cutting nature of the crystals. I turned my back to Togn and he stored the find inside the back pack, no doubt in a pocket of perfect size for it.

The discovery of the serpent skin caused a major change in how we moved forward from then on. There was no more stepping blindly between boulders or scurrying over smaller ones. We all started taking mindful steps, focusing intently on the immediate area around us while sometimes jumping back or sideways, startled by even our own shadows. It must have been a pitiful site, three would be adventurers, swords drawn, dodging left and right and sometimes backward at the sights of normal canyon objects. But our very intense scrutiny of what lay right around us, could not save us from the perils that lay in the larger view. If just one of us would have been looking up we might have avoided what happened next.

From the underside of a rock overhang a mass of young serpents dropped upon us! We were immediately covered in a slimy substance as the creatures slithered over us, wrapping themselves around our bodies, arms and legs. We furiously grabbed at them, peeling and pulling them from ourselves and flinging them. Swords were useless in this situation unless we wanted to add cuts to the mass of bruises we were receiving from their not-yet-fully-developed flesh ripping crystals. Their grips were horrendous once they wrapped around and they would begin to slide back and forth in a sawing motion. I could see how larger ones with fully developed crystals could easily cut a being in half. For now, we were just being painfully bruised. Togn got clear of his first and then busied himself helping Bril and I. We seemed to have gotten the brunt of the mass and once the last one was peeled from our bodies and flung away it was clear we would definitely be sore for a few glowcycles.

We leaned on boulders catching our breath in the narrow space. Not only were we heavily bruised from the serpents, but struggling in close quarters had also inflicted us with scrapes and cuts. None of them were serious, but they definitely added to our level of discomfort.

The glowstones were gaining brightness as we pressed onward, picking our way through the boulder field, alternating looking closely around us, and then also above and beyond our immediate space. The air was stifling and sweat poured from our bodies adding salt to our wounds and making our skin sting all over. We stopped briefly at a small tonc pool to drink some, and to splash some on our skin. When I told Bril and Togn of the healing properties I had discovered in one of those pools when treating Horse's bolt wound they both assured me this was not one of those.

Togn explained that healing pools were always fed from above through a trickle and that they only occurred where the tonc flowed from Divine Stone, a type that actually contained biologically active cells. Problem was Bril continued, not only was the Divine Stone very rare, but the springs that flowed through it to create the trickles, ebbed and flowed erratically, making it impossible to know when one might once again become active. I was disappointed in hearing how improbable it was I'd ever find another one of those pools, and it made me realize I'd have to be just that much more cautious.

We pressed forward and as we rounded a bend a new breeze wafted over us, carrying the faint scent of burnt grass. Then, after a few more paces, the canyon opened up into a huge bowl with unscalable cliffs sealing it off from the landscape beyond. At places on the steep walls, elongated sacks without bottoms, flapped in the breeze. Below, above, and all around them, carver worms busily devoured the cliff stone. At other places the sacks had bottoms and they hung heavily from woven tethers that were somehow fastened to the stone.

"Egg cases," said Bril. "The bottomless ones have already hatched out their worms, and they're at work on the walls. The others are yet to hatch."

"I wonder which type we're supposed to get the fibers from," I said out loud.

"We wouldn't want to disturb the carver worm incubations," said Togn, "So we should only take the ones that are empty."

The next problem was a tough one. How to scale the cliffs to reach the sacks. We slowly moved to the left, working our way to where a sack was nearby. It was at least five meters up the wall, too high for us, even if one stood on another's shoulders. The cliff wall all around it was covered with carver worms and there were no hand or foot holds. Then, Bril spotted something on the cliff wall across from us. It was a flesh ripper serpent, clinging to the wall while it tore into an unopened egg case and began devouring the worms inside. It was a violent act that made us cringe at its power and flexibility. As the serpent dined, sheets of the egg cases cascaded down the walls laying in heaps below the calamity.

"Well, I guess that's our answer," I offered. "If we can sneak below that serpent, we can grab the discarded pieces of the cases and then sneak away."

"It seems awfully busy up there," said Togn referring to the serpent, "Maybe it wouldn't care what we did down on the ground."

"But, remember what Oshya told us, that the best approach was stealth, so I vote that we use the backpack and become invisible," asserted Bril.

"You're probably right," I said. "There's no point in taking chances we don't have to take."

With that, we all held on to the pack at our designated positions and thought of our activation memories. Instantly we felt the floating feeling and it was as if we were looking through fog. Aware that our sounds were not invisible, we strode cautiously toward the fallen egg cases, watching the serpent's actions intently. We stopped at a place to the right of the serpent's tail end, where I reached out and grabbed a piece of egg case and handed it to Bril who used his free hand to open the back pack and stuff the case fabric inside. The egg case felt silky smooth on the outside and was coarser on the inside with just a slight coating of slime. I reached out and grabbed another piece, handing it off to Bril again. Bril whispered in my ear that the material packed really well and suggested we get maybe three or four more pieces. I reached out and grabbed another, and then another, each time handing them off to Bril. Togn kept his eyes on the serpent the whole time, watching for the slightest change in its position on the cliff. But none of us could have imagined what happened next.

In what could only be described as a single movement, the serpent was suddenly looped over the top of us, still clinging to the cliff face, but forming an arc above us. I rolled my eyes upward and saw its belly just centimeters above my head. The beast's face was circling in the air, its forked tongue flicking in and out wildly. We had forgotten about scent and now realized our smell was probably not invisible any more than our sound. Bril's eyes were wide as he slowly and quietly as possible began pulling his steel stone sword from its scabbard. Once his was free, Togn and I took turns gently removing ours and readying them.

The serpent's head swung wildly to the right bringing its eyeball, which was the size of my head, right in front of us. The tongue flicked more wildly. Togn's sword was well within striking distance, but we all held our breath, hoping that it wouldn't accidentally touch any of us and realize we were there.

Just then, I caught movement out of the corners of my eyes and I rolled them to the right to see what it was. To my terror I saw a second serpent slithering rapidly toward us. And then it was there, suddenly locked in mortal battle with the one arched above us.

The titans smashed their crystal-laden undersides together, each trying to encircle the other's neck. Then they would draw back, arch and slam into one another again, sending blood and scales flying through the air. We were mesmerized and frozen in place. The wild, gyrating motions of the beasts' heads all but eliminated the possibility of fleeing, and we definitely didn't want to inject ourselves into the middle of the melee.

A sudden bump on my head jolted me to a horrendous realization. The serpent above us was loosing its grip on the cliff face as its belly was now touching the top of my head. I shrunk down, but seconds later it was once again on my head. Togn, being shorter was now also feeling it, and Bril, who was standing in a low spot, rolled his eyes upward uneasily to see just how much further before it was on top of him. We all looked at each other knowing we had to make a move. Amidst the noise of the battle, Bril spoke out loud saying to wait until the serpent above us made its next attack and then to race to the right, around the serpent's tail. We didn't have to wait long and we made our move, hands clinging tightly to their assigned places on the pack and legs shuffling as fast as they could. On the other side of the serpent's tail we found a notch in the canyon wall to crowd into. It was just big enough for the three of us, side-by-side and had a rock overhang. As we caught our breath, we saw we had been detected.

The serpents suddenly stopped battling and both began circling their heads, tongues flicking, trying to pick up our scent. The one released its hold on the wall and slithered toward our nook. We scrunched down, swords at ready. The beast stopped just before us, flicking its tongue and twisting its head no doubt trying to get the smell to match up with a remembrance of a meal. The other serpent looped around our notch, its head rising above the overhang, peering down with its tongue darting wildly in and out. Several times the tongues barely grazed our swords, shoulders and heads. The serpents dripped blood from their battle and the splatters landed on us in large globs, practically drenching our clothes and hair. Suddenly, the beasts calmed down, stopped probing and flicking and appeared to be ready to retreat. As I looked down at myself and then at Bril and Togn, I realized the blood must have been covering our scent with theirs! Actually, a lucky break, even if it was kind of disgusting. A sly smile spread across Togn's face, and Bril grinned brightly.

The serpents moved away, one slithering back up the wall and the other heading to a spot with fresh egg cases just beyond it. Apparently their dispute was forgotten, and we, might actually be free to leave, but not without a couple more pieces of egg cases. As the serpent above tore into another case one of the pieces drifted down right in front of us. This time, Togn collected them, three more, and with Bril's help, stashed them in the pack. Satisfied we had enough, we inched our way from the safety of the notch and moved quickly across the canyon, working our way to where we had entered. Getting out however, was not going to be without its price.

As we began picking our way through the bolder field the young serpents we had fought off earlier began reappearing in frightening ways. Coiled between obstacles they would strike as we passed, flinging themselves onto us and wrapping around our legs, arms and bodies. Togn was in the lead and received more than his fair share of attacks, but Bril and I were assailed without mercy by the larger ones that came from the tops of boulders. We spent a huge amount of energy flailing about, peeling them from our bruised bodies and flinging them, or slashing them with our swords. The bruises on our arms turned to massive welts, and sores began opening on any unprotected skin. I loathed the creatures and at one point I began pulling them from me and hacking them mercilessly even after they stopped squirming from the blows. Bril was more measured in his approach, grabbing and flinging the ones closest to his head and neck first, followed by the ones that leapt onto his limbs and torso, methodically managing the onslaught with what seemed like an infinite amount of patience. Suddenly, it stopped. We didn't take any time to even acknowledge the change to one another, seeking instead to move as fast as we could from the wretched place.

We reached the main canyon and turned left, traveling back to the fork and just beyond to the tonc pool we had visited earlier. We were caked in sweat, our own blood, serpent blood and rapidly drying slime. Fortunately the pool was large enough for the three of us to get in at once. A steady flow of new tonc came in from a small, bubbling spring, and the pool then overflowed at a low spot, spilling down an incline and flowing through a hole, back below the floor of the canyon. The liquid felt wonderful and we splashed and scrubbed until we were exhausted and refreshed. The glowstones were at their full brightness and the canyon was awash in vibrant light. I lay back, floating in the pool staring up at the darkness that eventually swallowed the glowstones' light. In a rather strange moment of reverie I felt myself longing to see sky and clouds, and maybe even to catch a glimpse of a flying creature of some kind. It seemed so long since I sat on the shore of that lake, with Horse grazing contentedly and the water lapping nearby. Looking back it seemed like such a peaceful moment even though we had narrowly escaped the Tachina, and had been unmercifully chased since our arrival on the planet. I wondered about Horse, what she might have endured and if the end had been quick. I hoped so. Still, somewhere deep inside there was a light that I kept on for her, a sort of small flame that was ever watchful for her return. Then, I drifted into sleep.

CHAPTER TWELVE

The Pool of Memories

This time there was no hot breath cascading over my body from the mouth of a drac lizard to wake me, only the relatively peaceful sound of two adventurers practicing their swordsmanship. Togn and Bril, just a few meters away, dodged and feigned and took turns being attacker as they experimented with various moves to improve their abilities. I kept an eye on them as I pulled on my leathers and was rather impressed with their abilities for I knew they had little to no experience with these weapons. On the other hand, I was very familiar with them. I didn't know why because of the memory problem I had, but swords were definitely an item I knew, and knew well. With my scabbard on and my sword drawn I joined them and spent some time helping them to refine their offensive moves, while also showing them where their defensive stances and moves were leaving them open to damage. Of the two, Bril showed the strongest talent, but then he had youth on his side. I wondered if Togn might be better suited to a different type of weapon and resolved to explore that possibility with Ialeo when we returned to him. In the meantime, we had a few more deeds that needed doing.

We headed off toward Wind Silk Canyon but this time passing by its dreaded entrance and continuing on to find Crystal Cove. We didn't have to go far, for the canyon soon dead ended in a huge, oval-shaped area. Scattered across the floor of the cove were numerous pools and in many places the only passages beyond them were narrow bridges of stone, some arched above the fluid surfaces and others bisecting them. There was the faint smell of flowers in the air and a certain beckoning to the place that made us feel very welcomed.

"What is the essence of this place?" questioned Togn, clearly feeling euphoric and moving trancelike toward one of the pools.

"Not sure," replied Bril, reaching out and grabbing Togn by the shoulder. "We should wait, just a bit to get acclimated I think."

I was also feeling drawn to the pools as if something very familiar and comforting lay within them. The memory of Horse came back and I began to feel her presence again, as if she was nearby, and waiting for me. Then, a wave of longing overcame me as I remembered the woman in the clothing founden. I was sure she was nearby, and although it even sounded absurd to me, it was not absurd enough to think she might actually be in one of the pools. Suddenly, Togn broke free from Bril and sauntered to the nearest pool where he kneeled down and stared into the fluid, transfixed.

"Wait!" yelled Bril, racing toward him, while shielding his eyes from the fluid in the pool before Togn.

At that instant, Ataia's image flashed through my mind, snapping me from the altered state I had eerily entered.

"Look!" Togn was saying excitedly to Bril, as he stared into the fluid. "It's my mother! She's alive!"

I reached the two of them, grabbing Togn by the arm and spinning him to face away from the pool.

"Think, Togn!" I shouted. "You are in Ataia's heart, remember her? See her face in your mind! This is an illusion. You have to resist!"

Togn spun away from me, rising up and staggering backward.

"You've never been there for me!" he shouted back. "You only want to keep me away from my family just to help you save your own skin from the Tachina! You think I don't know what you're doing?"

"That's not true," I pleaded. "Togn, I've never expected you to do anything. I always thought you were being true to yourself. But think! Your family is dead. They died in the earthquake, a long time ago. Whatever you're seeing in that pool, it isn't them!"

It was then I saw the severity of our situation. Bril was now leaning over the pool, staring into it, mumbling and touching the fluid. If one or the other or both went into the pool I knew there would be no way to save them. Togn kneeled back down at the pool's edge and started stroking the surface. In desperation I tried the only thing I could think of. I stripped off the back pack and reached inside, finding the dread orb. I only hoped it might dispel the hold the pool had on them by filling them with fear and causing them to flee out of the cove. But, there was also the possibility it would drive them into the pool, so I raced around it, placing it between me and them. I placed the orb in my palm, holding it out toward them. The orb glowed blue and almost instantly the fluid in the pool turned from glossy black to grey. Togn and Bril seemed to be affected. They began to shrink back from the pool, from me. Then, in a flash of terror they both turned and ran, fleeing to the canyon beyond. I wrapped my fingers around the orb and raced back around the pool, grabbing my pack and out toward the canyon. Once away from the cove I stashed the orb in its pocket and headed out to find my two friends.

Back near the entrance to Wind Silk Canyon, they stood staring at the canyon walls, not talking. As I approached, they both turned toward me, looking confused and disoriented.

"Look," I said. "It's okay. That was a close call, and sorry I had to use the orb, but the two of you were really hooked on that pool. I was sure one or both of you might just jump in. Do you remember what Oshya said? It's nearly impossible to escape them."

Slowly the two of them began to regain their confidence and became more active.

"What happened?" Bril wondered out loud. "In just an instant I started seeing things in that pool and before I knew it I couldn't pull away."

Togn was on the verge of tears, mumbling about his lost family and how much he missed them. This was clearly a troubling result of using the orb, and the powers of the pools were unmistakably destructive, at least for Bril and Togn. I wondered why I had not been affected as much as they were. I had a momentary draw to the pools and flashbacks about Horse and my the woman might have driven me to linger and look into them, but it appeared my attraction to them was not anything like Bril's or Togn's. As I pondered the different outcomes we had each had I was drawn to memories, for it was memories that seemed to be what the pools used to pull unsuspecting beings to them. And that's when I realized it made perfect sense that I was not affected as severely as Bril and Togn -- I didn't have many memories, and the ones I had were not nearly as deep as theirs. It was right after that realization that I knew I would have to enter Crystal Cove alone to get the cloud crystals for Oshya and edge stone for Ialeo.

Togn and Bril were finally back to being themselves and Togn said he was sorry for the words he used in the cove, that he was on the journey because he wanted to be and that it was the pool that made him say the things he did. I reassured him that I already knew that. Then, I shared my realizations about the affects of the pools with them along with my desire to enter the cove alone to get the crystals and edge stone. Bril was at first apprehensive saying that if my theory was wrong I might not make it back out. But when I explained that I'd leave the dread orb with them and if they remained at the entrance to the cove, I'd stay in their view so they could respond if I lingered too long, he seemed to be less apprehensive. With that I handed the pack to Togn and the three of use headed back to Crystal Cove.

This time we all stopped when the cove came into view and before the smell of flowers struck us. Togn and Bril perched themselves on a nearby boulder that gave them an unobstructed view, and I headed into Crystal Cove. Immediately when the scent of flowers filled my nostrils, images and memories of Horse returned. I had an insane desire to run to the nearest pool and throw myself in, knowing I would find Horse there. But that was quickly replaced with images of my woman in the clothing founden with her scent and the way she smiled, and the feelings I had when I was near her. My mind reeled as the sensations intensified and I staggered toward the nearest pool. She was there, beckoning to me. Then, when everything could have been lost, Ataia visited me, placing herself between me and the nearest pool. Almost instantly the effect of my memories faded, the bodily sensations subsided and I was able to once again focus on the edges of the pools, looking for the glossy, black, edge stone columns.

It wasn't long before I spotted some growing at a corner where a pool met a stone walkway. As I neared, the columnar construction of that type of stone became readily apparent and I marveled at the way light played off its surface. It was as if it reflected and absorbed the light all at the same time so that portions appeared to be transparent while other portions appeared to be extraordinarily dense. The whole time I was in the cove, the memories of Horse were always there, like a constant nagging to see her in any one of the pools. I kept my eyes diverted from the pools and focused on the task at hand, but it took all of my will to keep that focus.

I reached the edge stone, selected a column that was about a meter long and that stood at the edge of a clump. Remembering how Togn had loosened the everstone I tried a similar tactic with the edge stone, using my palm instead of a thumb. The edge stone columns were triple the diameter of the everstone. With my palm squarely on the top of the column I began to slowly rock it back and forth. Perhaps because it was on the edge of a stand, it separated almost immediately. Then I slid my fingers down the back side all the way to the ground, snapping the piece off cleanly. During those moments of intense concentration I noticed the memories that made me drawn to the pools disappeared. But then, they were back, bringing a constant challenge to control my mind.

Scanning the area I looked for clumps of very clear crystals and spotted some immediately to my left. I crossed a stone bridge keeping my eyes off the surface of the dark pool and my mind focused on the crystal clump. But as I neared them I knew they weren't right. Their bases were also clear. I spotted another, went to it, but this time the bases were orange. Time and time again I would spot what I thought were sky crystals but upon getting closer find they were something else. When I remembered the journal shard and its ability to help locate items I regretted not bringing it with me. But, I also wouldn't have wanted to have lost it in there had I been unable to resist the temptations within the pools. I couldn't believe the variations in the crystals and wondered what all the different types of were used for. All those mental wanderings helped to keep memories at bay as I went deeper and deeper into Crystal Cove.

Nearing the rear wall of the cove I looked back and saw Togn and Bril as just two colorful specks in the distance. The air was refreshingly clean and the flower scent had grown intense during my wanderings. I scanned along the cliff wall and spotted another clump of clear crystals. This time, as I neared them I saw the unmistakeable cloudy bases and knew I had finally found the cloud crystals. These crystals also grew in an upright fashion in multi-sided columns. I reached the clump and chose a column on its outer edge. Very carefully I wiggled and pried with my fingers, finally breaking it free. Only the very top was clear and the rest of the nearly meter-long crystal was densely clouded. With the two objects in my possession I moved quickly toward the canyon, looking forward to being relieved of the constant temptations lurking in the place.

Bril and Togn bounded off the boulder as I approached, reaching to help me with the crystals. They were heavy and I must have been showing considerable fatigue, not only from their weight, but also from the constant struggle against the attractions in the pools.

"Let's get out of this place," commanded Togn, slapping my back with his very large hand.

When we reached the tonc pool Togn removed a piece of the egg case from the pack and tore a strip from it. Then, he set to work polishing the everstone, using the tonc water to help bring up the luster Oshya was seeking in the stone. Bril and I sat on the edge of the pool watching Togn but as it appeared the polishing was going to take some time, I switched my position to take advantage of a back rest and leaned into it. In no time I was asleep, dreaming of my horse and a woman, and a place and time we were all together.

On awakening the glowstones were dimming and Togn was finishing up the last centimeter of his polishing. The everstone looked amazingly different than it had and I was hopeful that its cream-like luster was exactly what Oshya was looking for.

"There," Togn announced. "One finely-polished everstone, ready to become a StarStone Scepter," he held the length of stone up, admiring it.

"Okay, nice work," said Bril impatiently. "Now, here, put it in the pack and let's get going."

Togn dutifully placed the everstone in its pocket, closed the pack and held it up for Bril to slip on. Then, Togn and I each grabbed one of the crystals from the cove and we set off up the canyon.

At Ialeo's weapon founden we delivered the edge stone, much to his delight and thankfulness. He immediately added the Sweet Water enchantment to our swords making them doubly effective against fire-based beings such as the kind we might encounter in Firston.

"You know," I said to Ialeo, "Togn here has gotten good with a sword, but I was wondering if you thought there might be a weapon more suited to his stature?"

"Hmmm," Ialeo murmured slowly while studying Togn's frame. "You know, I think he might really like an Obsidian Axe." He disappeared to the back of the space and quickly returned with a glass-like axe that had a half-meter-long steelstone handle. The handle was carved with a delicate curve and I could see right away that Togn could take advantage of that to really increase the power behind his blows. Not only that, the weapon was meticulously balanced as Ialeo demonstrated by resting it on the edge of his hand to show us it stayed perfectly level when placed on its center of gravity.

Togn took to the axe right away and I could see he had an innate understanding of how to use it. Ialeo handed him a belt sheath which Togn strapped on proudly and dropped the axe into. Togn probably didn't need his sword anymore, but I thought on the other hand it would give him more reach until he mastered throwing the axe. With that, we left our weapons with Ialeo and made our way to the Superterrestrial Order to find Oshya. Or rather, for Oshya to find us.

We placed ourselves in the courtyard of the Order in the same place we had previously been found by Oshya, and then we waited. And waited. And waited. The glowstones reached their lowest light and the crowds in the courtyard thinned out, leaving just us and a few others.

"Maybe we should just go look for him," said Bril, impatiently.

"Thing is, if we're moving about it might make it harder for him to find us," I offered.

As I watched Bril pacing I started wondering what was the source of this new impatience. Till then, he had always been very patient, almost too patient, so this was definitely a change. I liked him better with more patience though, so I found myself hoping this was a temporary thing. Meanwhile, Togn had drifted off to sleep and I started yawning a bit, no doubt still tired from the Crystal Cove experience, but also growing weary of the wait for Oshya.

Then, as if answering my own growing impatience he drifted into view in front of us, a ways off, and ambling in our direction.

"I have found you," he said admiringly as he approached. "Now, let me see what you've done with that piece of everstone."

First we handed the cloud crystal to him which he studied admiringly before placing it into a pocket on the inside of his tunic. Then, Togn removed the everstone from its place in the pack and presented it glowingly to him, his wide smile giving away the pride he felt in the polishing he had done.

"Magnificent!" exclaimed Oshya. "This will do very well."

With that he went into a trancelike state, removed a star-shaped, clear crystal from his shoulder pack, and moved it over the length of the everstone. Immediately it was as if the stone came to life. It began to have glowing, lightening-like strings inside it that gradually tamed themselves into straight lines running the length of the stone. Then, they went out. Oshya replaced the star crystal in his pack and returned his consciousness to the present.

"Now," he explained, "when you are ready to descend into a lower world you must hold the StarStone Scepter like this." He held the scepter from the bottom with it standing straight up.

"If there is any chance a passageway will open nearby, the scepter will light up with a very yellow light running through its center," he instructed. "Simply place it on its side on your flattened palm. One end will glow and will spin to point in the direction of the opening. Keep the scepter on your palm and proceed in the direction it is pointing. To ascend through the worlds, hold the scepter by its top, in a vertical position. It will glow blue, and you can then follow where it points."

With that he handed the scepter back to Togn and in a very fluid manner reached for the back pack.

"I have learned that you will be faced with challenges to your spirits," he began mysteriously. "These will not be easy things to overcome, and while it won't be ideal it will help you if this pack has the spirit fortitude enchantment."

Taking a yellow crystal from his shoulder pack he entered a trancelike state and moved the crystal over the pack. A yellow fog settled over the pack, and then disappeared. Oshya came back to the present and replaced the crystal in his pack.

"As long as you are within a couple meters of the pack, your ability to resist challenges to your spirits will be increased," he explained.

Next, Oshya used a very blue crystal to enchant the pack with the Resist Heat enchantment, and then used a pink stone to enchant it with the Strong Lung enchantment. He explained that resist heat would come in very handy in Firston because of the volcanic atmosphere. Strong Lung he explained would help to protect us from damage to our breathing from atmospheres concentrated with contamination, low oxygen and humidity.

Finally, he handed us a contact shard for Eana in the Land of the Misanthrope. He told us to be sure to visit her during our travels for she would be able to assist us. He turned and was about to slip away, but then turned back.

"You should know that those who seek you are not far from here, so it is important to move quickly," he counseled, seriously. "I have placed a distraction around you that will make you undetectable to them while you are near the Order. The farther you go from here though, the more detectable you will be, until at a point you will be fully detectable again. Make haste with your final preparations here and then go quickly from Micknok through Wild Wave Canyon. Once you are beyond the narrows begin using your StarStone Scepter to find you passage to Firston. And, one other thing. When you are in Firston, if you come across orb crystals it would be excellent if you could send some my way."

Before we could thank him, he was gone. And shortly after that, we were too, on our way with haste to see Ataia.

In the canyon the glowstones were reaching full brightness and the scene was busier than ever. People came and went from the multitude of foundens lining the canyon walls, carrying things in and carrying other things out. We picked our way through the crowds until we found Ataia's founden and stepped inside. In there too, things were very busy as beings searched through piles of material and finished packs of all imaginable sizes and shapes. We spotted Ataia at her workbench and made our way to her. She immediately looked up as we approached and jumped up with her arms outspread to embrace first Togn, then Bril and then me.

"I am so glad to see you," she smiled widely. "You look different somehow."

"That could be the result of facing down flesh ripper serpents and dark pools," quipped Bril.

"Oh, my, you have a right to look different then," she chided.

I removed the rest of the carver worm egg cases from the pack and presented them to her. I guess she was taken aback by the volume and she smiled broadly, obviously pleased.

"This is fabulous," she cried, "Once I turn this into thread and color it, it will be excellent for embroidery. You really should grab another pack while you're here. Long journeys have a way of filling these up."

Thank you," I said. "We'll do that. There is something I wanted to ask you about," I began, taking her elbow and steering her out of earshot of Bril and Togn. "First, it was amazing how being in your heart helped me at the dark pools and I thank you so much for that. They were far more formidable then I could have imagined. You actually appeared before me right when it seemed I could no longer resist the temptations of the pools. How do you do that?"

"It's not really a conscious thing on my part," she said, laying her hand over my heart and looking deeply into my eyes. "When we have the connection either one of us can appear to the other in times of spiritual stress."

"You mean I could appear to you?"

"Yes," she answered, and then surprising me, "You have."

"How do you mean that?"

"When I was young, a being came to me from one of the underworlds and he was able to show me exactly what I wanted to see, and to feel exactly what I wanted to feel. But, it was not genuine. It was more like spells he would cast just to get me to do things he wanted. Of course I couldn't see that and slowly, over several glow cycles I was doing things simply to please him. Then he brought other beings of his kind and they toyed with me until one time when they were all around me, you suddenly appeared before me. It was as if the spell was instantly broken. I looked around, looked at them, and really saw, for the first time, how far I had grown from myself. Thanks to you, I was able to just walk away."

"But if that was when you were young, I probably wasn't even on Octa, so how could that be?"

"These connections transcend space and time," she said matter-of-factly. "We don't know how, but they just do."

"Well, I'm sure glad they do," I said. "But there is something else. I've seen quite a bit of impatience in Bril recently and I wondered if you had any insight to offer?"

"Of the three of you, he has the greatest challenges in front of him from the spiritual perspective," she began. "His spirit animates him in mostly beneficial ways for himself and those around him. But, there is something there that can be easily bent, leaving him and those around him vulnerable to controlling forces. You will have to watch him closely for when his impatience begins to lead him away to where he is disappearing for periods of time, he will be at his most vulnerable. Especially before you reach The Mists you should deal with this. I have," her voice trailed off as she turned and made her way to a table in the corner. "Ah, yes, here it is," she said removing a contact shard from some randomly strewn on the table top, "You can try seeing Amoro in Firston, here's the shard," she said, handing it to me. "She will be able to help him to control those darker influences, at least until they subside as he discovers his true destiny."

"Is she a Spirit Familiar like yourself?" I asked.

"No, she is a Spirit Vixen and doesn't have any connection with others, so she can deal with spirit afflictions."

I thanked her for all her help and we embraced in a long, heartfelt hug. Then, I turned and found Bril and Togn among the crowd. They had each selected a pack and Togn handed the original pack to me which I slipped onto my shoulders. Then, the three of us left Ataia's founden, joining the crowds in the canyon. We walked quickly, feeling apprehension about the nearness of the Tachina. The crowds offered us some feeling of protection and so from that perspective we really weren't looking forward to being back out in the lonely canyons. But at that moment the best advice we had was to stay out in front of our relentless trackers.

CHAPTER THIRTEEN

Dropping into Firston

At Ialeo's founden we reclaimed our weapons and picked up a request from him to send back some steelstone, found almost exclusively in Firston near fire pits. We thanked him quickly, and set out, taking Wild Wave Canyon which opened up directly across from Ialeo's founden. Our steps took us into at first a very wide canyon, but as we descended, the walls began closing in. Our apprehension increased as the canyon narrowed perhaps because we were instinctively picking up on just how close the Tachina were.

Meanwhile:

At the tops of the cliff walls along the Micknok ridge, five riders raced toward Wild Wave Canyon. In the lead, Vortold the Tachina flicked the hairs along his shoulders and back, probing the air for the scent of his prey. His massive, faceted eyes detected light waves down to the minutia of intensities giving him a superior depth-of-field perception, while the hairs on his feet and hands fed a constant sensation of taste to his brain, in this case the taste of bridal reins and leather stirrups. His antennae floated out from the cavity in the middle of his face, constantly sending balance and direction signals to his brain while his proboscis hung limply from his mouth, as if ready at a second's notice to slurp up some food. He was a thinking, calculating hunter with extraordinary tracking abilities, and he prided himself in having always eliminated or captured his prey.

But, Vortold was more than a hunting machine as he could reason about even the deepest of subjects, even one as deep as the origins of his species. He appreciated his stature in the universe, a rare combination of human and insect where evolution had kindly kept most of the best attributes of each, and discarded the ones that distracted or weakened the organism. So, emotion and feelings were not things he was familiar with and that left him free to storm through his existence unfettered by their tempering effects. There were some things though that he cursed evolution for, such as the absence of wings. Two artifacts of those attributes still remained, protruding slightly from his shoulders, like forgotten scaffolds left standing at a completed structure. With wings he would not have to be dependent on horses, or any of the other forms of transportation he had encountered in his universal travels.

Nearby:

We stopped once again as Bril held the StarStone Scepter by its base, and this time it finally glowed yellow. Bril placed it on its side on his open palm and instantly the scepter moved, pointing out the direction of where a passage to the underworld would open. We walked in that direction until our way was blocked by one of the canyon walls. The scepter's glow had gradually increased in intensity and when we stopped at that point nearly half of its length was bright yellow.

"This must be it," I ventured.

"But how..." Bril stopped in mid-sentence in seeing the spectacle unfolding before us.

In a fluid-like motion, almost as if a blur, the canyon wall before us split open vertically and twisted, at first forming an arch, but then giving way to a circular opening with a tube cascading downward. In the next second a rush of hot air blasted over us, filled with the scents of fire and ash. The tube was littered with jagged rocks and though its angle was steep, there seemed to be ample toe and hand holds. We looked at one another, each searching in the others' faces for a sign of confidence. Instead, we all saw a mixture of fear and uncertainty. In the next instant though, our decision was made for us. I spotted movement above and when I looked up to the plateau at the tops of the canyon walls, there were the Tachina, already leaping from their mounts and grabbing for their crossbows. In the same instant, Bril and Togn also saw the scene and we all raced into the tube out of the range of the volley of bolts just beginning to rain down.

The tube moved like a serpent, shifting side to side and gyrating up and down. Our path was covered with rocks of all sizes and shapes and there was hot ash constantly raining down on us. I shouted to Bril and Togn to stay close so the enchantments on my pack would be in effect for them as well. The ceiling was low and we found that once we got our footing in the shifting enclosure we could move forward quickly, even reaching up to touch the ceiling to regain our balance as needed. The torrent of hot air rushing toward us was intense and we sweated profusely from the heat and the physical exertion required in moving over the rough terrain.

I stopped and looked back, hoping against all odds that I wouldn't see our pursuers. Instead I saw something much more immediately terrifying. The tube was closing! Bril and Togn had also stopped and were witnessing the same calamity rushing toward us. We all knew if we didn't stay ahead of the closure, we'd be forever sealed into the stoney fabric of Octa's underworlds. We turned and raced ahead with new resolve, and new speed. There were only two bright spots for us right then. One was that the Tachina would be delayed. And the other was the angle of the tube. It had almost leveled out so our forward progress was much faster. On and on we raced with the deafening sound of cascading rock crushing back against itself as the tube seemingly closed right at our heels. We were all fading, our lungs burning from the searing heat and dust as they tried desperately to supply enough oxygen to our legs and arms. Our hands were sliced from grabbing at the sides and ceiling of the tube, and our footwear was cut and torn. Just when I thought I might have enough nerve to look behind and see just how close the closing was to us, the tube shifted dramatically, spiraling almost straight down in front of us. Without thinking I reached out grabbing the strap on Bril's pack with one hand and Togn's shirt with the other. Then, I jumped into the abyss yelling for them to hold on. We went into a free fall and as I held tightly to them, they instinctively grabbed onto my forearms so that we were knitted together. I only hoped that slow motion would once again work its magic as I focused on the outcome I wanted.

Within seconds our fall slowed and not an instant too soon, for half of the tube opened up just below us, spitting us out onto the seared surface of Firston.

We stumbled for several meters, successively losing and regaining our footing until skidding to a stop. We had all managed to stay upright which was a good thing because the earth was a mixture or cinders and jagged rocks.

Slow motion had delivered us safely and now we stood where molten pellets of rock had once rained down. I looked back toward the tube, but the only thing to show that it had existed was a tall, arching column of seared stone stretching upward. I immediately felt very alone and vulnerable, and the scene around me was as desolate and uninviting as anything I had yet seen on the planet. Stretching as far as the eye could see there were vast rock undulations, giving the illusion that the surface had once been a sea of molten rock, its waves now frozen in stone. Jets of superheated gasses shot into the air from vents of all imaginable sizes scattered across the landscape and I could see places where the rock gave way to what appeared to be rivers of lava. The only thing that was slightly comforting about the place was the presence of the now familiar glowstones, giving off light ranging from dark red to pink. I looked at Togn hoping for some words of encouragement since this was after all his birth place and where he had spent his youth. I was not disappointed.

"Ahhhh," Togn squealed, stretching. "It's good to be home again!"

Bril and I, our eyes glazed over from the ruin we saw all around us, broke into laughter at Togn's seemingly disjointed observation. I think we were also laughing in glee and relief, after surviving what we had just been through.

"Togn," Bril asked. "How did your people ever survive here?"

"It's not that bad, really," Togn said. "This part is kind of desolate, but wait until you see the underground and some of the spire dwellings. Over many, many generations the Kech found ways to make life here very hospitable. C'mon," he motioned for us to follow, "I'll show you a great way to get around here."

And so, off we trekked, out across the barren, charred landscape, side stepping blowing gas vents and picking our way over jagged rock. Both Bril and I had received serious damage to our footwear and I found myself hoping there would be someplace to repair them. Togn's boots however, looked as good as they did before we entered the tube and so I asked him what they were made from. He explained that his people had discovered early on that rugged footwear was a must and so they developed special soles made from softstone, a kind of stone that had flexibility, with great resistance to cuts and tears. He knew of a place where we might be able to get some. My new hope was that it wasn't too far.

It turned out that Togn was an excellent navigator in a land with so much surface that looked the same. He explained that he got his bearings from watching how the gasses drifted coming off the tops of the vents and that he was very familiar with all the different landscapes of Firston. He said from reading the signs it wouldn't be long before we reached the banks of a tonc river.

Gradually, the charred landscape gave way to something more

ancient, with a moss-like covering that felt soft and cushioning beneath my feet. The vast undulations of seared rock disappeared, the air was not so heavy with fumes, and the gas vents thinned out. Now we entered   a cave-like land with multiple opportunities to go beneath Firston's surface. Our walk had begun to tire me and for the first time since I had arrived on the planet I had a ravenous appetite and could barely wait for a tonc pool of any size to slake my hunger. As luck would have it, my wait was very short.

We turned between two large mounds with openings facing each other, and there, in a sort of mysterious-looking place covered in thick moss, both the hanging kind and the close-growing kind, I spotted a trickle of liquid falling into a small, cupped-stone pool. There, we drank our fill, feeling rejuvenation course through our veins and the comfort of our appetites satisfied. We sat there for a long time, no one speaking, just listening to the trickle of the tonc and the whisper of a faint breeze that was very refreshing and not laden with the heavy fumes we had experienced so far. I found myself in a dreamy, serene mood, feeling secure and in the moment, completely. But then I noticed something that had been imperceptibly happening. My cuts, scrapes and bruises from the trip through the tube were healing up. We had found a healing pool! Bril and Togn suddenly woke to the same realization and we all broke out in laughter. It was indeed good fortune and the only other wish I had at that moment was for the pool to mend my tattered boots. But, that was not to be.

CHAPTER FOURTEEN

Cinder Strike

We all drank some more, and relaxed until the glowstones were brightening. As we sat there I took out our contact shard for Amoro, curious to see if we were close enough to her for it to work. Sure enough, a very faint glowing line appeared inside the shard, extending outward from its center. As I turned the shard the line turned also, so it always pointed in the same direction, much like a compass. But there was tension in the air.

"Do we have a contact here?" Togn asked.

"Yes," I replied. "She's a spirit vixen called Amoro, that Ataia supplied."

I avoided getting into why she supplied the contact, instead reaching into the pack and retrieving the journal shard, hoping to deflect any questions. I handed the journal to Bril who immediately pronounced curtly that one of our objectives was near. He said he couldn't tell which one, not knowing for sure how to use the device and I could see his agitation was mounting. It was almost as if he was going to loose control and run screaming across the landscape. I reached out to steady him.

"What's going on," I asked. He shook my hand lose from his arm.

"Don't touch me!" he yelled. "What kind of stupid device is this anyway!"

I reached out and grabbed the journal just as he was about to fling it.

"Whoa," I said. "Bril, relax. Here, sit down."

"I don't want to sit down!" he yelled.

By now, Togn had closed ranks with me, not knowing just what Bril might do. The two of us put on our best relaxed poses and tried to act nonchalant. Togn once again spoke about the tonc river he thought was nearby and how that would speed our journey. But Bril was not calming down. In fact, he had started to tremble and was muttering foul things about teaching us a lesson and cutting us just enough with his sword so we couldn't walk and would die long, slow deaths right there.

Togn and I stepped back unsure and confused about Bril's mental state.

"Bril," I said motioning to Togn and I. "You know who we are, right? We've never done anything against you."

I don't know if it was my tone of voice, the words or or something else, but I saw a softening in Bril's demeanor. Slowly, he relaxed, moving his hand from his sword's handle and then looking at us sadly.

"What's happening to me?" he wailed, throwing his arms side to side and then wiping his now-streaming tears.

"Bril," I said approaching and touching his arm. "Try not to worry about this. We'll figure it out. Maybe it's just the stress of the journey. I mean after all, we have seen some things so far, and dealt with life and death situations, and it's stressful. But we'll get through it. And you can depend on Togn and I to help you, just like we know you'd help us."

Togn had stepped up and was patting Bril's shoulder like a dog tapping his tail against his master's leg.

"He's right," Togn affirmed. "We've been together through tough times, and we'll see this through. It will be more difficult though if you run us through with your sword," we all broke out in nervous laughter at Togn's sneaky joke, "but even then, we'll make it okay,"

Bril, now his usual self, and still chucking from Togn's joke through tears and a runny nose, sniffed hard and threw his arms around our shoulders.

"Thank you," he said. "Thank you."

As we broke free I hoped our meeting with Amoro would be soon for I sensed there was something afoot beyond Bril's control, or even ours.

I knew so little about the place and the kinds of beings that might be lose there, that I felt very vulnerable. At the same time, I knew I had to be the strong one. Even though Togn was a solid being, he had a soft side that was always looking for guidance. And Bril, was barely experienced in life. Even though what I knew about life had no basis in memory, I sensed it was still more mature than either of their knowledge.

"Why don't we see if we can figure out this journal shard," I said confidently. "It can't be that difficult."

The journal shard, like all the contact shards, was translucent. The three of us studied its rather intricate upper surface and an interior surface below that one. The upper surface had two glowing red lines, one longer than the other, and each pointing in a different direction. The interior surface had two blue dots, seemingly randomly spaced and not really having any connection to the red lines on the upper surface. We eventually surmised that the upper surface lines pointed to our objectives, and that we could use them to home in on those, while the interior surface showed the total number of objectives. Apparently, the red lines only showed when we were within a certain range from the objective. It was all very mysterious, and we hoped we had made some correct assumptions. Otherwise we might be traveling to places we didn't need to go.

Then, on further study of both the journal shard and Amoro's contact shard we noted a small notch in each. By lining up the notches and laying the smaller contact shard over the larger journal shard we could look right through all layers and see how the lines on each lined up with the other. We were pleased to see that our path to Amoro lie in roughly the same direction as one of the red lines on the journal shard. We knew we should try to get both the steel stone for Ialeo and the orb crystals for Oshya but unfortunately we couldn't tell by studying the journal shard which blue dot corresponded to which objective. In the scheme of things though, we accepted the fact that our objectives would seldom line up as they had just done. And so, confident we had solved the riddle of the journal and contact shards we fixed our sights on a distant point of reference that lined up with the line pointing to Amoro, and headed off.

In a short while the land shifted even more to rolling hills and valleys punctuated by stone outcroppings and caves spewing their mists from below. Togn explained the caves were long-dormant lava tubes where flowing water and tonc were continuously being heated below ground, sending vapor upward where it was eventually released in a cool mist onto the landscape. The mist, he said, encouraged the growth of moss, and even though some caves released highly visible concentrations of the mist, from others it flowed out continuously, and nearly invisibly. For me, the landscape was welcoming after what we were initially dropped into on our arrival.

There was something very peaceful and relaxing about it and I hoped we could stay in it most of our time in Firston.

Our distant reference point was a spire that stood way above others in its area. Togn was unsure but he thought it might be one of a series of spires where some of his kind still lived, along with beings from all over Octa. The spire dwellings, he said, were first inhabited by his Kech people who put their mining experience to use when creating them.

Between us and the spire was a vast landscape only part of which we could discern. The glowstones in Firston were generally not as bright as the ones in Canyonlands had been, and so shadows were deeper and darker, and details off in the distance were harder to make out. We were definitely on our own as there had not been any signs of other reasoning life forms and there was a distinct absence of any signs other beings had moved through the area.

At a convenient location at the top of a rise in the landscape, I stopped to check our shards. With Amoro's contact shard laid on top of the journal shard I saw the lines had begun to diverge from each other. The line pointing to Amoro was still laying in the direction of the spire we had fixed as our reference point. But the brightest line on the journal shard, besides now being brighter, was also lengthening and pointing more to the right of our reference spire. It seemed we would have to decide soon which one we would head for first. And that decision was immediately made for us when we crested a hill.

We stood at the edge of a very steep cliff peering into a gorge with racing, churning water. The way to the right was more of the same and to our left, no difference. It seemed we had reached a major impediment to being able to continue in a direct line to our destination. The river was also a clear dividing line between the misty, lush landscape we had been traveling through and one much more like the barren, charred rock we had landed on when we entered Firston. For as far as we could see in either direction there were no places where we could get down near the river, and even though I thought about depending on slow motion, the best outcome I could imagine from using that would have been one where we simply ended up intact but in the middle of the torrent. Since one of our direction lines on the journal shard was veering to the right, we decided to go in that direction. In a way I was glad we were on the more lush side where we could at least travel more comfortably.

The terrain along the top of the cliff was a sort of transition land between the charred landscape across the river and the mossy one on our side. In many places there was no moss on the stone beneath our feet and the number of caves spewing their mist was greatly reduced. In their place we started seeing more vent holes, some large enough for us to walk right into, or fall into, just depending upon the severity of their angles to the surface. Even along the cliff top the land was gently rolling so there were times when we couldn't see into the next hollow. As we progressed those low points increasingly became cinder pits. Their bottoms were covered in round volcanic stones of many sizes with the smallest ones on top. As we walked on them our feet shifted and slid, not just front to back, but side to side as well, making it extremely difficult to maintain our footing. Even more treacherous were the pits that angled toward the edge of the cliff, often giving us the feeling that we might just slide right off.

It was while I was concentrating intently on maintaining my footing that I looked down toward my feet only to see what appeared like claws emerging from below the cinders. In the next instant they had wrapped around my foot and were holding me fast. I had been walking to the right of Bril and Togn who were also concentrating intently on maintaining their balance and continued their forward movement unaware I was trapped by something. All of this happened in the blink of an eye and my mind was still trying to fathom my predicament when the cinders all around me started rising up.

Suddenly, I was seeing a creature emerge from below, thrusting up through the cinders like something leaping out of water. The downward pressure on the front of my foot from what I now recognized as one of its paws went from intense to nonexistent as that same paw wrapped around the back of my leg. With fluid movement I unsheathed my sword and drove it downward at the arm that was now pulling me to the ground. As my knee struck the cinders a face appeared from below, a creature with a wide, flat snout, and red, glowing eyes set high on its head. Putrid smelling, hot breath shot from its mouth as it opened widely to accept the incoming meal. I watched in horror, struggling to move backward as three rows of serrated crystalline teeth sought out my midsection. In the next instant I felt the grip on my leg loosen and I fell backward only to see Togn and Bril struggling to avoid the flailing arms of the creature. The back of its head was facing me now and I could see where it had already received some substantial blows from my two companions' weapons.

As I struggled to my feet the creature got hold of Bril, its paw around his midsection. Togn circled quickly and brought a stunning blow across its arm, severing it. By now I was in motion again, raising my sword for an attack and aiming for the back of the creature's head. I didn't know what to expect since it appeared it was literally made of stone, but in the next instant I knew better. My sword dove deeply into the back of its head, traveling downward and into its neck. I quickly pulled upward on the weapon to be ready for a second strike, but saw it wouldn't be necessary. An eerily serene moment followed as the creature slumped forward, its arms dropping, head coming to rest on the cinder floor.

We all let out a collective gasp, staggering backward from the creature.

"What is it?" Bril shouted, through gasps for air.

"It's called a cinder strike," said Togn. "They hide like that for catching prey."

"Prey!" I said incredulously, still struggling to catch my breath. "What kind of prey? We haven't seen a moving thing since we got here!"

"You know all those caves we passed?" Togn reminded me. "Down inside of those there are what we call eekutchi. They're like a really big rat. They come out when the glowstones are right for them and they feed on moss and other creatures moving about at that time. You can see where packs have crossed the cinders," he said pointing to grooves in the loose surface. "Sorry, I didn't remember about the cinder strikes. There aren't many of them and it's been a long time since I lived here. Even growing up we never saw one, just heard about them."

"Well, that's no problem, Togn, I'm just thankful the two of you were here," I said. "Otherwise, I don't think I'd have made it. Whew! That was so close."

With our breathing back to normal we sheathed our swords and inspected the creature. What I had originally thought was a stone-like covering was actually octagonally-shaped scales that were overlapped slightly at their bottoms. Everything about the thing was round and featureless except for the wide, flat snout. There didn't appear to be any ears and its eyes were deeply sunken into very large sockets. The paws had segmented pads, much like fingers on their bottoms, with crystalline claws protruding from their tops. I was amazed when I checked the back of my leg that I didn't have any cuts on it and all I could figure was the creature's pads had been what gripped me and the claws were used when it folded its pads back, like making a fist. I returned to the back of the creature and peered at the fatal wound. The liquid that flowed from it was dense, like milk cream. Where it had dripped on the cinders it had turned to a solid.

"Look at this," I said, pointing for Bril and Togn to see the shiny, cream-colored blob. When I picked it up to inspect it closer I was amazed at how light weight it was, and aside from a few cinders embedded in its bottom it was like glass.

"That's its blood," Togn said matter-of-factly. He took it from me and twisted it into spiral shape. "See. You can bend it however you like and it doesn't break or separate."

"So what do beings do with it?" I asked.

"It also has very high healing properties," Togn continued. "You can put it on a wound or a burn, especially a burn, and it helps with pain and helps to heal it."

"This is definitely something we should keep," I said. So, we gathered up all there was and stashed it in our packs.

CHAPTER FIFTEEN

Finding Amoro

The cinder strike encounter was such a close call it made all of us feel on edge. Togn explained that while he knew about some dangers in Firston, he had spent very little time in the outlands away from his community and so he knew little about them. He then told us that there were subterranean levels to Firston where water flowed in streams and that his people had used the streams as a transportation system. Many of the caves and large vent holes were the tubes that connected the surface to the underground system of streams. Problem was, he said, you never knew exactly which tube would lead you to a stream and which to a dead end.

Avoiding tubes with hot steam would help to ensure we didn't venture into an underground lava stream, but otherwise it could be a trial and error process. There was always the chance that we might actually see a sign that would direct us to a tube that reached the stream system. The signs, Togn explained, had been placed long ago and as fewer Kech survived to use the system they deteriorated. Then too, he said, there were many places in outlying areas where signs had never been erected. He said signs would always appear on the upper right side of a tube and would be in the Kech language, a sort of abbreviated and elegant script. We resolved to check each vent tube and cave as we moved forward, and to avoid cinder pits wherever possible.

For almost a complete glow cycle we moved through the slowly changing landscape peering into caves and vent tubes and sometimes venturing into them to see if any connected to the network of streams we hoped would speed up our forward progress. At each cinder pit we worked our way around the lowest point, trying to keep shallow cinders beneath our feet. That in turn added greatly to our travel time. It wasn't that we were on a time table, but we knew the Tachina would eventually find a way into Firston and once here, with their fast moving mounts and keen hunting abilities they could be on top of us very quickly. Brukin's instruction to pay attention for a high pitched, rapidly vibrating whine as a sign they were near and potentially triangulating on me, was always in the back of my mind, like nagging reminder to always be alert.

Eventually fatigue set in as we hadn't rested and we hadn't found any tonc pools or streams in all the way we had traveled. We each took a piece of amber and chewed. It was most disgusting in flavor, making us screw up our faces as if in pain. Once swallowed though, we all felt energized.

Once again though, Bril's agitation was rising. It seemed as if whenever he was under stress his impatience would grow quickly and uncontrollably. There was little we could do except keep an eye on him and some space between us. As we rounded another cinder pit and crested the rise on the other side we were greeted by yet another cluster of cave and tube entrances. There was something different about these though and Togn knew right away what it was.

"Great!" he exclaimed. "I think we may have found what we're looking for."

Bril and I followed him to a tube with moss hanging over the entry and a light, cool mist escaping through its dense cushion of green. Togn reached high and moved the moss to the side at the upper right corner and sure enough there was a spot with the kind of script he had talked about.

"This is it!" he said, "Finally, maybe our luck will change."

Togn went first descending into what was complete darkness. I pressed my hand against the wall to steady myself and to keep a point of reference. The floor beneath my feet was very smooth and quite slippery with its accumulation of moisture from the mist. The mist was refreshing and I began to feel slightly rejuvenated. Our journey through darkness went on and on, turning corners, the floor undulating but always going down. Finally, I glimpsed some light and with a hundred steps or so we entered a spot with glowstones and a fast-moving stream. Togn squatted and squinted to study a vertical pillar of stone on the other side of the stream where more of the script appeared. Then he stood up and exclaimed we had lucked out, that we were on one of the main streams that would eventually lead us to a place he called Skelwora. Immediately I was conflicted. We had been trying to reach Amoro because of Bril's deteriorating condition, but if we now headed off to this community we might be going in the totally wrong direction. I pulled out the journal and contact shards and read them. Our destination, or Amoro, lay almost at right angles to the direction of the stream.

"Do these streams travel mostly straight?" I asked Togn.

"Oh, no," he laughed. "They have more turns and twists then you can imagine, and the direction they lay in in one place will most certainly not be the direction they line up with at your destination."

"So, it's kind of a crap shoot trying to use the shards down here because there's no way you can tell the movement of the streams," I said, stating the obvious.

"That's right," replied Togn. "What we know is that this one will take us to Skelwora and places in between, but that's about it."

"Places in between?" I questioned, thinking that meant there were some kind of stations, or stops along the way.

""Yes," replied Togn, explaining. "You see how shallow and slow moving the stream is here? Well that's because it sits at a high point which was no doubt constructed by the Kech when they were developing this system. When we leave here the water will flow much faster and be much deeper until the next spot where there's a chance to change directions or where there's a community. They're called exchanges. Only the main destination is shown on the placard at an exchange, but there are other placards along the sides of the stream that announce what's coming up."

"So, wait a beat," I said, trying to figure out just how we used the system. "So, what do we do? Jump in and get carried by the current?"

"No!" Togn laughed. "You get on one of these," he said reaching behind me.

There, along the wall of the tunnel were flat pieces of what appeared to be stone. I hadn't noticed them standing there because they blended in so well. Togn grabbed one by its edge and easily picked it up and dropped it down. It was about two meters long and half of a meter wide at the middle, but it was tapered front and back so it looked almost like what I knew of as a canoe, but instead of being hollowed out, it was completely flat. There were what appeared to be hand holds at various places, and Togn explained they were there so you could get a grip easily when going around corners. He simply called the piece of stone, a slab.

"So, this is a pretty fast ride?" I asked.

Togn laughed hilariously. "Oh," he said, "You're gonna love it!"

"What is this stone?" I asked, surprised at its lightness as I lifted it.

"It's softstone," replied Togn, "and just what we need to fix those boots of yours, and Bril's."

With that he used his sword to cut a slice of the stone from one of the slabs and dropped it down beside my left foot.

"Okay," Togn instructed, "stand on it."

When I did, he went to work cutting the stone following the outline of my foot. When he was done we did the same with the other, and then did the same for Bril. We stashed the cutouts in our packs. Togn explained we needed another item before he could make the boot repairs and that he hoped we'd come across it at a market. Meantime, my big toes were sticking through the fronts of my boots and my left boot was torn along the side of the sole. Still, they were definitely better than nothing.

"Well," I said, hoisting one of the slabs of softstone, "I guess we ought to try this. Any advice, Togn?"

"Okay," he started, "first of all don't try fighting anything, the currents are too strong and too swift. Just use the handholds and shift your body as you're entering bends, kind of like riding a horse. For those of us that might find we're ahead of the others, just stop when you get to the next exchange and let the others catch up. It's easy to stop at exchanges by just putting your arms out and touching the bottom. Right before the exchanges you'll feel your speed drop right off. To get going again, just use your arms to move your slab toward the exit of the exchange. Let's all stop at the first exchange we come to so we can see how everyone is doing."

With that we followed Togn's lead placing our slabs on the gently flowing, shallow water at the exchange, laying down on our stomachs, and using our arms and hands to launch. At first, the speed increased slowly for about 10 meters, but then suddenly it was like we had plunged off a cliff! The air and spray from the gathering speed made it almost impossible to see and the glowstones zipped past relentlessly, almost seeming like they were just one massive light. For a while we were going straight, but at the first bend I got a taste of the forces at work. My body was instantly thrown in the opposite direction of the bend, forcing me to hold on with white knuckles while my legs slid completely off the slab, my boot toes dangling in the torrent of the current. Ahead I could see Bril also struggling to hold on, all the while sending a wave of spray back toward me. We entered another bend, and another, followed by weaving in rapid succession from one direction to the next. The constant twisting and turning sent my body flailing side-to-side with so much force I was sure I was going to loose my grip on the hand holds. Suddenly the stream straightened, but then to my horror it dove downward on a long gradual incline, forcing me to stiffen my arms to keep from sliding forward and off the front of the slab. I held on for dear life wondering how far it would be before we came to an exchange. Fortunately, it wasn't long at all.

We rounded yet another bend and suddenly our speed dropped so fast that a rush of air was forced from my lungs and I felt like I was going to pass out. Then, it was over. I put my hands out and touched the smooth stream bed, coming to a complete stop. I looked to my left to see Bril roll off his slab and lay flat on his back, laughing hilariously along with Togn who had been sitting there when we arrived. I just stared at them incredulously, but slowly the realization spread over me that it hadn't been all that bad, and it sure was a quick way to get around. A smile spread across my face and I gave in to laughter too.

It was time to check our progress so I pulled out the shards and lined them up. Amazingly they now showed Amoro was very close. In fact, it appeared she might be within walking distance. We stashed our slabs and headed out of the exchange following the path through a tunnel and out through a moss-covered entrance.

The glow stones were bright and the landscape was now lush. Soft, spongy moss clung to the stones underfoot and the air smelled clean, moist and sweet. Off in the distance, and all around, the air above the landscape glowed reddish orange, no doubt from the volcanic activity in those places. We were in a slight hollow with what appeared to be a well-worn path leading to the top of a hill, so we struck off in that direction. Our energy was high from the rush of the trip in the stream system and I felt a strange sense of accomplishment from having managed to stay on the slab. At the top of the hill we beheld a beautiful site. There, nestled in a hollow with multiple colored glowstones shining from behind moss, sat a long structure, cradled in the side of yet another hill. The moss covered stone angled out over its front like a veranda and several pools of water, or tonc, or both, that were fed by small falls, overflowed into a narrow stream that disappeared below a nearby cliff. Immediately I felt at peace and began to really relax in Firston, for the first time since we had arrived. I checked our shards and sure enough, Amoro was there.

We walked to the front of the structure where we could see through its crystal windows. Inside, candles glowed softly and we could see yet another small waterfall cascading down one of the walls and ending in a large pool.

"There you are," we heard from behind us.

We turned to see a very wide and short woman approaching carrying a basket of moss. I could tell immediately she was of Togn's race, and when I looked at Togn I thought I saw a slight blush on his ruddy complexion.

Before any of us could respond, she said, "Don't be surprised. A messenger sent by Ataia came by and said to expect you," she stopped in front of Togn, dropped her basket and threw her arms around him.

"Ohhhh, it is so good to see you!" she cried. "There are so few of us left." After what seemed like a very long time, they separated and she turned to welcome us, not nearly as enthusiastically, but warmly nonetheless.

"Come inside," she instructed. "You must all be tired and in need of rest and nourishment." With that she led us through a large stone door that was so well balanced on its struts that just a slight touch of her finger sent it swinging open. Inside the air was light, and beautifully scented by the earthy perfume of the moss. Beneath our feet, a solid surface of smooth cinders reflected candlelight. The waterfall we had seen from outside dropped into a large pool and when Amoro saw us looking at it fondly she knew immediately we wanted to soak.

"The water is the perfect temperature," she coaxed us. "You will find it very relaxing so get in. I'll prepare some nourishment for us while you all relax." With that she sauntered off to another room.

We didn't waste any time stripping off our clothes and settling into the warm water. The fall constantly replaced the water, which overflowed and ran through a small hollow beneath the wall before flowing outside. There, with the soft sound of the water, the candles glowing and fatigue finally catching up to me, I fell into a deep sleep.

In my dreams I was with the woman from the clothing founden. This time though we were beside a dreamy pool of water surrounded by a thick fog. It was very warm and moist and we were both wet, like we had just climbed out of the pool. I studied her tattoo and then her appearance changed before my eyes. She grew much older and we knew each other very well, and she took my hand leading me into the water. As the bottom gradually faded away from my feet I felt a tremendous weight pushing down on my shoulders. Down and down we went, the water over our heads and deepening. She strode confidently and unflinching in front of me. Suddenly I realized I was out of air and I started gasping, swallowing water!

CHAPTER SIXTEEN

Then I was awake

Then, I was instantly wide awake feeling myself being lifted, air returning to my lungs and things coming into view through my water soaked eyelids. I was back in Amoro's pool with Togn's large hands under my armpits, holding me out of the water. I rolled to the side, grabbing the stones at the edge of the pool and pulling myself out.

"Oh," I gasped, "I was having this dream, being led underwater.... What happened?"

"I think Bril was trying to drown you," Togn said matter-of-factly.

"What!"

"I was half asleep," Togn said, "But I heard a struggle and water splashing and when I woke up I saw him pushing down on your shoulders, holding you under."

"Where is he?"

"He ran out when I shoved him away from you."

"Geez," I exclaimed, "Thank you, Togn! I was having this dream with that woman we both know, and she was leading me into deep water, and it got so deep and I was under for so long that I didn't have anymore air." I paused, my mind racing about what could be happening to Bril. "We better go find him," I jumped to my feet, and began pulling on my pants.

"No, no," cautioned Togn. "Amoro said to stay here. She went after him."

"Do you think she'll be okay, I mean, what with his mental state and all?"

"Don't worry," Togn assured me, "I'm sure she can handle anything Bril might do. Plus his sword is over there," motioning to a pile of our things.

"I just hope she can get to the bottom of this," I said wearily, sitting back down beside the pool and slipping into my shirt.

"Me too," Togn said hopefully. Then without hardly missing a beat, "Do you want to eat something? Amoro said there's food prepared back there somewhere," he gestured to the doorway leading to other parts of the structure.

I felt torn because I wanted to make sure Amoro would be okay, but on the other hand, she was a very strong looking woman and since she was one of Togn's race I relaxed and figured he would know best.

We rose and headed through the arched doorway and into a large area lit by glowstones with hanging moss drooping down walls having hundreds of carved niches. Each niche held natural things like dried flowers and crystals and many things I had never seen before. The room smelled of the refreshing mint-like aroma of the moss, blended with the terrestrial-like aroma of hot sunshine on rocks. To the right side of the room was a long, low bench hugging the curved wall. Its top was covered with what I assumed was Amoro's busy work. A sleek shard here, a pestle half full of unidentifiable materials there, and tools with finely carved handles complete with woven carver worm thread carriers neatly arranged. But what caught my eye in the menagerie of items was a glass-like substance. I ran back to the pool and retrieved my pack. When I got back to the bench I pulled out a piece of the cinder strike blood. It looked the same as the sample on the bench.

"Look here," I said to Togn. "Amoro might know what to do with this cinder strike blood. She's got a little of it here."

"This must be her damp room," Togn said. "She does her spells and enchantments here," he turned, studying the niches in the walls. "Maybe she has some firebrand so we can fix your footwear."

The next thing I heard was Togn's enthusiastic, "Ah, ha!" as he pulled a five centimeter square cube from a niche. He dug into the pack and removed the softstone cutouts he had made. He placed one on the floor and told me to remove my boots. Then, with boot in hand he dropped the cube of firebrand onto the softstone. Immediately a flash and intense white flame spread across the stone's surface. He waited as the stone softened and immediately after the flame went out, he pressed the sole of the boot on to the softened stone. Pressing down on the boot's top he made the stone rise up along its edges. Then, he used his sword to form the stone to the sides of the boot. When he was done, the boot had a new sole that was impervious to most anything.

"Here, try it on, and walk a little in it so it picks up the pattern from the floor." he instructed.

I slipped my foot into the boot, feeling heat still rising from the sole, laced it and took a few steps. It felt incredibly light yet strong, and as I walked I could feel the boot sticking just a little to the cinder floor, no doubt creating little dimples in the sole that could improve traction. Togn motioned for me to hand the other boot to him and he went to work on it. I was amused by his childlike joy as he went about the task. It seemed that no matter what came our way he was incredibly resilient and I was very glad for his knowledge. I slipped on the second boot, walked to add the impressions, and then we went through the doorway to our right.

Now, we entered a very light and circular room. A large, clear glass circular window sat above a serpentine stone countertop with orange, yellow and red swirls. There was a pot sitting on one of the red swirls with steam rising from it. Togn went to it, sniffed and smiled broadly.

"Mmmmm," he said with glee, "syphoria!"

I stood beside him and let the aroma fill my nostrils. It was like something I had known but I couldn't describe it, or remember it. The scent made my mouth water and my stomach growl! Togn wasn't wasting any time. He filled two stone bowls with the stew and handed one to me with a stone spoon. At first the taste was slightly sweet and salty. As I ate more though enjoying the berries and what seemed like potatoes, I started feeling incredibly energetic. Togn saw it in my eyes and he smiled ear to ear.

"It's got moonberries and momoroot! And of course some tonc and moss," he explained. "You will be ready for anything after one bowl of this, and after two you probably won't be able to sleep for a glowcycle, at least."

Even though I had no memories of food, the lack in variety of food since my arrival on Octa had troubled me a little. Tonc was easy, quick and seemed to nourish me just fine. But there was something pleasant about using my teeth, and having the feeling of solid food in my mouth. We ate like we were famished and even had seconds. Finally, my thoughts went back to Bril and Amoro.

"Maybe we should go look for them," I half-asked, half-stated.

Togn agreed and so with our new found energy we stepped back on to wild Firston. Togn called out in a rumbling, echoey vocal blast. Again. And Again. Then, we heard a faint response and set off in the direction of the sound. Our trek took us up the rock cliff that formed the back portion of the hollow behind Amoro's house. On top of the rise we could see for kilometers in all directions. There, just a few hundred meters away we spotted the pair and set off with speed to reach them. But as we approached we saw another being.

Hovering just above Amoro and Bril a dark, wispy, almost smokey entity held Bril in a seeming trancelike state. Bril's head was back, his arms hanging limply at his sides and his feet were just inches off the ground. Amoro was standing to the side of Bril moving dancelike while waving a fluted shard. She was chanting something and her tone was deep and stern.

"It's a Cinder Spirit Wraith," whispered Togn in my ear. "It's got Bril pretty good and Amoro is trying to break the spell."

"What can we do?" I asked, my voice cracking.

"The pack!" Togn blurted. And he was off, racing back to Amoro's house to retrieve our main pack. For just a moment I was confused, but then I remembered the pack had the Spirit Fortitude enchantment and if we could get it close enough to Bril it might help in Amoro's struggle. I moved closer to Bril, testing to see if the wraith responded in any way. Sure enough, when I was just a meter away, my fortitude was drained. I was thrust into a darkness I had never experienced. My will turned to mush and I felt my confidence, even about living, draining from my being. I sank deeper and deeper into nothingness as a weight bore down on my shoulders. I was about to give up on my will to live until I saw Ataia before me, smiling, knowing. My confidence rose. She gestured for me to follow as she turned and walked away. I could see a beam of light around her and extending behind her, and I stepped into it, following. Within a few steps, the darkness on me lifted, Ataia vanished and my will to live returned. I spun around, now a few meters away from Bril and the wraith.

By now, Togn was back and he threw the pack to me. I put it on and took the few steps to Amoro, standing close to her with my hand on her shoulder. I felt an amazing rush of energy, all golden, warm light covering me. The light started ascending and spreading out to cover Bril until he was completely immersed in it. The wraith started making a high pitched screaming noise, and moved excitedly back and forth. Amoro held her ground and continued chanting faster now. I started to rock back and forth with her and the golden light encircling Bril expanded, getting brighter.

There was a moment when the wraith seemingly made a last stand, gyrating wildly, screaming at an unimaginable pitch. But, Amoro and our enchantments were too much for it. In a gesture of defiance, it threw Bril to the ground, dashing his head into the cinders and sending his body into convulsions. When it was done, it disappeared into the wind.

I raced to Bril lifting his upper body up out of the cinders and wiping them from his bloodied face. He was incredibly pale, unconscious, and breathing heavy, fitful breaths.

"We need to get him in the wet room," Amoro yelled.

Togn moved in and lifted Bril on to his shoulder with my help, and we raced back over the cinders, down the cliff and through Amoro's massive front door. In the wet room, Amoro went to work, gathering substances from various niches and blending them together using two stones. Togn and I gathered pieces of moss from the pool area, soaked them in the water and used them to bathe Bril's body in hopes of bringing down the fever he had developed.

When Amoro was finished with the preparations she approached and knelt beside Bril. She fitted a golden, dough-like substance to his face and formed it all around his head. Then she opened a hole in the substance near his nostrils and another one at the very top of his head. Next, she lit a wad of dried mosslike material with a small piece of firebrand. The material flashed with white hot flame and then gave off a golden, sweet smelling smoke. We made room for her to move as she waved the smoking materials just above and all along the length of Bril's body. The smoke hung in the air just above Bril and it developed long, tiny filaments that reached upward a meter or more, and downward, seemingly into Bril's skin.

Meanwhile, Amoro knelt at Bril's head, methodically chanting a series of musical sounds. Her tone was much different than the chanting she used with the wraith. It was a coaxing and seductive chant and I could see Togn was visibly moved by the sounds and the tone. But it was Bril's response that startled me. As if he was being animated, his fingers and toes started twitching, causing his hands and feet to gyrate. Then his arms and legs wobbled and his torso started rising and falling, undulating with the chanting. The filaments of smoke seemed to penetrate all the way through his body, and by now they reached all the way to the ceiling and I suspected also beyond. I would learn later that this was a spirit retrieval ceremony where this mysterious smoke worked with the chanting to seek out and draw back lost spirits. It seems the wraith had scattered Bril's spirit across the land and somehow it would be drawn back with this process.

Amoro continued chanting for a long time as the smoke filaments worked their way around Bril's body. Then, the filaments suddenly seemed to realize something. They began banding together and spinning themselves into a rope like form. Once the rope of smoke was about four centimeters in diameter it drifted to the top of Bril's head, sought the opening in the dough-like material and dove through, disappearing inside. Suddenly, Bril convulsed and sucked in air through his nostrils. It was like a first breath, and at that moment it was immediately familiar, as if it was something I already knew.

Slowly, Bril moved his head, first side to side, and then raising off the floor as if trying to look around. He mumbled something. Amoro lifted the dough-like mask from his face.

"You're back," she said softly.

For a moment though we weren't sure. Bril looked confused and curious at the same time.

"Do you remember me?" Amoro asked, "Them?" gesturing to us. Then, a flicker of recognition followed by a big smile. He was back.

I felt a rush of gladness and gratitude. Togn offered Bril his big hand. Bril grabbed it and stood up with his help.

"Whoa,"Bril said. "What happened?"

"Do you remember the wraith?" Amoro asked.

Bril was stunned for a moment, then I could see his memory coming back. His face grew grave.

"What is it?" Amoro probed.

"I remember now," Bril began, "and I saw things. Things that were terrible."

He told us that the wraith had come up from the cinders directly in front of him and almost immediately he felt his life force draining. Once it had a lock on him he could no longer resist and he entered a very dark place. No longer able to see, he was thrust into a black void where images raced in front of him. He said he saw me in a kind of web and these large fly-like creatures were sticking their proboscises into me and drawing out blood. Then, in the distance he saw himself, standing by and watching, almost as if he was working with the flies. He turned away from us, tearfully murmuring, shaking. Togn went to him, put his hand on his shoulder and spoke, comforting. Amoro drew me aside.

"The beings that are tracking you have enlisted the help of the wraiths here in Firston," she counseled. "This won't be the last time they prey on Bril's weaker spirit to delay, intimidate and locate you.

The spirit fortitude enchantment on your pack will definitely help, and," her voice trailed off as she surveyed the niches along the wall, "I was going to say that I could enchant your weapons with a mist bender enchantment, but I don't have enough cinder strike blood."

"Wait," I said and went to the pack retrieving the cinder strike blood we gathered from our earlier battle. "You mean this," I held it out to her.

"Yes! With what I have this will provide enough for at least four enchantments."

I went to gather our swords and obsidian axe. Togn had taken Bril to the pool so he could bathe in the healing substance. Seeing the bruises and cuts on his body, I wanted to use a portion of the cinder strike blood to help him heal. But, I reasoned that our long term survival was more important, and if we encountered more of those wraiths, we'd definitely better have all the help we could get.

I took the weapons and placed them on Amoro's work table. She combined the pieces of cinder strike blood by flashing them with a cube of firebrand. Then she meticulously cut and formed it into four shapes matching the cutting edges of the weapons. Next, she gathered 12 compounds from the niches, blended them together and used the paste to coat the insides of the strike blood forms. The final step was to chant a series of 12 words while sliding the forms along the edges of the weapons. As she did so, the weapons glowed a ghostly black. When done, she turned and sat on a low stone stool, dropped her head, and seemingly went to sleep. I deftly collected the weapons and went back to Bril and Togn.

"New enchantment," I said to Togn, handing him his sword and axe. "Now, they will be effective against those mist and smoke types of creatures."

Togn beamed, strapping on his sword and axe sheaths and fitting the weapons to them. For a long time we relaxed, and shared some more syphoria, hoping to boost Bril's energy and reinforce our own. Amoro slept on the stool even as we passed by to replenish our bowls.

The three of use talked about our next plans. We still had to find some orb crystals and steel stone for our friends in Canyonlands. Above all, we needed to find the drop point that would get us into The Mists. We also talked about the delicate issue related to Bril's spirit. When Amoro awoke we asked if she had any other ideas for fortifying Bril against spirit benders like the wraiths. She confided that we would get all the answers we needed, once Bril reached The Mists because it was there that he would meet the being who would guide him to his destiny. She handed a contact shard to me, and said she had been having visions about Bril and that once in The Mists we should see the being Uraya. She said it, genderless Uraya, would be able to take Bril on an astral journey where he could learn of his destiny. Once that was done, he would be forever changed because he would have insights that would make him certain about the choices he makes.

Amoro gave me four cubes of firebrand and what looked like a rope made of moss. The rope though was only about 10 centimeters long and she saw my puzzled look. I couldn't imagine why we'd even find it useful. Then she held out her hand and I gave the little piece of rope to her. She looked across the room, focusing at the other wall and suddenly, the little piece of rope extended to cover the distance.

"It will work for you too, or anybody," she said.

I took the rope in hand and looked at my hand, imagining the rope fitting there. Sure enough, it collapsed to its original size. It was seemingly similar to what I was experiencing with slow motion. The act of focusing my intent now had new meaning. Togn took the rope and played with it, sending it out all the way into the damp room and then bringing it back, chuckling the whole time.

"This will definitely be helpful," I told Amoro as I stashed the firebrand in the pack. "I don't want to overstay our welcome, or ask for too much, but you wouldn't have any idea where we could find some orb crystals?"

She smiled a broad smile, throwing her arms around me and giving me a powerful hug. "You can never overstay or ask for too much, and yes, you can find orb crystals in the fire cove just before Skelwora. You can't miss it, on the right with a bit of a green glow rising from it's darkness. But be careful, there are lots of eekutchi in there and they like those orb crystals for nests. They're not too upset if you take some, but if you take some that are near their nests they will get belligerent."

We rested some more while Togn made the repairs to Bril's boots. Shortly later we stepped back out on Firston's fire-ravaged ground and headed for Skelwora.

CHAPTER SEVENTEEN

Skelwora

Rested and energized we took the path to the Exchange, boarded the softstone boards and took off on another wild water ride. This time I made the mistake of being directly behind Togn and was drenched with spray for most of the journey. We stopped momentarily at each Exchange to monitor our progress and check for any old signs that might provide clues about our locations. Sure enough, at the third Exchange Togn announced we were close to Skelwora because the sign actually announced the distance remaining. Togn said that probably meant that we'd be in Skelwora at the next Exchange. But, we needed to get the orb crystals for Oshya, and that location was before Skelwora. So, we dutifully stood our softstone boards along the rough hewn stone wall and headed out of the Exchange.

When we emerged the glowstones were at full light, casting sharp shadows and lighting everything in a soft yellow light. The air smelled putrid and as my eyes adjusted to the light I saw why. We were standing in a foul-smelling liquid that was flowing from a rise to our left and passing by the entrance to the Exchange. We all realized the problem at the same time and jumped in unison to higher ground.

"Whew!" I said with disgust "what is that?"

"That is eekutchi excrement, and while it smells awful, I used to know people who swore by it as a cure for aches and pains," Togn informed.

"Yuk," said Bril, "Well, regardless of that, I won't be rubbing any of that on myself, that's for sure."

Togn laughed while I just chuckled.

"Okay," I said. "So I guess we follow the stream of that stuff and we should find some eekutchi and hopefully some orb crystals."

Bril and I pulled out swords, while Togn hoisted his axe. We walked on the higher ground and followed the stream of excrement. It was clearly flowing from a hollow just 30 or so meters ahead. The landscape here was quite different from other places we had been in Firston. There was more solid rock and it occurred in coarse, distorted forms with many niches and crevices. It was dark gray to black and it had a burnt smell. Moss grew haphazardly from the holes and cracks. We stepped cautiously because the same jagged material was underfoot. I was glad Togn had fixed our boots and when I stopped to look at the bottom of one, I saw the sharp stone was having no effect on them. But, having stopped for a moment, I felt like something was watching me and I was sure I caught movement out of the corner of my eye.

In the next instant I saw what it was, and it was on the attack! The creature was long and slender with scales. The body was at least a meter long and the snout made up almost a third of that length. All I saw were two very long rows of razor-like teeth and my sword was nowhere to help! In the next instant, it's head was separated from its body by a single blow from Togn's axe! The head flipped upward and struck me in the chest on its way to its final resting place. All I could do was shake my head in disbelief. I couldn't believe I had missed its approach and been caught off guard so much that I didn't even have time to use my sword.

"Wow!" I managed. "Togn, thanks yet again for saving my life, or limb, or whatever I might have lost there.!"

Togn chuckled, "You wouldn't believe how many of these I dispatched when I was growing up. They are dumb as rocks, but they are stealthy. Once you get used to them though, you kind of get a sixth sense when they are going to attack."

Bril went to the head to study it. "Wow, those are some weird teeth," he observed. "They are not really pointed, but more flat, like knives. Hey, look, one of them came out." Bril pointed to a flat, ivory-looking item about five centimeters long and two centimeters high. He picked it up, shaking off the black blood and studied it.

"Pretty sharp" he announced. "We should keep it." He scouted around and found a thick piece of moss root. Then, he pressed the sharp side of the tooth into the root. "There, I didn't want it to cut up my pack so that should work until I find something more permanent." With that, he found a just-right-size pocket in his pack and plopped the tooth into it.

With the shock of the first attack behind us, we readied our weapons and moved forward, our heads turning constantly to see all around. I was glad the glowstones were bright because the light definitely helped us to focus on the shadows. As we rounded a corner we saw a large cove that backed into a wall of blackish red rock. Fire cove, I thought. All along the upper edges of the rock we saw round crystals embedded in the rock and also hanging by crystal threads. All along the base of the rock we saw eekutchi, laying about, resting. I whispered my disappointment to Togn and Bril who looked at me with the same level of concern. How could we manage to get past all of them while getting up high enough to grab some of the orb crystals?

We scouted the area around us to see if the crystals might also occur in other places. But, no luck. It was Bril who whispered what we all were thinking. Why not go up on top of the rock and reach over to get the crystals? With that, we inched our way to the side of the cove. Bril and I took the lead as Togn walked behind with his back to us to prevent an attack from the rear. We crossed back over the stream of excrement and started up the rocks on the side of the cove. But then, the unplanned happened. Bril stepped on a mass of the crystals hidden beneath the moss, slipped and fell. Before I could help him get up, there were three eekutchis bearing down on him coming from seemingly nowhere. Uh, oh, I thought, a nest. Togn swung into action bringing his axe down on the lead eekutchi, while I swiped at the second one. Meanwhile Bril struggled to his feet and stepped backward to avoid the mouth of the third animal. Togn and I dispatched it in unison. Now, other eekutchi were streaming toward us.

In a brilliant move, Bril knelt at the nest and started prying orb crystals from it with his sword. Togn and I stood against the onslaught, flailing mercilessly at one after another eekutchis. Bril yelled that he had two crystals in his pack. At that point I yelled for them to grab on to my pack and we all remembered the event we learned to activate Absence of Presence. Once invisible, the eekutchi kept bumping into our feet and gnashing their teeth in the air, but we stepped skillfully and quickly enough to avoid being caught in their jowls. After another few steps we were beyond the mass of them. Still, we maintained invisibility until we were well away.

"Whew!" I said. "Everybody okay?"

"Don't see any blood," Togn announced.

"Me either," intoned Bril.

"Well, that was a lucky break. I couldn't believe how fast you dug out those crystals, Bril," I said, laughing.

Togn laughed agreeing.

"It was actually a stroke of luck," Bril said. "At first I didn't think so when I fell, but when they came out so easily I knew we'd be okay."

We bounded away toward the exchange. Once inside we grabbed the boards and took off on another thrill ride. This time I managed to stay in front of Togn. We stopped briefly at two exchanges, but neither was the exit for Skelwora, so on we went. At the fourth exit, Togn announced we had arrived, and so had many others. We were in a large oval shaped underground room with tunnels coming in from all sides. The tunnels disgorged beings seemingly constantly so we were suddenly in a crowd. We followed Togn and the others to the exit and then out into Skelwora.

Things were not like Canyonlands at all. The stone ceiling was much lower so that the canyon walls met it at just a couple of meters. The street was arching and the coarse stone of the walls was hollowed out to accommodate foundens, places to eat, and residences. The feeling was very closed in, and protected. There was also no place to turn in our weapons and many of the individuals were carrying swords, axes, long knives and daggers.

There was an amazing mix of beings. Most had the familiar human form but that's where the similarities stopped. I could see many of Togn's race, with their short, wide forms. But I also saw some very tall beings with elongated faces and noses. There were some who had extremely exaggerated features like deep crevices in their faces and bulbous cheeks. There were many that looked like Bril and me, only in different heights and weights. With all the variety I started to feel like I belonged, like it didn't matter what you looked like, everybody seemed to be accepting of difference.

As we passed a weapons founden, a man approached us, stood in front of our path and spoke.

"I believe you have something that must get to Oshya in Canyonlands, so give it to me," he said very sternly. As Bril was removing his pack to retrieve the orb crystals, I asked the man what items he was expecting us to have. Before Bril had the orbs out of his pack, the man answered correctly. The exchange happened quickly and the man disappeared into the crowd.

"Well," quipped Togn, "that was very efficient. We didn't even have to search for him."

I agreed and then reminded my friends that we still needed to find some steel stone for Ialeo before we could drop out of Firston. We continued down the street taking in the sights, sounds and smells. Ever since I had arrived in Firston, my senses had been assailed by the unfamiliar. I thought that it might be partly due to my loss of memory, but I also thought that Firston being sandwiched between the lighter Canyonlands and the heavier Mists, was a place of exaggeration. Smells, sounds and even sights seemed to be condensed into their raw basics.

The pace of life was also concentrated and it felt as if the beings inhabiting the place were larger than life. And, as if I had asked for an instant example, we were confronted by a being with a most commanding presence. Her skin was silken, her face captivating and her stature alluring. I had to catch my breath so I wouldn't look so enthralled that she had appeared before me. Then, she spoke.

"Catching you three in my sight, made me wonder if we had known each other before this moment."

Bril, Togn and I exchanged glances among ourselves, shaking our heads side to side in unison. None of us could speak.

"Come, come, dears, I'm sure you can speak."

Finally, it was Togn who managed a chirp-like "no," surprising me almost to laughter because his voice was always much deeper.

"Well at least one of you has a voice," she chided. "There is just something very familiar here. Maybe with just one of you?"

I searched my memory but had no recollection of her. Having found my voice again, I inquired if she recalled a place or circumstance.

"No, I do not," she affirmed, and then added, "for it is in illusion we arrive and in illusion we leave."

The words reverberated inside me. They were the same words carved on the first obelisk left behind by the ball creature upon my arrival on Octa.

"Wait!" I motioned for her to stay. "What you just said, is very familiar to me," and then as if we were exchanging coded messages I said, "Do we have but moments to become as momentous," mouthing the words from the second ball creature obelisk.

She regarded me through squinted eyes, and then said, "You know, I'm in need of an eekutchi tooth because when dulled they become wonderful garment closures," she fondled one on the front of her long, flowing, veil-like robe, all the while eyeing Bril. I could see Bril blushing as he studied her thinly masked feminine figure just under the cloth.

Bril swung his pack from his back and opened it, pulling out the eekutchi tooth and handing it to her. "Here," he said, dreamily. "I don't have any use for it."

Togn and I exchanged eye-brow-raised glances, smiling at Bril's seduction. Then, she reached into a hidden pocket near her shoulder and withdrew a contact shard. She handed the shard to me, saying, "When we arrive from above, we must leave from below." In the next instant, she was gone.

Togn and Bril looked quizzically at me and I realized then that it was time to fill them in on the messages from the ball creature obelisks. It turns out they had wondered why I had asked them about messages from the ball creatures they had encountered, and Bril said that when I didn't explain he was suspicious. I apologized for keeping it secret and I recognized that given how much we must rely on each other, that anything undermining trust could eventually work against us. I told them from that point on, I would be open with everything, and I hoped they could be as well. In another way I was glad they also knew the words now and maybe we could all share in the process of discovering what it all meant.

The shard the woman gave me had the name Alechay and since she didn't tell me what part of the underworld to look in, I took out the journal shard and lined up its notch with the notch on the contact shard. No luck. No line showed on the contact shard. But, while I had the journal shard out I noticed a glowing red line that went all the way to the end of the shard. I assumed that represented the path to the brood foot plant we had to get for Ataia in the Mists. The other red line stopped short of the edge of the shard, and must have been to show the direction of steel stone we needed to get for Ialeo. We already knew it would be found near fire pits so it seemed likely there wouldn't be any of those in Skelwora.

Next I dug into my pack and found the contact shard for Uraya, but Togn stopped me.

"The line will be to the edge for that one too," he said. "Amoro told us they were in the Mists."

"Oh, right," I remembered. "I guess we could get rid of that journal shard since we have you to keep track of all this stuff," I said to him jokingly. He laughed with me as he always did.

We continued down the street, considering our needs as we passed each founden. My leathers were in good shape but both Bril and Togn were practically wearing rags. We went into a fabric and cloth founden and started searching the racks for leather.

Togn and Bril each found some nice pieces. Togn's were honey-colored and Bril's were a burgundy. At the back of the room they got scanned and punched the buttons. In short order they stood in front of me looking like a couple of professional adventurers, weapons and all.

"Now that is an improvement," I said, "And, that leather will protect you a lot better than that old fabric." I felt a sense of pride to have such faithful, well-appointed companions on such an arduous quest. I only hoped they could stay with me.

Back outside and just a few doorways down the street the rangers were breaking up a fight. That was the second time since we had been there that we noticed altercations among beings. When I asked Togn about that he reminded me about the rynd and that it was much more prevalent in Firston and the Mists than it was in Canyonlands. Plus, he said, the weapons didn't get checked in Skelwora, so there was that added issue. Still, he assured me, the rangers always had extra presences near places where rynd was available so they kept disagreements from growing into something larger.

As the glowcycle wore on we continued down the street, enjoying the sights and sounds, and not having to be on guard for surprises like cinder strikes and eekutchi all the time. The glowstones were at that soft golden glow when we stopped in front of a rest founden. Togn's nose detected tonc stew and he went quickly inside. Bril and I followed without hesitation because we were all very hungry after our travels and the events that had accompanied them.

The large hall was very quiet with just a few beings milling about and helping themselves to the offerings in the pots. Togn and I got bowls of tonc stew, but Bril went for the rynd. Togn's eyebrows raised when he saw that, and he pulled me aside.

"We should keep a close eye on him if he's going to eat that," he said seriously. "It makes people warlike, and he's already got that problem of his."

I nodded agreement and suggested that when we went to rest that we take turns staying awake. We all sat at a long stone table on stone benches, savoring our meals and enjoying the warm, secure feelings of being in that space. I felt a sense of peace come over me as the tonc stew worked its mellowing magic. Finally, I told my friends I needed to rest and nodded at Togn with my best, "wake-me-up-when-you-are-ready-to-rest," look. He smiled and nodded back. I went to the back of the room, found a freshly covered moss bed and sank into it, falling deeply asleep.

A sharp shaking of my shoulder woke me with a start. It was Togn.

"He's gone!" Togn said desperately.

CHAPTER EIGHTEEN

Vortold's Delight

Meanwhile:

The band of Tachina stood around Amoro. The stout woman was tied to a roof post in her house. Numerous lacerations oozed blood that Vortold lapped up with his proboscis. She was defiant and Vortold was merciless. Being the hunter of his fame meant always getting your prey. He felt no concern for any being he encountered and was totally compassionless with those he thought held answers for his quest.

Amoro squinted through tears of pain, chanting tones and words that bolstered her defenses and resistance. Vortold grinned, slime dripping from below his proboscis. His open mouth showed teeth, an evolution as the Tachina arose from the dark matter of a developing galaxy. His multi-faceted, bulbous eyes reflected the glowstone and candle light and his hands, another evolved aspect, opened to reveal small, sharp barbs. He raked the three fingers across her face, drawing more blood.

"You will tell me when they were here, and when they left," his voice rasped and crackled. Amoro remained defiant, chanting. Vortold sucked some more blood from the new wounds. He liked the taste, a nice salty, sweet treat, and he delighted in the knowledge that soon he could drink his fill. But first, she must talk.

Meanwhile, in Skelwora.

We raced outside to the full glare of the glowstones. It was almost mid glowcycle. We looked left and right, starting in both directions, then stopping. There were so many beings and I was barely awake.

"Where, why, would he go?" I asked Togn in desperation.

"That rynd!" fumed Togn, disgusted.

"Okay, wait," I said, trying to inject some logic into the situation.

"He didn't take his pack, right? So, maybe he's just gone for a stroll?"

"A stroll?" Togn looked incredulous.

"Okay, wait, what about that woman he was smitten with? She had some kind of knowing because I could have sworn she knew Bril had that eekutchi tooth. Maybe she somehow influenced him and he went looking for her," I offered.

"Well, stranger things than that have happened on this trip," Togn said thoughtfully. "There is no way we are going to find him by wandering around. And standing here isn't going to do anything either."

"Okay," I said, "but just so we don't overlook the obvious, let's just scout around here. You go that way and I'll go this way. Maybe he's still in the area. Let's meet back here after we've checked around."

So, we set out. I looked back a few times until I could no longer see Togn, all the while watching the crowd of passersby and darting into and out of the foundens. When I had traveled far enough up one side of the street, I crossed and started back down the other side. Along the way I came upon a slot canyon leading off the main street. I hadn't recalled seeing it before, but reasoned I was probably overwhelmed by all the activity and had simply missed it. I ventured inside and saw that it was a sort of disposal place where the foundens got rid of unusable items. It was as if they were bound for something because everything was sorted into piles of like items- cloth here, leather there, different types of stone separated out, glass in another pile, and piles of other materials I knew nothing about.

I continued deep into the canyon, beyond the piles, coming to another slot canyon going perpendicular to the main one. And there, my heart sank. Sitting, back against the stone wall, head in hands was Bril. His sword was on the ground covered in blood, and laying nearby was a Gurji man, a being from the Mists, who was not moving. I raced to him and checked for a pulse, but he was already cold and gone.

Shaking my head in disbelief I went to Bril. He was trembling, head in hands, muttering to himself. I put my hand on his shoulder.

"Are you okay," I asked, wondering if he might be wounded. He didn't look up, he just sobbed. I turned my head, surveying the scene, trying to piece together what must have happened. The Gurgi man's axe was still in his hand and his clothes were dirty and disheveled, not from any recent misadventure, but like they had been that way a long time. Nearby I saw a small pool of blood and a trail of blood leading off up the canyon. I turned back to Bril who was head up now, staring straight ahead.

"Okay," I said, planning, "We need to get out of here. There's nothing we can do for him," motioning toward the man. "This could be big trouble if some rangers show up here." I stood up and retrieved Bril's sword and was about to hand it to him, but in seeing the blood decided to wipe it off as best I could on the dead Gurji's clothes. By now, Bril was up so I slid the sword into his sheath. Then, I looked him over really well and to my relief saw there were no injuries, other than a few bruises on his face and hands.

"C'mon," I counseled, "Let's just walk out of here, real natural-like. No running or calling attention to ourselves. Once we find Togn, we'll grab our stuff from the rest founden, and go find a quiet place to talk about this."

"Okay," Bril muttered, and we stepped out of the canyon, being our best casual selves.

Once back on the main street we found Togn right where he was supposed to be. Without telling him any details, I urged him to come with us, get our packs and leave. He adopted his best efficient and serious demeanor and we went inside. Fortunately none of the small-headed beings with the rounded ears had gone by to refresh the moss on the beds so our packs were untouched. I made a mental note to ask Togn and Bril about those beings, in case they someday figured more prominently in my life than just as moss refreshers.

Back outside we continued down the main street, passing the slot canyon that led to the place of Bril's recent problem. We kept walking, eyes ahead, acting casual, chatting nervously to each other. After a while the canyon street opened up, growing wider and with a much higher ceiling. The space in the middle of the street was bounded by long blocks of the colorful serpentine stone that were about a meter tall. This created a sort of park-like area with tonc and water fountains, seating, and tables where beings played some sort of game. We entered through an opening in the stones and found a few seats off by themselves, well out of the earshot of passersby. Bril and Togn sat on one seat, while I sat across from them, leaning forward, resting my forearms on my thighs. Togn, having sensed something all along, now grew more serious.

"Okay," he said, "what's going on? Where were you," speaking to Bril.

Bril leaned forward, staring at the ground. "I don't know," he started and then stopped. "Well, I mean, I don't know what happened.

It's like I woke up in the middle of a nightmare...didn't know where I was... and these three beings, Gurji, I think, were jostling me about, trying to get my sword. I thought I was dreaming, and a hand brushed my face...and all I could think was I wanted them off me...to leave me alone. I felt the sword handle in my hand and I drew it and struck at the one closest to me. The blade struck across the side of his neck...and then blood, a lot of blood. Another one grabbed my arm, but I kicked him, and, I don't know. It's all a blur after that. But, then they were struggling away, up the canyon, one holding the other up. I tried to wake up but realized I already was. The man on the ground was gurgling, shaking, but there was so much blood. Then he was quiet. I fell back against the stone wall and just sat there, not able to understand how I got there, or how they got there. It is all just a series of moments of clarity and a bunch of moments of just darkness."

I looked at Togn, relief showing on my face.

"Okay," I started. "It was self defense. You were just trying to get them to leave you alone and there were three of them, so you would have naturally thought they might do you some grievous harm. The way you described it, it seems like you weren't intentionally trying to cut that guy. You were just lashing out, trying to get them to leave you alone."

We were all quiet for a while. Then, Togn, seemingly needing to bring some clarity, said that he wondered if the three Gurgi, were the same ones we had seen earlier in the altercation with the rangers. He said because they were outside of the rest founden that they had probably been eating rynd. He said the Gurji were notorious rynd lovers and in fact it was they who had introduced it to the rest of the underworld. He spoke in long, slow sentences, as if telling an ancient tale to be remembered.

When the Gurji brought animals to the Mists in the early years of habitation, they did so mainly for the milk and the foods made from the milk. But over time the animals multiplied too much and so they started to slaughter them. They got a taste for the meat, and because of all the energy it provided, they became aggressive because they had more energy available than they needed. Meanwhile, the animals saw what they were doing and so the animals carried fear in their meat. The Gurji ate that, and that fear infected their bodies. He said that explains how the Gurji became aggressive and fearful, all at the same time. Based on what Bril remembered, Togn thought there was no other way for the event to have played out. Either they were going to hurt or kill Bril, or Bril would have to do that to them.

It was then that I thought it was time to address a potential underlying issue, Bril's problem and rynd.

"Look," I said, turning to Bril. "Maybe the rynd right now is not a good idea for you since you are already having a problem with frustration and anger." I watched for his reaction because I knew he was a bright person and independent, and he might not like me telling him what to do.

Togn chimed in, "And, actually, I know I go on at length about rynd, and I know it is kind of a negative thing in my culture, but it's probably best if we all avoid it for now. The tonc and tonc stew and of course syphoria, all give us what we need. Maybe we save the rynd experience for when we know we have to fight a lot."

Bril was already nodding his head in agreement, obviously relieved that others thought his actions were in self defense, and seemingly recognizing that the rynd may have played a part in the events of the previous night.

"I don't ever remember losing time like that," Bril said, "except when that wraith had me."

Togn and I both raised our eyebrows in wonder, thinking. Amoro had warned that the wraith was in concert with the Tachina and would try again to use Bril to find us. Maybe once the wraith was in contact with Bril, somehow the Tachina could home in on it to locate him, and ultimately me. What I didn't understand was why it had let go of him. Perhaps when he started defending himself against the Gurji, the wraith spell couldn't overcome his will. Or, perhaps the wraith was using a different type of spell. Regardless though, if the wraith was involved, the Tachina were probably closer than we'd like them to be. I felt a new sense of urgency to finish our business in Firston and find the passage to the Mists.

I looked across the street and saw a weapons founden and had an idea.

"Do you think that weapons maker would have steel stone we could send back to Ialeo, and skip the step of going to find a fire pit?" I asked Bril and Togn.

"We could see," replied Bril, "but he'd probably need something from us in return, and then we're back to having another item to get."

"But," Togn said, "maybe they would know the best place to find the steel stone." All our faces lit up at the same time and the next instant we were crossing the street.

Inside the weapon founden we met Ukino, a very tall, athletic female with muscle-sculpted arms, long ears and enticing eyes. She regarded us wide-eyed and seemed immediately taken to Bril.

"You aren't from around here," she half-questioned, half-stated, while surveying Bril's face.

"No," Bril stammered, "we are just passing through."

"I see," she said dismissively. "Too bad," she paused, taking on a sort of bored look. "So, what do you need?"

Since Bril was already the de facto spokesman, Togn and I let him continue.

"We need to find a fire pit so we can get some steel stone. You don't happen to know where we might find one?"

"You said you were passing through. Where are you going?"

"We are on our way to the Land of the Misanthrope," Bril stated boldly.

Ukino smiled, "Well, you've got nerve. I'll give that to you." she hesitated before continuing, "So, when you get to the LoM, it would be generous of you to send back a few blood stalker diamond point scales for me to use for the very finely crafted and custom spears I make. You might be able to find them just laying around down there because the blood stalkers do shed them from time to time. Otherwise, you just need to kill one of them."

I looked at Togn to see his reaction and it was like mine, disbelief. But, Bril didn't reveal any qualms. He just shook his head yes, smiled and asked, "So, where might the fire pits be?"

Ukino told us we would need to leave Skelwora by following the main street. Once beyond the city a kilometer or so, she said to watch for a tall spire with a very pointed top on the left. She said we would see black smoke and flame arising behind it in the distance. There would be a low cliff we would have to scale and once on top we could continue on a plateau until we reached the edge of the fire pit. Once there we would have to find places where the fires along the walls had cooled and that's where we'd get the steel stone. She said to look for the shards that had black, crumbly bases because they would be the easiest to remove.

We all thanked her in unison and went for the doorway.

"By the way," she called after us, "there are some rumors about cinder shell titans and smoke striders out that way. They aren't rumors."

We looked at each other shaking our heads, while Ukino burst out laughing as she walked to the rear of the founden. I assumed Togn knew about the titans and the striders, but I just didn't want any more bad news right then. So, I held my questions for later.

As we continued down the main street the ceiling gradually started rising until it became imperceptible in the distance. The glowstones were the brightest we had seen in Firston, illuminating everything in a yellow, red light and creating deep dark shadows wherever the light couldn't penetrate. I was feeling reasonably optimistic about finding and getting the steel stone. But, I was still concerned with Bril and trying to think of ways we could stem the attacks from that wraith if they started again. Other than the spirit fortitude enchantment on my pack and Ataia's heart blessing, we were left with just the mist bender enchantment on our weapons. We also had the dread orb which we hadn't used yet and knew nothing about how it might affect a wraith, so that was a kind of wild card we'd have to play if or when everything else was failing. A more positive appraisal occurred to me though. Once we got the steel stone, we could immediately start using the StarStone Scepter to find a passage to the Mists. That would delay the Tachina from catching up, but even so, I began feeling that I was increasingly delving into wishful thinking.

When the street neared the end of town there were few beings moving about. Within only a few meters we were once again on our own, venturing into unknown and potentially hostile territory. The path was not hard to follow because it had changed into mostly hard, smooth, black stone. Unlike the cinders we had walked in for much of our journey in Firston, this was almost a pleasure to walk on. All around us there rose up weird-looking rock structures. Some reminded me of mushrooms and others looked like squash. I wondered how I knew about those items, and more how could I even know how they tasted, but I knew I did. My missing past was now just a part of who I was. I had given up trying to remember, instead preferring to let it be and try to hang on to any new memories my mind was creating.

Eventually we spotted the spire and the black smoke rising in the distance. Walking along, we scanned the cliff for potential rock slide areas we could use to get to the top. At one place Bril pointed out a logical path that angled up the face of the cliff. It was boulder-strewn and the rocks were sharp, but when surveying the rest of the cliff, that looked like the best option. We started up, Togn in the lead, followed by Bril and then me. I reached out to steady myself by putting my hand on one of the boulders and suddenly, it was moving!

The noise it made was ear piercing, throwing Togn and Bril off guard and stumbling backward and sideways to regain their footing. I had backed up several paces to get out of the way as the boulder grew larger and larger until an animated stone figure stood in front of me. It rocked back and forth, seemingly dazed, as if it had just woken from a sound sleep. Bril was aghast, scrambling to hide behind a boulder, while Togn was looking slightly bemused. Then, everything came to a standstill. The stone creature just stood there, looking through black eyes and smelling the air with its cylindrical snout.

"It's okay," Togn yelled at me, seeing the terror in my eyes. "It's just a titan. You woke it up."

The titan then turned, raising its right, stoney leg while swinging to the left. I saw the stone foot flying toward me and fell to the ground. In the next moment the titan was moving away, taking deliberate steps with its snout just a meter off the ground. A few meters away it stopped, dropped to its stone knees and started to bury its head, snout first into the rubble. Then, it was quiet.

Togn was laughing hysterically as I got up and went about checking for damage to my arms, legs and stomach from the sharp stones. When I caught up to my companions, Togn explained that cinder shell titans used their snouts to smell volcanic gasses. When they found a vent of the gas they buried their heads in the stones and then used their mouths to consume a sort of liquid ash that coats the insides of the vents. Many times, he said, they eat their fill and then just fall asleep with their heads buried.

"So," I complained, "here I was, worried about these titans ever since Ukino mentioned them, and you knew all along they were harmless?"

"Well, not completely harmless," Togn corrected, "You almost got stepped on!"

I had to chuckle at that while letting a feeling of gratitude seep through the previous feeling of terror. It was a relief to know that not everything in this strange world was hostile.

We continued our climb, being much more cautious about where we stepped and where we put our hands. At the top of the cliff, a vast plateau stretched out in three directions. All along the flat expanse there were many glowing holes with smoke rising from them. The air was hot and heavy carrying the smells of fire, molten rock and many different substances all combined in one. The holes were not evenly spaced, but they did appear to get more numerous farther away. I estimated the nearest one was probably within a kilometer. I mentioned to Bril and Togn that they stay close to me so they could benefit from the strong lung and resist heat enchantments of my pack.

The ground below our feet was a form of cooled, molten rock. It was entirely black with many potholes and undulations. Walking was not difficult, but we did have to pay attention where we stepped, especially since Togn told us about the heat sinks. These, he said, were places where the original molten rock had solidified over gas bubbles. If the gas had eroded the underside of the rock over time then the surface would give way easily when walking on it. He told stories about losing friends of his in heat sinks. Not all were deadly because sometimes the gas pocket was very shallow so the worst that happened was the being would fall into a hole they could easily get out of. But, many of the heat sinks were anywhere from a few hundred meters to kilometers deep. From those, there was no coming back. Togn warned us to watch for rock on the surface that was shiny like glass. That was a telltale sign of a heat sink.

Over the next few hundred meters we stepped around at least a dozen potential heat sinks. I realized that if it hadn't been for Togn, Bril and I would have probably perished in Firston, long before getting this far. It seemed like such a stroke of luck that he had found me right after I had lost Horse and then that he had decided to accompany me. I couldn't just assume it was coincidence but that made me wonder just how much of my experience was beyond my control, and ultimately whether I had any control at all. Ever since blasting through the dark wall, my life had been a series of what I could only think of as amazing events. I wondered how much of my current experience was somehow linked to a previous, unremembered experience in another place and time. It seemed like every time I visited this topic I only ended up with more questions and few answers.

Meanwhile, back at Amoro's house.

Vortold withdrew his proboscis from Amoro's stomach for the last time. He added a defecation to the countless others littering her cinder floor. His four companion hunters lazed along the edges of the pool, their hunger satiated by Amoro's blood and flesh. The Tachina had taken numerous small bites from her arms, legs and stomach. She had hundreds of lacerations from Vortold's barbed hands, and all of her fingers and toes were gone. Vortold looked upon her almost admiringly, wondering to himself why she would go through so much for some weak adventurers she hardly knew. But, he was grateful for the nourishment she had provided and he fully intended on taking some of her to go. Who knew when they'd find food as good, and his companions, at a minimum, needed to eat or he would face a certain mutiny.

He went outside and emitted a high pitch squeak in three short burst, then he waited. In time, a smokey, billowy figure emerged in front of him assuming the shape of the wraith. Vortold squeaked the question about the wraith's efforts in finding Bril. The wraith assured him he was on the trail and would have the boy by the next glow cycle. In the meantime, the wraith suggested Vortold should go to Skelwora because he had received information that the trio had been there. The wraith disappeared and Vortold went back inside, delighting at the task of harvesting the rest of Amoro, and then getting on with his hunt.

CHAPTER NINETEEN

An Unlikely Ally

Nearing the fire pit I noticed a dark haze moving toward us. It appeared to be a rainstorm, although it was much darker than the storms I was familiar with. Togn turned up his nose, smelling the air and then screamed.

"Ash rain!"

The leading edge of the storm was just reaching us, dropping random drops here and there. Togn and Bril pressed in close to me.

"Touch my pack!" I yelled.

It was not a moment too soon because as the main force of the storm reached us the invisible Cover enchantment activated, creating a see-through domed covering that deflected all the drops of ash rain. It felt like sheer magic being able to look up at nothing above while seeing the acid drops smash, disintegrate and flow around us to the ground. The drops left tiny pock marks in the molten stone all around us before quickly disappearing into a low hanging mist.

The storm lasted a very short time, and when it was over the mist seemed to congeal and then slowly flow into the nearest fire pit, disappearing into the abyss. Togn and Bril released their holds on my pack and we all let out a collective sigh.

"Did you notice the smell?" Togn asked us.

Bril and I both nodded and I understood then how Togn had sensed the danger. It wasn't until the storm was right on us that I picked up on the sweet, sickly odor coming from the rain. Togn however, being a native of Firston, had a heightened sense of smell for just such dangers so he was the first to recognize it, and lucky for us he had. Otherwise we would have been riddled with burning holes in our skin.

Once again I was immensely appreciative of having a native of

Firston along with me. I was also keenly aware that if all went well, we'd be dropping into the Mists soon. Who would help us avoid the perils there? None of us had any experience in that underworld, and so I started to wonder if we had missed an opportunity somewhere along the way to adopt a new member to our team who could guide us in the Mists. But, I was brought back from my wonderings by the edge of the fire pit looming in front of us.

We stood before a vast cauldron, easily 100 meters across. The sides angled inward toward a bottom that was 50 meters deep. The bottom was a fast flowing river of lava, with steam rising and hissing. I cautioned Togn and Bril to stay near me so they could be covered by the Resist Heat and Strong Lung enchantments on my pack. We leaned in, straining our eyes to see signs of steel stone. The sides of the pit were a mixture of cinders and boulders, and for at least 25 meters down they looked cool. No signs of fire, or lava, or even glowing edges. The misty smoke rising from the deep had a very pungent, mineral smell, like coal burning in a blacksmith's fire. Blacksmith, I thought. Where did I know about that from? Then quickly dismissed the thought as just another mystery of being me.

As my eyes adjusted, I noticed a couple of meters down there were patches of a different material. Instead of the black, crusty look of the cinders and the boulders, this material was smooth and reflective. I pointed out the patches to Bril and Togn.

"What do you think," I asked. "Is that the steel stone?"

"You know, I don't see anything else down there that isn't cinders and lava boulders," Bril said.

"Well," I started, "I guess we just head for the closest one, staying close together."

We stepped over the edge and immediately saw this wasn't going to be easy. Our footsteps caused the cinders to bunch up and slide, us, along with them. Togn and Bril held on desperately to the straps of my pack, the three of use looking like drunken sailors walking on a ship's deck in a storm. Every step I took caused the leading foot to slide, forcing me to quickly step forward with my other leg to keep from failing on my ass. Multiply that spectacle by three, and you get a picture of how comical the scene must have been.

By now, the misty smoke was so thick that we could taste it. It was bitter and it seemed to accumulate at the back of my throat, no doubt due to the action of the Strong Lung enchantment. When we reached the patch, I took one last step and let the slide bring me to a sitting position. My legs were trembling from the descent and finally sitting down felt really good. Togn and Bril sat on each side of me and we studied the patch.

"Yep," said Togn, "there's the crumbly base Ukino told us about," as he grasped a shard with both hands and rocked it back and forth until it popped out of its socket.

He handed the shard to me and went to work on another one. The steel stone was like other shards we had harvested in that it rose from the ground in spires and had multiple fissures where it could be broken apart in equal vertical pieces.

"It will be easier to carry if we keep them in chunks instead of splitting them apart," Togn said. "That way too, Ialeo can separate them in thicknesses that fit what he's making. How many should we get?" he asked.

Bril and I were acutely concerned about adding too much weight to our packs, and backs, so we all agreed that three would be enough. After we stashed them securely, one in each pack, we got back on our feet and began the slippery task of climbing back out. It seemed like we were going two steps forward and three backward. After awhile I looked back and we had only advanced a few meters. Not only that, our strength was being sapped and muscles pushed to their fatigue points. It was then that Togn had his brilliant idea. He told me to wait while he went rummaging in my pack, eventually pulling out the piece of moss rope. He scoured the edge of the crater for a suitable anchor point, then held out his hand and imagined the rope wrapped around it. Like a trained snake, the rope extended to the selected boulder and wrapped itself around the base where it would bind between the boulder's base and the ground when we pulled on it.

"Well, I guess it doesn't know how to tie a knot," Bril said, yanking on it, "but it's wedged in there pretty good, so let's give it a try."

So, we set out, pulling ourselves hand-over-hand up the sloping cliff of marbles. Once at the top we sat down and rested as the environment was so toxic it was draining our strength, even with the enchantments.

As I peered across the vast expanse of blackened rock, steam, and the red glow of subterranean fire, I was sure I saw something moving toward us. It wasn't taking a straight path, but instead wandering in our direction. As it neared I noticed it had an elongated human form especially the lengths of the legs and arms. There was a slight mist swirling around it but underneath it was waxy looking, and very light toned, like almost pure white. I nudged Togn and pointed in its direction. His words were not reassuring.

"Uh, oh," he murmured.

"What," I asked concerned.

"I think it's a Smoke Strider," he said resignedly. "They are not really a being from Firston. They're from the Mists, but they have to come here to finish their metamorphosis into wraiths. They start as a Heat Marsh down in the Mists, then they come up here and once they complete their first kill they become a Smoke Strider with that wispy mist all around them. With each kill they add a new spirit to their collection. After they kill enough, they end up being a wraith. From then on, they only steal spirits from the beings they encounter, leaving behind a trail of spiritless beings who are bound to them."

Great, I thought, another peril. When would they end?

"This shouldn't be too big of a problem," Togn said rising. "We've got a couple of good enchantments on our weapons, and there are three of us. Just don't let the claws get you. They have a substance that opens holes in your fortitude, not to mention your skin."

Admittedly we had some advantages, but, because only my pack had the environmental enchantments, we would have to stay close together, making it impossible to surround the creature. We formed up like the head of an arrow, with Togn's hulk as the point and Bril and I at each side of him. The Strider seemed to be assessing the risks, staying a few meters away, dancing slowly side to side. Fortunately, it was still ground bound so we wouldn't have to deal with it in the air. In the next moment, it had apparently finished sizing us up for it sped directly at Togn!

Togn struck the first blow, lashing one of the creature's arms as it swung with claws extended. The Strider shrunk back, spewing a white liquid from the wound. It seemed to be reassessing but I couldn't tell if it was figuring a different attack, or was considering a retreat. It regarded us through narrowed eyes, and then it did something totally unexpected. It spoke, and we could all understand.

"Well, well, what have we here? Three accomplished adventurers, or three ignorant idiots?" the Strider chided.

It was Togn who responded. "Why don't you try that again and see for yourself!"

"If you were a little bit wider, I wouldn't be able to see your friends," the Strider derided Togn.

At this point I wondered what was actually going on. The creature first attacks us, and then when it gets wounded it starts insulting us.

For some strange reason it was Bril who broke through the impasse.

"You are conflicted about who you are," he said to the Strider. "What is it? Do you not wish to become a wraith?"

"Whatever could you mean," the Strider replied adamantly. "Of course I do. After all, that's what all Heat Marshes do, they become Smoke Striders and then they become Wraiths. What a silly supposition."

"Oh really?' questioned Bril. "Why then are we talking and not fighting? Is it because you just don't have the stomach for it? If so, I don't blame you. From what I understand you have to kill and eat flesh while taking spirits, and who knows how long you have to do that. It just seems like a waste. After all, there were probably so many neat places and fun times in the Mists, and then you had to come to this desolate place and spend you time fighting things and killing them. All this smoke and stink and heat. Doesn't seem like much of an existence to me."

Suddenly the tough exterior of the Strider crumbled and I thought it was going to start crying. It stood there looking forlorn, holding its injured arm, looking everywhere but directly at us and clearly shrinking in size.

"You're right, you're right, it's a terrible existence. I absolutely hate it. I hate it here, I hate what they say I have to do, I hate everything. You know, back in the Mists, I had a nice little glen with a stream, and yeah I had to steal some of the animals from the farmers, but it was a good life. But here, ugh, it's just desolation, and it's desolation on me too."

I started feeling bad for the creature. It certainly seemed sincere and if it was faking those crocodile tears it was an excellent actor. What a strange turn of events. Togn and Bril looked at me, and the three of us just shook our heads with raised eyebrows. Finally, I decided to see if we could just end the confrontation.

"Well, look," I said as gently as I could. "Sorry to know you have this conflict, but we really need to get going. So, can we assume you won't attack us again?" I realized I was putting a lot of faith in the creature to be honorable, but I hoped I had read the signs right.

"Go," the Strider said resignedly, removing it's hand from the wound which had now closed up. Wow, I thought, a fast healer.

Togn, Bril and I started side stepping in unison, keeping our formation while still facing the Strider. Once we were a safe distance away we turned and started walking back toward the cliff, looking back every few steps. None of us spoke. Each one left wondering about what had just happened. It definitely made me more aware of the individuality of creatures and beings. It seemed we made a lot of assumptions about entities just based on their characteristics, but doing that was probably limiting our experiences. It was Bril who stopped and broke the silence.

Looking back at the forlorn creature he said, "I just feel like I want to help it."

Speaking of which, I wondered just what 'it' was because there were no outward signs allowing me to fit it into a gender. Meaning it was maybe not prone to the hormonal type of emotions expressed by beings with gender. So there was that curiosity, and then Bril's words that made me more confident in something I had been thinking about. The descent into the Mists with none of us having experience there meant we would be really at the mercy of the perils. What if we had someone with us who knew the Mists? I wasn't sure if it would work because of things like whether the creature can stop its development and what all the consequences might be. But, it seemed worth exploring.

So, I broached the idea to Togn and Bril that we invite the strider to go along with us. Bril was immediately in favor, but Togn was very uncomfortable with the idea.

"It attacked us," Togn offered. "I'm all for helping creatures but how can we ever trust it? Especially since it's basically a wraith-in-training, and we've already not had a very good experience with those creatures."

"But," countered Bril, "it's not a wraith yet, so there is no issue about it attacking our spirits, especially mine because of my current condition. And, we really are going to be flying blind in the Mists."

Togn was thoughtful, looking back at the cowering creature, assessing, measuring. He remembered being helped by strangers a few times in his life and how much he appreciated what they had done for him. He was also very aware of the potential dangers lurking for them in the Mists. It was a tough decision but he knew it was worth the try.

"Okay," Togn shook his head. "If it wants to come, then it's okay with me. But, at least initially I think one of use should walk behind it, just to keep an eye on it." We all agreed. Bril called out to the creature, motioning for it to approach. When it sauntered to within a few meters Bril told it about our quest and asked if it wanted to go with us. At first the Strider seemed unsure and I could understand why. It was already on an evolutionary path that was deeply imbued in its genetics and spirit. To turn its back on that would be stepping out into the unknown. But then, it's countenance changed, as if it realized that continuing on its current path was just too uncomfortable.

"Okay, okay, yes," the Strider said with a tone that was mixed between resignation and acceptance.

At this point I thought it might be important to reinforce the creature's place in our group and even try to get it to pledge its support of the group. After all, we would probably have to depend on it in whatever fights lay ahead so we had to be at least a little assured that it wouldn't break and run, or worse turn on us. Of course I knew it was probably a long shot to even think that such a creature would understand the concept of loyalty, but still, we were operating in the space of "why not." First though, we had to see if it had a name.

In a very guttural voice the creature said its name was Rarik. I explained to Rarik we were traveling to the Mists and thought it would be good to have someone with us who knew the land and the creatures living there. Rarik understood immediately and seemed to brighten at the prospect of being looked to for answers. I told Rarik that when we have had to fight that we all help and we watch out for each other. I asked if it would pledge its loyalty to us as we would to it. It said it would, and added, that it was very grateful for the chance to become something other than a wraith. With that, we settled into being a party of four, with Togn, at least for now, taking up the rear.

Once we climbed down the cliff and got back on the road, Bril pulled the Star Stone Scepter from his pack. Holding it from the bottom, with its tip pointing straight up, he watched intently for a yellow glow. At first it seemed like nothing was happening, but then an ever so faint yellow line appeared running through its center. Bril laid the scepter across his palm. The end closest to him glowed red immediately and the scepter spun to the left and stopped.

"Looks like we might be getting to the Mists," Bril announced. Off we marched in the direction the scepter pointed. It immediately took us off road and through some rough terrain with sharp volcanic rock underfoot. Bril and I were relieved we had the new softstone soles which so far were literally undamaged. Rarik walked on some sort of fleshy feet that had great, thick callouses on them so we didn't hear any complaints from him.

Our path took us through lands of spires and then places with more cinders, and finally into a little cove with water dripping from verdant moss. Underneath the moss overhanging the upper edge of the back wall of the cove there was an opening. I immediately thought it was part of the old Firston water tube system, but Togn assured me it was not. We went into a cave with dim glowstones as in a vein along one wall. Deeper and deeper we went. Gradually, the sound of rushing water grew louder. Then, we were standing in a tunnel beside a fast moving, shallow current with the scepter pointing into its darkness.

"Well," I said, "Looks like we're going to get wet." There were no softstone boards to ride on, so Bril stashed the scepter in his pack and we all stepped up to the edge of the water. We had no idea where the flow went and for how long we'd be in it. We didn't know if it would plunge us off a cliff into a treacherous waterfall, or bounce us off rocks and fling us against the tunnel walls. Of course there was also the possibility it would do all those things and more!

Meanwhile.

Vortold and his accomplices defecated in a narrow canyon in Skelwora. On the ground was a Gurji who had been killed in a blade fight. By now it was well worked over by the Tachina with their telltale bite marks and scrapes from their hand barbs. Vortold licked his chops and flipped his antennae up stiffly, sensing the air. His horse was laden with two additional bags now, both holding portions of Amorro.

"That creature had some sweet flesh and blood," Vortold winked at his helpers. "Hopefully we'll find some more of them in our travels." Vortold's accomplices licked their proboscis in unison, a sort of tribute to their leader and one they hoped would please him. Vortold was unpredictable when it came to how he treated them, so they always sought opportunities to make him feel important.

The lead Tachina chirped a series of sounds and waited. In time, the wraith appeared. He told Vortold that his prey was about to enter the Mists. Vortold flicked his proboscis violently, assailing the wraith for not stopping them before they left Firston. The wraith shrunk back in fear and then Vortold uttered a series of high pitched shrieks. The wraith dropped to the ground. Its wispy, smokey cloud settled around it as black soot revealing the pale body of a Heat Marsh.

"It's so hard to get good help in these times," Vortold complained.

With that, the group jumped to their mounts and raced off to find an opening the the Mists.

CHAPTER TWENTY

Sailing Into the Mists

We stood at the edge of the fast flowing water, looking at each other while trying to get up the nerve to take the plunge. Then, Togn stammered a suggestion, no doubt sensing the trepidation we all had about going headlong and very quickly into someplace we could not see.

"Maybe we should link ourselves together with the moss rope," he half-stated and half-asked.

"Wow, good idea," I said.

Togn pulled the rope from my pack and focused on making it wrap around each of us just below the shoulders. Then he did something none of us had thought of doing. He was the last in line and he tied the rope around himself using a slip knot. A collective surprise came from myself and Bril. For some strange reason we had assumed the rope couldn't be knotted. So now, it had even more uses!

"Okay, so now what? How do we do this?" Bril, who was in the lead, asked the very question on all our minds. It was Rarik who shed some light for us because it had traveled between the Mists and Firston before. It explained that because we had traveled downward for such a long distance in the cave that we were no doubt very close to an opening to the Mists. So, it said the transition would be quite smooth and we'd probably arrive in the Mists without even realizing it. We just needed to go with the flow and once we came out of the tunnel we'd be there. Togn, Bril and I all looked at each other questioningly. So far, transitioning from one underworld to the next hadn't been anything we'd call smooth. But, we were all willing to hope this one would be.

We all crouched to get ready to jump in on cue. Bril started a countdown and on three, we all dove into the rushing water!

Everything went black and almost immediately after, everything lit up. We were dumped into a large lake and into a totally different world. We were in the Mists.

We worked our way out of the current and over to the shore where we de-roped and stood in awe. The environment was so different from where we had just been and incredibly different from anything I had seen so far on Octa. We stood in almost waist deep grass. Just a few meters from us there was a sharp rise like a plateau with dense foliage running all along the edge of the lake. When I looked downstream, I could just barely make out the far lake edge. Everywhere I looked, I just saw dense foliage. The glowstones were exceptionally bright, even brighter than any I had seen before. Then, there was the smell. It assailed my nostrils with moisture and the heavy, musty smell of decaying plants juxtaposed against the fresh fragrance of flowers which covered the gradual rise going from lakeside to top of the plateau. I looked at Rarik and could see the pleasure on his face.

"Well, how does it feel to be back?" I asked it.

"Oh, it is a very special feeling," Rarik replied. "This is where I belong. Not in that desolate fire place."

I noticed Rarik had lost some of its misty appearance and seemed to be more like what I imagined a pure Heat Marsh was, instead of a being in between a Heat Marsh and a Smoke Strider. When I asked, it told me that the longer it stayed in the Mists, the more it would revert to being a Heat Marsh. Apparently the environment wouldn't support a transition from solid to mist. Then I asked it the one question that was probably on everyone's mind.

"I wanted to ask you, Rarik, about something that's difficult to bring up, but, something that has a direct bearing on your survival, and possibly ours. Normally, you'd have to eat flesh, so you can understand our concern about making sure you have enough to eat. We don't want you to be hungry enough to be tempted by our flesh," I managed a chuckle, "We mostly consume tonc. And an occasional stew. Are those items you can also survive on?"

To all our relief Rarik confirmed that tonc was an acceptable food. However, it said that occasionally it had to eat from an animal because the tonc is missing three important nutrients that its form requires. Rarik assured us that there would be ample opportunities in the Mists to capture small animals that would serve its needs. Rynd was also one of Rarik's menu items, although we wanted to avoid that for Bril, at least until his anger issue was sorted.

We decided to use the contact and journal shards to see if any of our objectives was nearby. I started with the journal shard and saw a blue dot with an arrow pointing from it to a red encircling ring. This was new. We had never used the journal shard before to find a messenger for turning in one of our objectives. I turned slowly and saw the arrow moved according to my movement. It was then that I saw the arrow was pointing to the notch on the journal shard's end. I held the shard in front of me with the notch pointing away from me and turned slowly. The arrow moved away from pointing to the notch. I turned back until the arrow pointed to the notch.

"Well, " I said. "It looks like a messenger is in that direction," I pointed in the direction of the notch and the arrow.

Next I noted the red line, supposedly pointing to one of our objectives. It was very short which made me think that our only material objective, Broodfoot plant for Ataia was nearby. The red line was pointed a little bit to the left of the notch. So, I turned to the left until it lined up with the notch and told the others to follow.

Tramping through the tall grass was difficult as it would wrap around out legs and ankles as if trying to hold us back. I asked Rarik what was going on with that and it said it was Grasp Grass, and not to stay still for too long or we might not be able to get it to release. Rarik told us the Eekutchi hunt in it often because how it holds unsuspecting prey while they simply finish them off. With that piece of information we all pulled out our weapons, and started walking a lot faster. Already our alliance with the Heat Marsh was paying off.

After a few hundred meters we moved out of the Grasp Grass and into a more normal grass that was short growing and fragrant. By now, the red line on the Journal Shard was practically gone, so I stopped. I asked Rarik if it knew what Broodfoot plant looked like and it stooped down, plucked a plant stem with oval, plump leaves and held it up. We all looked around us and saw a whole mass of those plants. So, we started collecting some. Once we had several bunches we stashed them in Bril's pack.

Now when I looked at the Journal shard there were two arrows pointing in almost exactly opposite directions. Because we had to see Uraya and Warr in the Mists, I laid their contact shards on top of the Journal shard, one at a time. The red line on Uraya's contact shard was the shortest so I turned until I faced its direction. Unfortunately that placed it somewhere in the lake, or on the other side. That was disappointing since we had no way to tell the distance represented by the line. We only knew the shorter the line, the closer our objective. After much discussion we decided to take the shortest route around the lake and on the way we would watch the line's length and where it pointed. From that, we surmised, we'd probably get a good idea about the location of our objective.

We made our way back toward the tunnel we had arrived through. It stood like a large cave going into the side of the plateau, disgorging white frothy water. It was shaped like an open mouth and on each side there were white boulders, giving the appearance of a face with its mouth wide open. I laughed to myself because it seemed at that moment to be hilarious. My humor break though was soon dashed. As we rounded the corner to go up the side of the tunnel's opening, six Eekutchi attacked from all directions!

Bril got bitten on the leg as he flailed with his sword at the biter. That Eekutchi went down, but the other five got more aggressive, snapping, dodging attacking, in a random, chaotic melee. They were ferociously fast leaving most of our stabs and swipes simply cutting through air. Fortunately, Rarik's long arms and sharp claws made quick work of two more of the devils, while Togn's axe ended another. I managed to wound the last and it crept away, screaming.

As we recovered, adjusting ourselves from the chaotic battle, I noticed Rarik was gone. Togn was checking Bril's bite which was pretty awful looking. It was like a chunk of his skin and muscle had been removed, leaving a bloody, stringy mess.

"We need some Shalow Root," Togn announced, "And some vine to tie it in place."

About that time, Rarik showed back up with leaves having red veins and a length of willowy vine. It handed the materials to Togn who went to work covering the wound and lashing the leaves in place. Wow, I thought. Yet another good reason for befriending Rarik. Maybe we had lucked out.

Togn explained that he and his people had often traded with beings from the Mists to get Shalow Root because it helped to rapidly heal many different types of injuries. His people often had injuries from the work they did. At his urging we all followed Rarik to where he found the plant, and then stashed some in our packs. While there, I noticed a fresh skeleton of one of the eekutchi we had just fought, laying a few paces away in the taller grass. Apparently Rarik had been hungry for some flesh. I was pleased that it chose to satisfy this hunger in private just because the process of ripping flesh from bones was not an appealing activity to me. I hoped some time we could all sit around a fire at a rest founden and share a meal of rynd for him and anybody else wanting some, and tonc stew or syphoria for me.

With the latest calamity behind us we resumed our trek, Bril with his arm over Togn's shoulders, to favor his injured leg. When we reached the top of the plateau my senses were assailed by a sea of colors, cascades of butterflies, singing, flitting birds, and the sweet fragrance of a never ending expanse of flowers. For as far as I could see the flowers dominated every space. Inhaling the smells made me feel light headed and euphoric, and I saw it was having the same effect on everybody else too. We had been through a lot, the glowstones were dimming and we were tired. A few hundred meters into our fragrant walk, the past overcame all of us. The last thing I remember was slumping down and rolling onto my back in an impromptu bed of moss, grass and sweet smelling flowers.

CHAPTER TWENTY-ONE

Learning the Lay of the Land

I awoke refreshed and sat up to see my fellow adventurers still sound asleep. The glowstones were dim now, giving the landscape an eerie appearance with the sea of flowers dropping shadowy reflections across the ground. There was something about the scene that reminded me of an old feeling, something lost to time. I could sense the nature of the feeling, but recalling it in all its glory was beyond my reach. What was it? Was it regret? Was it a feeling of loss? But of what? There was a heaviness to it, and deep, golden light that amplified the over riding feeling of sadness. But like an ending without a beginning, whatever was locked in my heart seemed content to stay there.

Across the field I saw the beginnings of a rain shower. It started as a mist rising up to the full height of the stone sky, gathering inward and then flowing outward like a flock of starlings dancing in unison across the sky at twilight. I wondered where that memory came from. It was so odd how so much of my life was a mystery to me, yet I would have these fleeting instances of sharp clairvoyance. As I watched the gathering storm get darker and spread farther across the sky, it carried with it an emotional darkness. Like a finger plucking a string, a sliver of dread crept over me, amplifying my earlier feelings of sadness. What was this new anomaly that seemingly spread hopelessness?

But then, very quickly, I started to spin downward even more, spiraling to a place where life was too painful to continue living. There was nothing but darkness around me, and a gathering pain built from dread upon dread. I struggled to understand this sudden shift in consciousness and the overwhelming sense of hopelessness that was filling my stomach. Then I felt an agonizing emotional pain searing through my body as it seemed my life was being sucked out of me.

There was a void, a dark mass that was welcoming me. It was a place of refuge where all of my torment would disappear. I realized the void was death and I longed for it. To just be free from the pain, from the emptiness and hopelessness, was now everything I wanted. I reached for my sword, bringing the blade to my throat. I had to end it. It was all too painful.

Suddenly, I was on the ground with Togn and Bril struggling to get me to release the sword! My determination to end my pain was only getting stronger. Why were they interfering? Couldn't they also see there was no point?

"It's a rain wraith!" Rarik yelled against the incoming calamity. "It's feeding on his hope."

Rain crashed down in sheets, drenching everything in just seconds. Togn and Bril were pulling on my arms with all their strength.

"Get his pack!" yelled Bril. "Bring it close to his head so the enchantment is strongest!"

Rarik grabbed my pack and brought it above my head, holding it just inches from my face. In that instant I could feel my resolve weakening along with my strength. As the rain poured down on us, I could feel my arms weakening and the darkness lifting. To my right I glimpsed the edge of the storm, and hanging off it like a misty curtain was a being like the one that had attacked Bril in Firston. It was wispy and elongated and having more substance than the rain. It was also very dark, and then I saw its face, gleeful, determined, hungry. I turned my head away and stopped struggling with Togn and Bril. Togn pulled the sword from my hand and tossed it. Then the three of us collapsed from fatigue, each laying where we stopped struggling, breathing heavily, rain pouring off us. Rarik sat down resignedly, looking in the distance, the rain stirring some long lost memories.

The downpour continued for a very long time, and when it stopped, the water was flowing around us, rushing to the lake. I couldn't remember ever feeling so wet and exhausted at the same time. I didn't want to move, not even lift my head to keep water from running into my ears. I was drenched, and spent. Once again, darkness overtook me as I fell into a deep sleep.

I would learn later of Rarik's explanation for what had happened. It told Togn and Bril that Rain Wraiths almost always accompanied rain storms, along their edges. They fed on hope, and when they got near a being who is struggling with sadness or depression, they home in on them and start feeding. The more hope they steal, the stronger they become and the weaker their victim. Eventually, if the wraith isn't deterred, the victim almost always kills themselves. Rarik also explained that its kind, Heat Marsh, were unaffected by most wraiths although they were also highly ineffective in a battle with wraiths. So, we shouldn't depend upon it for much help in defeating attacking wraiths.

As I slept, Bril and Togn used the journal and contact shards to scout along the edge of the lake. As they followed the arrow pointing to Uraya, they discovered the destination was fortunately not in the lake, but somewhere on the other side.

I was sitting up again when they returned. The feeling I had been analyzing when I last awoke was the trigger that caused the wraith to home in on me. Even though I usually had an abundance of hope, that one little instance of exploring an unknown sadness was all it took to become a target. It was clear that here in the Mists it was extra important to be mindful of our spirits. I was glad Bril hadn't been awake as the storm approached or he might also have been attacked. The outcome might have been very much worse.

So far in the Mists, we hadn't found any tonc water and my body was feeling the effect. Remembering the Nourish enchantment on my pack I reached in and found several pieces of amber which I shared with Togn and Bril. Rarik was still energized from its last small animal snack.

After having our amber and beginning to feel the rejuvenating effect, I asked the obvious next question of Rarik.

"Tell us, Rarik, what other dangers lurk here in the Mists?"

Rarik began by telling us about the Phase Glades. Apparently not all the land in the Mists could be trusted. There were clearings surrounded by trees and shrubs that rapidly appeared in your path. Like a mirage, they were there, then not, then there again. The Phase Glade was not a place you wanted to be caught in because it was nearly impossible to escape. The phases of the glades were totally random and unpredictable so it was difficult to see a pattern that would allow you to escape.

We watched Rarik with intense interest as it settled into a story telling mode, complete with exotic eye movements and symbolic hand gestures. Next Rarik explained about Mist Catchers. This particular evil was one of the earliest lifeforms in the Mists and so they were particularly well suited to fulfilling their survival needs. Those 'needs,' were to feast upon the aspirations of beings. Rarik told us that early in the daily glowcycle, when the light was dim, they commingled with the mist that usually hung over everything. They were very astute at blending in and moved rapidly through the fog in packs. Once they beset an individual, they surrounded it and rapidly pulled out filaments of the individual's goals and dreams. When they were through, the victim was directionless, losing its focus in life and wandering aimlessly. Those beings damaged by the Mist Catchers often ended up as slaves, doing meaningless work for animal keepers. Many times they also ended up in recipes enjoyed by rynd lovers.

By now, the glowstones had lighted the terrain enough for us to safely continue. Following the arrow and line on the contact and journal shards, we walked with Rarik in the middle, who continued telling us about two other entities to be concerned about.

The first one, Rarik called an Elemental Mushroom and said it was a multi-being. Normally, it was a giant mushroom of about a half meter tall. But when sentient beings were within range, it changed form, becoming the same type of being as its intended victim. Then, the perpetrator would tune in to the victim's fears and begin amplifying them, while pretending to be a concerned friend. Once its monofilaments were connected to the victim, the Elemental Mushroom released chemicals that broke down cellular walls allowing it to slowly feast on the victim. Beings with an attached Elemental Mushroom would gradually lose their life force because they couldn't get enough nourishment to replace what the mushroom was feeding on. The mushroom posing as the victim's friend would of course stay with them to 'care' for them until they died.

Rarik then told us about Spirit Snatchers. These entities were like Rain Wraiths on steroids and much faster. They could appear as any type of being, even non-sentient, and once they locked on to the victim they rapidly drained its spirituality. Without their animating force, the victim then dies physically.

"We also have eekutchi, which you've already experienced, and dark pools," Rarik finished his explanation.

"Oh, yes, we are familiar with dark pools," intoned Togn.

By now, and amazingly, Bril was able to walk on his own, with only a slight limp. I resolved to always try to keep some Shalow Root in my pack.

As we started down the opposite side of the lake our footsteps suddenly began falling on a well-worn path. Like a very wide animal trail, the path led us down the side of the lake until branching, with one route continuing beside the lake and the other moving off to the right. We checked the journal and contact shards, and took the branch going to the right. After traveling only a few hundred meters I noticed a blue dot had developed a very long arrow, meaning a messenger was very close. And, sure enough, within another few meters the path branched again and a being was approaching from the right.

It was a strange being in the way it moved and how it seemed to interact with the environment. But as it got closer I saw that it wasn't a sentient being at all, but instead a machine. It was tubular with five stacks equally spaced along the top. It moved on a system of wheels that had a wide belt wrapped around them, giving it a footprint that was almost as long as its body. The stranger thing was that it was eerily quiet.

When the machine neared us, the journal shard's red arrow and blue dot disappeared and the machine stopped directly in front of us. On its side there was a patch of material very similar to the contact shard that ran the length of the tube. Below each stack, the material showed a confusing array of dots and arrows. I assumed that somewhere in that chaos there were probably dots and arrows, or just dots, that represented our journal shard, or the machine probably wouldn't have stopped.

We stood there studying the dots and arrows at each stack until a sort of buzzer rang out and a high-pitched voice started speaking.

"We are here to collect. Please place the items in the appropriate stack."

We all looked at each other questioningly. Which stack? I looked to Rarik, since it was native to the Mists, but it shrugged its shoulders, looking as puzzled as the rest of us. After much more pondering and studying, it was Bril who came up with an idea.

"Look here," he said, pointing to the second stack from the left. "It shows 12 blue dots with arrows, and two blue dots without arrows. And look, all the other stacks only have blue dots *with* arrows. So, I think the blue dots without arrows on the second stack must represent the blue dots we used to have on our journal shard related to the steel stone for Ialeo and the brood foot plant for Ataia. There are five stacks, and there are five levels to Octa. Starting from the left, the first stack represents the surface and the second represents Canyonlands, the third Firston and so on."

"So, we put everything for Ialeo and Ataia in the second stack," enthused Togn.

"Yes!" Bril shouted, having a eureka moment.

Rarik, being the tallest of us, hopped on to the belt that ran around the wheels. Then we all started handing the steel stone and brood foot plant from our packs to it, which it dutifully stuffed down the stack. As it did that, the blue dots went away. Then, I asked the obvious question of all my friends.

"Since you are all native to Octa, and messengers travel across all the levels, how come none of you have seen a messenger before, and knew how to use one?"

"Well," began Togn, "We've never seen *this type* of messenger before. There are many kinds, but the most common are simply human-form beings with facial tattoos that identify them as messengers. They sometimes have carts, or even horses drawing carts just depending on how much material they have to move. So, this is just a different type than we've experienced before."

Rarik and Bril nodded in agreement. In the next instant, the machine moved away, continuing down its solitary path doing its solitary duty. I was slightly in awe of the whole system, especially considering how big Octa was and the challenges of sorting materials across multiple levels and no doubt thousands or more individuals. And just how the journal shard and the messenger machine were able to communicate their dots and arrows was a great mystery. I wished I had Brukin there with me because he might actually know that answer.

After aligning Uraya's contact shard with the Journal shard we struck out in its direction. As it turned out, that meant following the messenger which had turned sharply to the right a few hundred meters after leaving us.

We now left the flower field and entered a dark wood. Glowstones along the ground and on canyon walls lit our way as we traveled through thick stands of twisted-trunk trees and brush displaying an array of flowers and berries. Every now and then an animal would scurry out of our path. Once, after this happened, Rarik disappeared for a short while and then rejoined us with a burp. It seemed it was either stocking up on its flesh nutrient needs, or it needed more than I had been led to believe. But, it was no mind because it had shown its worth to us in spades, and so far had been trustworthy.

On we went, deeper and deeper into the forest until we came to a long chasm cutting through the land in front of us. It was here that the arrow to Uraya pointed away from the path we were on. It pointed to the left and appeared to follow the edge of the chasm. Getting off the well-trodden path was uncomfortable for me, but the others seemed to welcome the change. We scrambled along the chasm paying close attention to staying well away from the edge. Then, we came to a large flat rock jutting out into the chasm with no way around, other than to cross it. Of course, we had to stop to peer down into the chasm, just out of curiosity.

Right at that moment and strong wind rushed at us from the right followed by a wall of frothy, rushing water. Fortunately, the water was several meters below where we stood, but as it flowed past we saw several things caught in its torrent including a lifeless being that Togn thought was a Gurji. The scene reminded me of my last times with Horse and I asked the group if it was possible that the rush of water was from releases of holding ponds like in Canyonlands.

"It is so," answered Bril. "The water moves through the underworlds with each level managing their own accumulations. Canyonlands' releases go first to Firston, making their way through that environment and then on to the Mists, and finally what little is left ends up in the Land of the Misanthrope."

Togn could see I was thinking about the possibility that Horse could still be alive and on one of these other levels. He put his big hand on my shoulder.

"It's not likely," he said comfortingly. "That first drop was a long one."

I knew he was right, but, I was a more hopeful person than most, so I kept the possibility alive in my heart. We finished crossing the flat rock, stepped around the trunk of a very large tree and stood face to face with a small man who also looked like a woman. When the being spoke, it became clear who it was: Uraya.

CHAPTER TWENTY-TWO

Finding Purpose

"You are welcome, follow me," Uraya instructed. They turned, took two steps and a doorway opened. It was like a hole in the scene before us that revealed a large, bright room with incredibly high ceilings.

As we stepped through, one by one in awe, we were now standing in a very large structure with white walls and three large openings looking out to a vast expanse of sea set below two suns and multiple moons. There was the faint scent of salt and the earthy smell of stone baking in sunlight. It was all very familiar to me, although I couldn't remember when I had experienced those sights and sounds before. All along the shoreline of the sea there were rock structures with amazing details carved into their faces. Some were tall, some short, some elongated and others perfectly round. The designs carved into them were intricate and wildly colorful. The raised portions used bright colors while the subdued portions used darker colors. A large flat stone in a star shape jutted out over the drop-off outside the openings.

I wanted to run out, stand on that stone and take in all there was to see for I hoped it would stir a long-lost memory about a real sky, a real sun and real clouds. But, out of deference to our host, I restrained myself, only to be surprised when they looked directly at me and told me to go out on the stone and look around. I wasted no time.

I walked all the way to one of the star's points and looked down hundreds of meters to the water lapping more of the carved stones on the beach. The sunshine felt so good and the fresh, salt air was a treat to my nostrils and lungs. I had an immediate feeling that I wanted to just stay there. Stay there forever.

When Togn, Bril and Rarik joined me, I could see the place had awakened their senses too. None of them had ever been to the topside of their planet. So a sky, suns, clouds and fresh sea air was a totally new experience for them. So we stood there, for a long time, silent, experiencing, feeling like we were drifting in and out of consciousness. We didn't know until later that was exactly what Uraya wanted us to experience.

Eventually, we heard them call to us, softly jolting us out of the reverie and back to the task at hand - Bril's problem. I was so hopeful that Uraya could finally help him discover his destiny and maybe even help all of us in our journey ahead.

When we went back inside, Uraya stood beside an elongated tube with a clear cover that was open.

"Get in," she said to Bril.

"Whoa," Bril protested. "Wait a bit. What is that?"

"It is for your journey, to make sure your spirit and body don't separate, for that would be disastrous," they replied.

"But, journey to where?" Bril asked.

"There are places in the universe that hold answers to a being's origins. As for everyone, your origins go back much further than your memories here on Octa. You have been on a never ending journey, but certain portions of that journey are hidden from you until the information will have meaning for you. Now, is the time for you to discover what direction your destiny lies in. This device will not go anywhere. It will stay right here, with your body inside. But, your spirit will go somewhere and when it returns, you will have all your answers."

Bril looked nervously at me. I gave him my best reassuring smile.

"This is what you've wanted, right? From an early age you sensed your answers lay here, in the Mists. Because Amoro sent us here, I trust Uraya. But, that is me. You must decide if you also trust them. If so, then a trip in that box will likely be life changing, and in a good way. But, it is your choice," I counseled.

Bril looked back at the tube and I could see his resolve building.

"Okay," he said. "What do I do?" he asked as he approached the tube.

"Do?, Uraya asked back. "You don't 'do' anything. You just be. You will feel like you are in a dream, and you will see strangers living lives. But, they won't be strangers, they will be the previous vessels you used for your spirit. They will be you. After this review, you will begin seeing you as you are now, and you will see the life path that most matches your spirit. It will all be over in the blink of a glowstone.

When you come out, the 'doing' will begin, as you start to do things to perfect yourself to the purpose you have chosen."

"Wow," Bril mumbled, half-heartedly. "But what if I don't like the being I'm supposed to become?"

"That never happens," Uraya said confidently.

Bril turned to us and offered a weak wave, "Okay, my friends. Say good bye to the Bril you've known. I sure hope you like the new one." He smiled.

"Of course we will," encouraged Togn, waving enthusiastically along with Rarik and me.

With that, Bril climbed into the tube and Uraya closed the lid. Several glowstones on the side lit up and then a line of lights illuminated and started to very slowly go dim from one end. Uraya told us the process would be complete when the line of lights were all dimmed out, and that it would take some time. On seeing our curious looks because they had previously told Bril it would be over quickly, they explained that was his experience, but that ours would be much longer. It had something to do with us experiencing time in our bodies, but that he was experiencing spirit time.

"In the meantime I sense you could all use some nourishment and maybe rest?" Uraya asked.

Without waiting for an answer they motioned to follow. We went through a long hallway with a solid stone wall on one side and round holes in the ceiling. At the end we entered another room that was dim and cozy with moss beds, warming glowstones and a feast that included, rynd, syphoria, tonc and crispy uenthy moth legs, gathered only from those already perished, they assured.

Once we started eating we couldn't stop. It seems we had forgotten just how hungry we were. Rarik went for the rynd while Togn and I enjoyed the syphoria and tonc. Once we sampled the uenthy legs we couldn't stop eating them! They had a very delicate, sweet flavor and were slightly crunchy, making them an excellent dessert to a very satisfying meal. We ate without talking and gradually the nourishment and the mystical aspects of syphoria took over. I could barely make it to one of the beds before falling into the moss, soundly asleep.

When I awoke it felt like I had only slept for a short time, but I was well rested. Togn and Rarik were talking quietly nearby and when they noticed I was awake they stopped, looking at me with curious grins on their faces.

"What's so funny?" I asked

"Well, you've got a moss spider web in your hair!" replied Togn, laughing along with Rarik.

I quickly leaned over with my head between my knees and fluffed my hair with my hands. Besides stringy webbing, out fell a hairy spider about the size of my fingernail.

"What the..." I mused as the little thing dropped to the floor and scurried away.

Rarik filled me in, telling me those spiders often mistake hair for moss and once they nest in hair once, they start looking for it because where there is hair, there is also usually warmth, and they really liked being warm. Sometimes, Rarik confided, the being might not even know the little things were in their hair because they often built their nests deep below the hair surface. People with long hair might have a spider in there for many glowcycles, just depending on how often they washed their hair. I already knew that for many beings in the underworld of Octa, regular hair washing was not a thing.

"Rarik was just telling me stories about its times here in the Mists," Togn said.

"Yes, it's such a different place from the other underworlds," I remarked, hoping to spark some more from Rarik. And, it worked! Rarik was actually quite a talkative being, and it seemed to enjoy story telling.

Rarik launched into a story about its early years as a Heat Marsh and how knowledge was imparted to it. Heat Marshes are spontaneous beings, with no parents, and are themselves, genderless. They develop from the combination of several minerals and proteins that exist in boggy marshes. When two particular proteins combine and register in their DNA, the Heat Marsh goes through a transformation which leads to a highly developed intellect capable of picking up languages rapidly, and having an innate and deep understanding of the physical world and how to manipulate it.

Rarik then told us that their entire catalog of knowledge was transferred to them from the ancient mitochondrial DNA that exists in the substances of the marsh. That DNA receives information from the water that flows around it, and that water in turn carries the knowledge of the universe. So the knowledge every new Heat Marsh receives is the most recent knowledge of the universe, accounting for trillions and trillions of changes that happen in a cascading timeframe. Rarik said that it only needs to spend a short time in a boggy marsh to get its knowledge refreshed and updated.

So basically, I thought, Rarik was a universal genius capable of always having the latest information about anything! It was a realization that propelled my mind into new territories. Could the Heat Marsh know about the Tachina, and know maybe even more than Brukin knew? Could Rarik have the information that would give me, and us, an advantage in defeating the Tachina? As much as I wanted to explore the possibilities, I felt it was too soon. Selfishly, I didn't want to scare Rarik away by revealing what was chasing me, us.

"Well," I said casually, "We should plan on getting you to one of those boggy marshes for your upgrade, when we happen near one."

"Yes," replied Rarik, "That would be excellent."

Rarik was launching into another story but Uraya interrupted, saying Bril was back. We all grabbed our packs and went anxiously down the long hallway. In the open area we saw Bril sitting on the edge of the tube he had spirit-traveled in. He looked remarkably refreshed and he exuded a calmness I had never seen in him before. In the next moment I found out that calmness was the result of an amazing new bounty of confidence. He had a commanding presence, but not borne of power or control but of supreme confidence in his own abilities.

"Hello, my friends," he smiled broadly. "I have had the most amazing experience and I now know my path. I will share that with you in time, but for now I hope you will allow me to still accompany you, with a few detours along the way. Just so I can reach my full potential, which I think you are all going to appreciate."

"Yes, yes!" we all replied in unison. I could see everyone was relieved that Bril hadn't turned into some sort of controlling being, bent on changing all of us into a carbon copy of himself, as often happened when beings had deeply personal spiritual experiences. Once again, I was surprised at having that piece of knowledge, but I resisted the temptation to explore its origins. It was just for me to accept at that point and hope that maybe someday I would have the answers to my own origins.

"Now," Bril said enthusiastically, sniffing the air "where is that syphoria, and is it Uenthy Moth legs? I'm famished!"

We all returned to the room with the beds and food. There we feasted yet again, although Bril dominated that activity. We filled him in on our new information about Heat Marshes and talked about next steps. Besides surviving, we only had to see Warr for some updated weapons, and accommodate Rarik's visit to a bog, and then make whatever stops Bril needed so he could reach his full potential. Then finally, find the opening to the Land of the Misanthrope. It all seemed so simple when talking about it, but ever since this adventure had begun nothing was ever simple.

After awhile we bade farewell to Uraya but not before they drew me aside with some words of caution.

"When you meet with Warr, the armorer, you must ask him for a contact shard to Skelak. I will notify Skelak that you are coming. Otherwise, he might not accept Bril for training. In the meantime, watch him closely for he is still vulnerable, especially to wraiths."

Then, the door to the Mists opened and we stepped through.

Meanwhile...

Vortold sensed the air with his proboscis. He knew he'd be able to pick up the subtle difference in air pressure that existed near an entrance to another underworld level. His mount shifted under his weight, its flanks scored red from the Super Being's barbed legs. Vortold's accomplices waited, on edge, not wanting to move a muscle lest they disturb their master's concentration. The leader moved his horse closer to an elongated ditch covered with thick moss. Suddenly the opening appeared and the crew raked their horses sides with their barbed legs diving into the expanding abyss leading to the Mists. Now, Vortold thought with glee, his prey was finally within ready reach.

CHAPTER TWENTY-THREE
Finding an Old Friend

As we stood there on the stone overlooking the rushing water below, Bril and Togn manipulated the journal and contact shards, and I reflected on our latest experience. I regretted that I hadn't asked Uyaya if I too could get into the tube so I could rediscover my own purpose, but more important, rediscover my own memories. I wondered if it would have worked and I would have found out who I was, before I was a guy who was named Keln by a guy named Togn. Or would I have needed some other kind of motivation before the thing would have worked for me? The rushing water below had no answers, but Togn and Bril did. They had gotten a line on Warr, the armorer who would give us some weapons more suited to these lower levels.

So, off we went, dodging through brush, thistles and dead tree limbs until we finally emerged in an open field. It was a wonderful sight to behold after clamoring through so much foliage. We were covered in leaves, spider webs and no doubt a few bugs between our clothing and our skin. But we were in luck because in just a few hundred yards we came upon a small pool with water flowing in one side and out the other. We all stripped down and enjoyed a refreshing bath. Well, except for Rarik. It didn't wear clothes, and felt more comfortable in a pool of mud than one of fresh water. We had gotten used to its waxy, human-like, featureless form, and the fact that it constantly shed its skin so it always looked mostly clean. Somewhere in the few memories I had, I remembered a small being that lived near water that had a face similar to Rarik's. Unlike Rarik, those beings hopped around and were much smaller than Rarik. I wished I could remember a name for them, but all I had in my mind was the image.

Amazingly, right at that moment, one of them jumped from the edge of the pond! It was only airborne until it met Rarik's claw-like hand, and then it was gone, down its mouth. Bril and Togn saw my surprised expression and burst out laughing. It seems I was becoming the group's jolly jester. When the humor settled down I asked my companions what they called that little creature. Their answers were each different. So we settled on the one that was easiest to say; frop.

Refreshed from our bathing and light hearted moments, we continued following the red line in the shards leading to Warr. The field was immense and the glowstones were at full light and with so many of them directly overhead the shadows were almost nonexistent. The grass was tall with heavy seed heads causing many to bend down from the weight. I could smell the sweetness of the green things all around and the ground under foot was soft to step on. It was much easier walking than in Firston with its rolling cinders and sharp rocks.

In the distance I saw what looked like a ring of trees and it made me think of a safe place, secure from attacks by the next monster that might happen upon us. I was intrigued by it and I would have liked to see it up close but it was not in our path. I looked to my left and saw the woods we had left receding with each step. It seemed so long ago since we had seen Uraya, yet it was just a short time.

When I brought my attention to the field in front of us, the ring of trees was now in our path.

"Did we turn?" I asked everybody.

"No," said Bril, now known in my mind as the keeper of the shards.

"Well I could have sworn that ring of trees wasn't in our path just a few steps ago," I said.

"I didn't notice," chimed Togn, seemingly distracted by something.

Rarik was dallying behind, enjoying its homeland, running its fingers through the tall grass and occasionally plucking a flower to smell, and then eat. I asked Bril if we were still on the right track and he assured me that he was now a master at using the shards. Meanwhile, Togn started talking about the ring of trees. Only now the trees were practically upon us!

"Phase Glade!" yelled Rarik.

But it was too late. Bril, Togn and I were inside the glade. It was a very surreal feeling. It was as if I was in a dream and everything was slowed down. Even the trees moving in the breeze, were swaying almost musically. There was a slight hint of coolness and the shade was everywhere. All around the bases of the trees there were low growing grasses and right in the middle there was a little rock pool that had a small waterfall at its center.

"Wow," murmured Togn. "This is very nice in here." His voice was mystical and lilting and it caused me to laugh out loud. Then Togn was laughing and then Bril was laughing.

"Oh, " I said. "I want to stay here awhile."

Our laughing subsided and we stood there in awe. It was Bril who then started to react differently. He stood contemplating, like he was calculating, struggling against something and trying to figure something out.

"Hey!" Bril yelled at us. "Wake up! We're in that phase glade. We need to find a way to get out."

"Oh, I see," said Togn dreamily, "Now I know why nobody gets out of these things. They like it in here," he laughed gleefully.

Bril grabbed Togn by his shoulders and shook him.

"No," Bril said, "Come out of it. Try to fight it."

Togn adopted a serious face, but then sputtered and started laughing again. I started laughing with him, and I couldn't stop. We fell on the ground and when we stopped laughing we just lay there, looking up at the leaves fluttering in the breeze and enjoying the delicious scents and sounds. I wondered what I was doing, almost forgetting why I was in the Mists and what was important for me to do. I began to think that in time Bril would get used to the place and we could all just be there, enjoying the peacefulness and security.

As my reverie continued I could see Bril becoming more desperate. He started digging through his pack, searching for something. Then he began wandering around the perimeter of the glade, looking for something. His face was all serious and I could tell he was fighting something in his mind.

"Why don't you relax and come over here and lie down," I called dreamily. Bril stopped his frantic movements momentarily, looked at me wishfully, but then continued roaming around the perimeter of the glade, searching, probing.

Everything was just so perfect, the temperature, the time, the humidity, the light, and best of all there were no creatures trying to attack me. I watched Bril as he stopped his searching around the edge of the glade and resumed digging through our packs. Then, he had the moss rope in his hand. He sat down and closed his eyes, imagining. The rope began to extend, longer and longer, until it finally extended through the trees at the edge of the glade. Time seemed to stand still. I was at peace, dreamily watching Bril and the rope. The rope seemed to be dancing, and then Bril got up quickly and came toward Togn and me.

"Here," he said, "wrap the end of the rope around you, both of you."

Togn and I struggled to achieve the simple task and the process was so funny we couldn't stop laughing. Finally, Bril mustered us all on to our feet and wrapped the rope around us two times before tying a great big knot to secure it to our bodies. Then he yanked on the rope once, really hard. The rope bounced up and down and then I felt tension against my skin where the rope was wrapped. It was pulling us. The sensation was so strange that Togn and I started laughing as we walked in response to the rope's pulls. Ever so slowly the three of us approached the edge of the glade with me and Togn laughing hysterically, as Bril fought the desire to do the same. Instead he kept a serious face and focused on the rope, managing the packs and keeping us moving along.

Before I knew it, we were out of the glade and there was Rarik, the rope wrapped around its body as an anchor with its long arms pulling the rope which dropped in a coil at its feet. In an instant, all the previous humor disappeared, and Togn and I stood there in disbelief of what had happened. I couldn't believe how quickly the glade had changed position and swallowed us up. We had complete memory of the events, even of all the laughter, although at that point we could no longer discern what had been so funny.

Bril collapsed on the ground, clearly exhausted.

"That was pretty amazing what you did," I said to Bril. "How come you weren't as affected?"

"I don't know," Bril said breathlessly. "But I've noticed that since I came out of that tube, my head is more clear. Maybe that has something to do with it."

"Well, thank you!" said Togn. "We would have probably never gotten out of there if you hadn't thought up that trick with the rope."

We wondered what happens when beings stayed in there. Bril said he found a lot of skeletons as he was looking for a way out. He said there were all types, from human forms to eekutchi and others he couldn't make out. He said he thought they just ended up providing energy for the glade as they decomposed.

Not to overlook its part in getting us out, we all thanked Rarik, enthusiastically. It seemed to enjoy the praise and said it was glad it could help because it couldn't imagine not having all of us with it. The event cemented Rarik's place with the group, and if any of us had any lingering doubts about its loyalty, they were gone.

By now, the phase glade had moved on, but we knew how closely we now had to guard against being drawn into one, and how quickly that could happen. Bril lined up the shards and off we went, once again, to find the armorer, Warr.

After almost a complete glowcycle in the open fields, we saw a low area coming into view that had trees, bushes, and a stream. As we neared the peaceful scene we saw fences with animals inside them. They appeared to be goats, sheep and cows. There were troughs supposedly to hold some sort of food for them, but they were empty. A little closer and I saw the animals were pretty thin, having bones showing through their hides. Their heads were down and when I was close enough to see their eyes, I glimpsed despair.

We stopped at a safe distance.

"Togn," I asked, "do you know what's going on here?"

"Well," he replied, "looks like a holding area where they put the animals before they slaughter them, But, these animals sure don't look like they'd have much meat on them. Of course many of the Gurji are more interested in the bones and the meat in the centers of the bones as deeper flavoring for their rynd."

Rarik agreed, looking on with disgust. "There's not a good meal among them," it said.

My heart was immediately struck by the cruelty I saw before me and I knew that all those animals could eat grass, yet they were fenced into a small space where the grass was picked clean. Meanwhile, just on the other side of the fence, there was ample grass. As I studied the scene I noticed one of the larger animals was laying down on its side, and when I pointed it out to the group we all moved closer to get a better view.

I got right up to the fence and suddenly the animal got up and came right over to me. I'd have known that animal anywhere, and in any shape. It was Horse! Horse shook her head and let out a hoarse greeting. She sniffed my hand and snorted her recognition.

"Oh, girl," I moaned, "What have they done to you?" She was very gaunt and had multiple cuts and scrapes on her legs and haunches. My heart was breaking, and then the anger came. I just started tearing away at the fence, pulling the timbers apart at their connections, determined to get her out. In an instant, Rarik, Togn and Bril joined in.

We made quick work of the fence. The other animals watched with interest, and once Horse was out we moved away from the opening. The other animals slowly started leaving and hungrily eating the lush grass just outside the fence. I knew it would only be a brief meal for them because somebody was probably going to notice them out. So, I urged my friends to help me drive them as far out in the field as we could. We used all sorts of tactics, from scaring to prodding, but eventually they were well away from their prison and feasting on sweet grass.

Brill got the shards lined up and they pointed us back in the direction of the holding area. We decided to veer to the right to go well around the scene of the crime, but after a few hundred meters two Gurji came from the holding area at full speed toward us.

"Hey there!" yelled one, "Stop! That's our horse!"

We stood our ground, swords at the ready, Horse well behind us. When they came close enough I told them they were mistaken and the horse was mine, lost in a Canyonlands flood, several glow cycles ago.

The other one screamed at us about all the animals being lose.

"They needed food," Togn said calmly. "And you obviously couldn't see that."

Then, without provocation they both pulled their swords and ran at us. Bril and Togn broke out to the sides while Rarik and I received their first strikes. Rarik caught the sword arm of one, twisting it, causing the sword to fall to the ground. The other one's sword clashed with mine, but then Togn and Bril stepped in grabbing his arms and throwing him and his sword to the ground.

I placed my sword tip against the leader's throat.

"The horse is going with us because she belongs to me," I said resolutely. "If you try to follow, it won't turn out well for you."

With that, we gathered our packs, sheathed our swords and walked away, leaving them laying in the lush grass.

CHAPTER TWENTY-FOUR

Deeper Into Mists

Within a kilometer of our encounter at the Gurji holding pens we came upon a large pool of water with wonderfully succulent grass all along its edges. We stopped and rested letting Horse drink water and eat some grass. I didn't think it wise for us to linger and I also didn't want Horse to eat too much of the rich grass after having been starved for some time. She would need time and rest to recover from her experiences. Unfortunately, we needed to keep moving so any extended rest would have to wait.

As we moved on, the land started changing. We entered a large valley and in the distance we saw tall rocky cliffs punctuated by sections of very large trees. The valley stretched out to our left and right. A very wide stream of water ran through it at the lowest point and I saw many places where the water seemed to disappear, as if flowing underground only to reemerge farther down the valley.

The glowstones were growing dim and I started feeling the fatigue that came with not having enough nourishment. Except for Rarik, the others were also slowing down and stopping more often. I noticed Rarik had briefly disappeared a couple of times since we had left the Gurji holding pens, no doubt grabbing quick snacks, as I had seen numerous little beasts scurrying about in the grasslands. We rounded the corner of a low rock escarpment and discovered a small waterfall. The water flowed out from underground and the refreshing smell told me it was a tonc stream.

We drank the tonc thirstily, feeling it rejuvenate our bodies and spirits. Horse grazed contentedly, alternating between the grass and quick sips from the tonc pool. When our hunger was slated we removed our boots and let our feet soak in the pool as we talked about the things we'd seen and done. It was a time of warm camaraderie among adventurers thrown together for some unknown reason. Perhaps it was just the randomness of the universe, but I preferred to think it was all exactly as it was supposed to be. Each one of us was acquiring, in some way, the experience we needed, and we all needed the others for it to happen. It was well I didn't know the challenges before us and how our bonds would be tested, for that would have spoiled the enjoyment of those moments. As the glowstones dimmed, so did we, falling into deeply needed slumber.

I awoke to the sound of talking. Togn stood a few meters away from the pool talking to what looked like another of his kind. What a coincidence, I thought, another Kech, here, in this valley. I was immediately curious about their story. Most interesting would be why they were there and where they were going. But, I didn't want to be too obvious and interrupt so I just arose, knelt and washed my face in the pool and took several hands full of tonc for breakfast. Nearby, Horse was grazing and I was heartened to see she appeared in much better spirits. She grazed voraciously, her tail swishing from side to side. I didn't see Rarik and assumed it must be off getting some of its preferred nourishment. Brill was just stirring, gradually awakening like he always did.

As I picked up my pack and slid my arms through the straps, Togn and his new friend came over. Togn told me and Brill that the newcomer was Dogn and was indeed of Kech origin. I could see Togn was excited about being in the company of one of his own kind. He told me that Dogn had been catching him up on some of the news about the few remaining Kech. I was still mystified as to how and why Dogn was there.

"Where are you on your way to?" I asked him.

"Well, Togn mentioned you are bound for the Land of the Misanthrope and as a traveler myself, that's always been a place I've wanted to see," replied Dogn.

"And you just happened to be traveling our here, in this valley, where there are no roads?" I inquired more directly.

Dogn regarded me quizzically and then smiled and said, "There is something pleasant to me about being out in the wild so when there are no roads, that's where you are more likely to find me."

I thought his response was deceitful and I looked at Togn to see if it registered with him. But it didn't.

"What do you two think? Can he come along with us?" Togn asked me and Brill.

Brill was almost always brimming with confidence and enthusiasm since his spirit journey and he didn't disappoint in this instance.

"I think he should definitely accompany us," Brill quipped, slapping me on the back. "After all, you never know what we might run into out here and another set of hands could be helpful."

I couldn't disagree with that, but I still held suspicion in my heart. About that time, Rarik returned and immediately drank a hearty serving of tonc before standing up, acknowledging us and then realizing there was a new being in the group. Togn introduced Dogn to Rarik and filled it in on the newcomer's interest in accompanying us. I could see that Rarik harbored similar misgivings as me, but I think being the newest member to the group it probably didn't want to take a chance of alienating any of us.

So, Rarik just nodded and said, "Okay."

Dogn didn't have any weapons so Togn gave him the sword he carried since he also had the obsidian axe. He remarked jokingly that it would lighten his load not to have to carry both. That only increased my unease. First, a total stranger shows up out of nowhere, and then we arm him. It seemed like a recipe for disaster, but I needed to honor the group's wishes. In one way I was glad for Togn. He seemed to really like talking with someone who had similar life experience.

Brill lined up the arrows on the shards and we struck out with Horse following along. We were in high spirits, well rested, well nourished and now a party of five. As we moved through the valley with the glowstones gradually getting lighter, I noticed a refreshingly cool air passing over us. It was fragrant, like flowers, and it seemed to have the just right amount of moisture. I was growing to like the Mists. Well, except for the dangers that lurked there.

Togn and Dogn walked together in the lead, chatting constantly and occasionally breaking out in laughter about some silly event, or time they remembered. Bril and I formed the center of the group, while Rarik and Horse took up the rear. We were moving along at a good speed until we entered a patch of the nasty grasp grass, and this patch was particularly vigorous. We had to constantly wield our weapons against it to get it untangled from around our legs. The task was particularly difficult because the grass wrapped quickly around our ankles and then tightened fast. Rarik, being from the Mists, and having four sets of razor-like claws, was very practiced at cutting the grass, and even fast enough to keep freeing all of Horse's four legs. But for the rest of us it was exhausting. And then came the eekutchi!

This time we were beset by more than I could count. All we could do was stay standing in the grip of the grass and flail away at the little beasts. Eventually we all managed to get turned so we were back-to-back in pairs, except for Rarik, and that made defending ourselves much easier. Rarik again excelled at eekutchi killing, and even Horse got into the act, raring up on her hind legs and stomping down on the aggressors. The noise was tremendous because the eekutchi had a very high pitched scream they used when attacking, and then when we wounded them their screams became deafening. After a few more blows we started to focus more on killing them by either separating their heads from their bodies, or dealing a death blow to their vital organs, so we could reduce the terrible screaming. As the bodies mounted some of the eekutchi stopped attacking us and started tearing into their brethren. I don't know how many we killed, but when it was over, the ground was piled with them, while scores of others then ignored us in favor of feasting on the defenseless dead and dying.

We caught our breath and then quickly continued hacking our way through the grasp grass. Eventually, we could see where the patch ended and made a fast break once we were free. We literally ran for a kilometer before slowing down to to a fast walk. Our first encounter with grasp grass hadn't been extreme enough to make us watch closely for it and go around. But after that experience we changed our strategy. From then on, when we saw the telltale twisted stalks, we detoured as far as necessary to stay out of its grip.

The glowstones were reaching full illumination and all the stress and physical exertion had taken its toll. We stopped at a rock outcropping and checked my pack for amber, hoping the Nourish enchantment had sensed our depleted energy stores. It had, with ample pieces for all of us, excluding Rarik who had feasted on some eekutchi. Then we checked ourselves for injuries and were amazed at how many bite marks, scratches, cuts and bruises we had. We took turns applying Shalow Root to the worst of our injuries. When I checked Horse I found she had a serious wound to her flank. It was not a place where I could just tie Shalow Root over it. So, I did my best by cleaning the wound with the plant juices and then pressing a leaf in place, hoping the combination of plant fluid and blood would form a temporary bandage. I held it in place for a long time and then it seemed to stick. So I was hopeful it would keep the wound clean and prevent further blood loss.

Once again, Brill lined up the shards and we set off with hope to find Warr. We also were staying alert for a muddy bog where Rarik could get an update.

Our journey took us out of the valley and up the side of a small mountain. The terrain became more rocky and the landscape went from grassy to bare dirt and stones, with sporadic stands of trees having feathery filaments for leaves. The filaments danced in the slightest breeze and were iridescent, changing colors within the glowstone light. It was all very magical and I wanted to stop for a time beneath the trees, lay on my back and look up through the branches to watch the feathery leaves from below. But, nobody else seemed taken by the scene so I stayed the course, content to imagine what that experience would have been like.

At the top of the mountain we overlooked another valley, although this one was much deeper with what looked like a town right in the center. Rarik looked around as if searching for a landmark. It pointed to a deep canyon that cut through a mountain to our right. It said the canyon was called Narandier and that it was the source of much of the tonc in the Mists. Because of where the town was in relation to the canyon, Rarik said the town was called Tiffovan, and also said that it would not accompany us into the town.

"Why won't you go with us?" I asked.

Rarik explained that his kind, beings of the Raphicia order, also included all the wraith beings. Because they are are spirit eaters and spirit benders, they are largely confined to the outer areas of the Mists, but will only enter towns to feed when they are desperate. Rarik said it was risky for them because one order of the rangers specialized in identifying them and neutralizing them, and they focused their efforts in and around population centers. Rarik said neutralization was a hideous and very painful process that ultimately drove the victim to devour its own fleshy parts over a period of glowcycles.

"Well, you have been a loyal friend to us, Rarik, so we will do our best to protect you, and understand you not wanting to go into the towns," I said on behalf of the rest of the group.

"Oh, no," Togn moaned. "You don't think the rangers will do that to us, do you?"

"No," Bril said assuredly, "Why would they do that to us, we're not Raphicia?"

Togn's face took on a more worried expression and his voice wavered, "But we've been traveling with Rarik and maybe they will know that, and then torture us to get information about it."

"Look," I said, "That's nothing to be worried about. Lots of beings come in contact with Raphicia, either knowingly or unknowingly, so there's no way they can detain everybody. Plus, nobody in their right mind is going to be traveling with one, so Rangers won't even think of that."

"Well, I should stay here with Rarik and not take the chance," said Togn.

"Yeah, and I'll stay with him," Dogn announced.

It was all very strange because I had never known Togn to be much of a worrier, so I was a little concerned. Still, there really wasn't any reason for him to go into Tiffovan and he along with Rarik would be formidable opponents to any beings up to no good. Dogn, I was unsure of, but, he had performed well against the horde of eekutchi so I gave him the benefit of the doubt.

After ensuring Horse had plenty of grass and access to water, Bril and I headed toward the town. I thought the break from walking would give Horse a longer rest so she could heal from the recent abuse, and from the eekutchi wound.

I was anxious to see Warr and get some better weapons for what lay ahead. I was also hopeful that Bril would get the rest of his answers and the training he needed to continue toward his destiny. But in the back of my mind I also hoped it wouldn't mean losing him, because we really needed his help. Actually, it was me who needed his help. I realized that I needed to keep reminding myself that the journey all began because of me being chased by the Tachina and trying to find a way to survive, and maybe even defeat them. Everybody else, except Bril, were going along simply to help. I owed them a great debt and I wondered if I could ever repay it.

As we approached Tiffovan we landed on a road that was mostly packed clay, and it was a relief from walking in grass and having to side step stones and holes dug by various creatures. Entering the town was a gradual process of passing by a building here and another there. The structures were a mix of stone and wood, with both materials used generously together. The stone portions were used on the lower parts of the buildings and then logs were placed on top of the stones in layers, making everything appear very solid looking. Stones and trees mixed casually around the buildings creating the illusion that the buildings were rising from the land in a sort of unplanned fashion. The air was light and delicate with an amazing range of floral scents.

I could sense the excitement in Bril, who was now very close to finally becoming the being he was meant to be. His confidence was almost contagious, making me feel a little heady and supremely sure of myself. We checked the shards and sure enough, the line for Warr was very short. Within a few hundred meters we entered the main part of town.

Tiffovan was small, and laid out in a circle, so no matter which way you turned on the main street you always ended up back where you had started. We took the branch to the right and within a few meters we stood in front of a narrow building with three stars inside a half circle over the open doorway. The line on the shard disappeared, so we went inside.

The walls were stone from top to bottom and there were a vast array of racks attached to them holding all types of weapons. There were swords, daggers, crossbows, steelstone bows, axes, lances, spears, darts, shotstones, hatchets, vials, all the necessary accessories for all of them, and many items I'd never seen before. The walls were barely three meters apart so wherever you stood you could practically touch everything on either wall.

Suddenly, a being floated down from above and hovered in the air, in a sitting position right in front of us. He had long white hair and a beard that dropped in a point from his chin. On his chest there was a large medallion with the word WARR in big letters. Although his appearance was definitely male, Ialeo had told us that he was a neut, which I assumed was either a male or female that simply had no use for sex. When Warr spoke, it was like a lilting melody and it seemed that everything he said was incredibly interesting.

"When you walked through that door," he started, pointing behind us and exhaling a long, slow breath, "you brought with you some serious spirits that I have not seen in a very long time."

Bril and I looked at each other with raised eyebrows.

"I am just amazed by the two of you, out here, facing the dangers of all four underworlds, and yet, you seem steadfast and confident," Warr continued with enthusiasm. "It is an honor indeed to serve you, for two of your kind, seldom grace my presence."

"Well, thank you," offered Bril, trying to emulate the same enthusiasm for being in Warr's presence. "We have heard that you specialize in weaponry that is more fitting to the Mists and the LoM, than the types we already have."

"You have heard correctly, stalwart one, and since you have far to go in your quests, I will apportion some items to you as suggested by Uraya, who is such a dear heart."

With that, Warr took from a pocket in his cloak a handful of small, but lethal looking darts. He explained they were faze darts and that they caused confusion in any being struck by them, so that they lose direction and their will. Fortunately they were reusable so all we needed to do was reclaim them from the docile, stricken foe.

Next, he produced a shade stone, which he explained was a type of shot stone that punched multiple holes in a being's spiritual resolve. Immediately after, Warr waved a deep purple stone over the shade stone and recited some words that were meaningless to Bril and me. He explained that he had added the life force deplete enchantment to the Shade Stone so the holes it punched in a being's resolve would also simultaneously drain their life force. I was so wishing we would have had one of those when we were dealing with the wraiths that had attacked.

Then Warr became very serious and stared intently at each of us in turn, holding his gaze for an uncomfortable amount of time. He then reached to the wall and removed two flawlessly smooth round stones from a shelf. As he held them in his hands I saw stone dust flying and heard a high pitched whine as an energy busily carved designs in their tops. He handed one stone to each of us and when we looked closely, each one had a different design. Warr called them stones of primary essence and said they were ward stones that would protect each of us from spirit attacks. He warned us to stash them securely in our packs, and not to get them mixed up. If that happened, and one of us was carrying the wrong stone, there would be the opposite effect and we would become seriously vulnerable to spirit attacks.

"You have others in your party," Warr said mysteriously. "One of them has been with you," he stared at me, "a long time."

He took another smooth stone from the shelf, carved it and put it into a stone box wrapped with a vine to keep it closed. He handed the box to me.

"This is the other one's stone of primary essence, you must leave it in the box with the vine securely in place until you give it to him." Then he became very serious again.

"You have two others in your party and one of them is a Raphicia, which is one I cannot help. The other one is not what he pretends to be, and is also beyond my help."

I was not surprised by his last comment and it helped to reinforce my ongoing suspicions about Dogn. I also suspected that Rarik, being of the wraith bloodline, would be less susceptible to attacks from those of its own kind.

Warr then floated upward into a loft and disappeared to the back of it, saying as he moved, "You will find Skelak on the little island just beyond the city. I alerted him that you were on your way so don't delay."

Bril and I looked at each other with surprise, turned and left.

Outside, we wondered out loud how to find the island, and mysteriously a passersby said, "Follow me."

So, we did. The being was amphibian-like but with refined features and very finely cut scales so that they almost appeared to have typical human-like skin. But the scales were iridescent making them very easy to distinguish from other human forms. She had arms, legs, hands and feet but there was a webbing between her toes and fingers. There were also small slits on the sides of her neck, like the gills of a fish.

Our new leader must have seen us studying her.

"You have never seen one of my kind," she stated. "I am the Ericota, and we are key to helping manage water in the Mists, but across all the underworlds as well. We also serve as water transport for beings who have to cross spans of water that are too deep and far to walk or swim across."

She led us to a sleek watercraft that had intricate carvings across its sides. It was made of wood and there were no sails or methods of powering it. I was intensely curious about just how it would move through the water. Once on board, Bril and I went to the front of the boat and stood looking out at a vast expanse of water. Nowhere could we see an island, but by now, our host was lost to the details of getting others aboard, and managing the movement of containers on and off the vessel.

Before long, a horn sounded, long and low, and suddenly the boat lurched forward. We were underway.

CHAPTER TWENTY-FIVE

An Island

I had no direct memories of ever having been on a watercraft. But, I knew what they were, and I knew that they usually used the wind to move across the water. On this vessel though, there were creatures just below the water, chained to anchorages on its sides, and they swam, pulling the hulk along. And, they swam very fast. Standing at the front of the boat, looking down through the water, we watched transfixed as their team of lithe bodies swayed rapidly side to side, driving their very large tail fins. There were no less than 24 of these magnificent creatures, each one a copy of the next. Their strength and endurance were incredible, and the speed our boat reached was fast enough to cause a spray of water to rise three meters into the air above the ship on each side of the pointed bow. The wind in my face, laden with moisture and the coolness of the water, felt strangely familiar and comfortable.

As I turned my attention to the deck of the ship behind me, I saw beings of several different types. The Guji were the most populous, but I also saw other Ericota as well as some beings that were very human-like but having an elevated posture and presence. Their "in-charge" postures of hands on hips and all-knowing expressions made me ask a nearby Ericota about them.

"They are Culliam," he replied, "and they mostly control city and town management, and are very powerful."

"What does that mean," I inquired further, "You mean they can control other beings, or they have special powers?"

"They decide everything about how the communities operate, including who uses which structures, what the structures are used for, how many rest foundens there are," his voice trailed off, "basically everything necessary for the community to function."

"How does one become one of them?" Bril asked casually.

"You don't become one," laughed the Ericota, "You have to be one. They came from the star system of Virgo, on a planet connected to the star Zavijava. Their ability to manage complexity is well known across the galaxies. Before an expedition of them arrived centuries ago, everybody here was pretty miserable. They had to toil all the time, there were constant shortages of nourishment, there was a lot of fighting over materials. But they convinced a few communities to let them manage things and soon more of them arrived to work in all the other communities. They are the smallest group in the Mists, and across the underworlds, but they have a very large influence."

"So they are originators of the foundens, transportation systems, messenger system, water management and all the other community needs?" asked Brill.

"Right," said the Ericota, "they arranged it all, and still manage it."

It was nice to finally know how all the systems came into being. I had pondered it many times and never imagined it was just because of a group of star travelers that happened to be good at managing things. Of course, I didn't have anything to compare it to since I couldn't remember where I came from, or how things within that society got managed. But, I appreciated how things worked in the underworlds, and felt some gratefulness for the Culliam and their efforts.

Looking out across the expanse of water my mind wandered to my tattooed woman friend. I felt such a strong draw to her that it seemed we surely had history together. Ah, yes, history, the thing Keln, or whoever I was, knew little about. That damn dark wall, I thought. Besides me, how many other innocent souls had passed through and found themselves without memories in a strange new world? But then, slowly, like discovering some deep secret with layers of complexity, new questions arose.

Could the woman also have come through the dark wall? And if she had come through around the time I did, then that could very well explain our connection. My mind raced at the possibilities. Had we known each other before we even arrived on Octa? That would also explain our familiarity with each other. And had we been involved in the same affairs that had drawn the Tachina after me? If so, then she also might be in their crosshairs. The thought made me anxious and fearful for her, and I felt a strong new sense of purpose. Besides escaping the Tachina, and even defeating them, I needed to somehow find her again. The more I thought about it, the more I became convinced that she was the answer to so many unanswered questions.

Bril tugged on my sleeve and pointed to a massive rocky mountain jutting up from a very green island. All along the island's coast I saw a formidable barrier of vines growing several meters high. Sandy beaches meandered between rock outcroppings and there was a single dark cloud raining on one small patch of land at the bottom of the mountain.

The ship's pilot approached and told us it was time to get off. Bril and I looked at each other and then back at her, questioningly. She said she had come as close as she could and we would have to swim and walk in from there.

Bril looked at me, laughing, "I guess we should have gotten a boat from Warr as well," he quipped. We went to a ladder rope at midship, climbed over the side and stepped our way down to the water. Then, we jumped in. My feet couldn't touch bottom so we swam for a few meters and finally reached a depth where we could walk in from there. By the time I turned to look back, the vessel was disappearing into a humid haze. I wondered how we'd get back, but decided it wasn't worth the time to think about that.

Once on the sandy beach we walked along the water's edge, looking for an opening to the rest of the island through the viney barricade. We didn't have any tools but our swords, and the thought of having to hack our way through vines with stems 10 centimeters thick and larger, was too daunting to even consider. The rocky patches along the water were well worn from the water's movement, having smooth sides and rounded shapes. But, they were tall and scaling their slippery sides was out of the question.

We walked a few hundred meters and then Bril spotted a cave. We headed for it and at the entrance we strained our eyes trying to see how deep it went. Since it seemed to go on a long way, we entered. The first blast of darkness made me stop and wait, trying to get my eyes to adjust. Eventually we could see enough to make our way, haltingly and carefully. The bottom was rock strewn and there were big holes filled with water that we had to avoid. All the while, I'm thinking we might be on a wild goose chase. After all, we simply took the pilot's word that this was the island Warr was talking about. I struggled against a nagging feeling that we were wasting our time.

On and on we went, tripping, stumbling, literally feeling our way. My hands were cracked and bleeding from their encounters with sharp rock, and my legs were feeling very tired and heavy. But, I was incredibly thankful for the softstone boot soles because they were definitely saving my toes from a lot of potential injury. I could tell we were climbing up, and every now and then there was an opening above, letting in slivers of light and making things much more visible. I started to hope that might mean we would emerge from the cave and into glowstone light at some point soon.

But, on we went. I was growing more and more wary about our predicament and was about to ask Bril if he was feeling the same way. But right then, whoosh! Something went whizzing by me and crashed into the rock wall behind. Whoosh! Whoosh! Two more somethings flew by, delivering a blast of air as they went. Bril dodged to the right and took cover behind a boulder. I wasn't far behind him. Then seven more objects hurtled through the space, crashing into rock behind us. By the sound of them, we were sure the flying items were stones. I looked at Bril, no doubt with my most horrified face, but he was more mystified than horrified. More flying items whizzed by and crashed into the stone protecting us. Then we heard a most hilarious laughter. It bordered on deranged and absurd, and it rapidly rose in pitch before descending to a final baritone. I saw a smile cross Bril's face, and then he stood up and stepped out from behind our shield. I reached to pull him back, but he was gone.

The laughter continued on and off, but no more stones flew by. I stepped out after a safe while. Bril just stood there, smiling and looking up through the cave, as if trying to see something that he knew was there. Suddenly, we heard a voice behind us!

"Hehehehe," it started hilariously again, "Have I got a treat for you!"

We spun around and faced a very tall man wearing some sort of helmet and holding a staff that looked like it was made from StarStone, the very same stone we used for finding the entrances to the under worlds.

I was totally dumbfounded, but Bril was grinning ear to ear.

"Is that you, Skelak?" Bril asked.

"Give that boy a trophy!" shouted Skelak insanely. "He's a smart one, he is. But let's see just how smart he is."

Skelak caused a stone to rise up by waving his staff from side to side. Then as the stone floated there in the air, he formed his lips into an O, and sent a blast of air at the stone, which took off like it was shot from a canon, crashing into the stone wall just beyond where we stood.

Then, Skelak handed his staff to Bril and said, "Okay, your turn."

And so, Bril's lessons had begun. He would later tell me that when he went on his soul journey, he learned that his destiny was to be a wizard. A wizard who could motivate things in the natural world, make force fields, manipulate gravity and even summon something called an Enderether for assistance when in life threatening situations.

But for now, I found the most comfortable seat I could find and just watched as Skelak tried his best to teach Bril the finer points of throwing stones by breathing on them. It was a painful process to watch because it required Bril to channel previously expansive and unfocused energy into extremely compressed units, and do it over and over again in rapid succession. It was also exhausting and I fell asleep for a long time, only upon awakening to see the two still at it, Skelak demonstrating and Bril attempting.

After a long while Skelak led us out of the cave and we dined on syphoria and tonc stew. Then when the glowstones were dimmest, we slept. When I awoke, the two of them were some ways off, making trees bend and throwing all kinds of objects by simply blowing on them. I was amazed at how quickly Bril was progressing and began to think I'd really appreciate all of his new skills. In fact, those skills could be lifesavers for all of us. That was only if Bril, with his new skillset, wanted to still travel with us. My hope was that Skelak would guide him to finish walking his current path before starting in a new direction. But of course, I also allowed the choice to be his. I didn't want anyone risking their life for my cause if they didn't want to.

One glowcycle turned into two and then three and eventually I lost track of how long we were on the island. My glowcycles were filled with syphoria and tonc stew, sleeping, exploring the island and then sleeping some more. Bril's were full of Skelak, and channeling his energy and focusing his concentration and practicing the hundreds of tactics he'd need to know to begin his journey as a wizard. Skelak made it clear, that what Bril was doing was only the beginning. He would need to practice and learn for the rest of his lifetime, because as Skalk said, "A wizard is for life."

On one particularly bright glowcycle I watched as Skelak retrieved a length of StarStone from an old iron locker set into the side of a huge boulder. As Bril and I watched, he caused it to float in the air and spin. After awhile of spinning faster and faster, I momentarily thought my eyes deceived me as the spinning got so fast it was almost like the stone disappeared. But then, the spinning stopped and what had been a very basic piece of stone was transformed. It was now cylindrical, about a meter and a half long, with a bulbous top that was carved to resemble flames. Its sides were carved in spiral fashion with glistening tiny crystals in the grooves, and its color went from gradient hues of blue to gradient hues of orange from bottom to top.

Skelak ceremoniously handed the new staff to Bril saying, "This staff will serve you well as long as you adhere to the wizard's code."

Bril grasped the staff firmly, planted it on the ground and beamed a big smile from ear to ear.

"Now," yelled Skelak, "let's teach you how to use it!"

And off they went into the forest. This time, they were gone for several glowcycles. Meantime, I explored some more, feasted on syphoria, practiced my swordsmanship against the vines along the coast, used the pack's golden threads to repair several holes from my journey through the cave, and slept.

Eventually, I began to grow weary of the stagnation and wanted to move on soon. I wondered about how Togn and Rarik and Horse were doing, and I hoped they wouldn't think something had happened to us and just leave to go on with their lives. It was always a possibility, and the wild card in the mix was Dogn. I was still suspicious of his intentions and was anxious to get back and get to the bottom of it. Weighing on my mind also was the tattooed woman. I hoped she was okay, and that wherever she was, her journey was somehow on track to coincide with my travels.

At the beginning of yet another glowcycle I decided I should leave, get back to the others, and wait there with them until Bril was finished. I went to where the two were talking and was just about to announce my intentions when Skelak let out a hideous laugh, pointed in the water's direction, and told us to go away. He did it in such an immediate manner with wild eyes and forceful tones that we wasted no time and started running to the cave entrance. As we went, clods of soil flew past us and one hit me in the back. Bril immediately turned around, waved his staff at an incoming clod and sent it flying back toward Skelak, hitting him in the chest. Skelak let out a hearty grunt, and then broke into one of his hilarious laughs. It was still echoing in my ears as we entered the cave.

CHAPTER TWENTY-SIX

Betrayal

We navigated the cave quickly and were soon on the sandy beach walking toward the spot where we had arrived. I didn't know why, but it just seemed like going back to the arrival spot might have something to do with getting picked up for the return journey.

As we walked I couldn't help but notice a profound difference in Bril. If he had been confident before, he was now even more. It gave me a feeling of security, something I had seldom felt since arriving on Octa. It just seemed like being with Bril meant not having to worry about anything. It was a very nice feeling and one I didn't want to be without. So, I was feeling uneasy about what Bril's plans were, now that he was a bona fide wizard.

"So," I began, "What are your plans now, Bril?"

"What do you mean?"

"Well, you are a wizard now, and I while I don't know exactly what that means, I assumed you might have quests or something you have to do."

Bril stopped walking and turned to face me.

"One of the most important things Skelak taught me was to honor those relationships where I am needed. Do you need me?"

"Well, yes, it seems more than ever."

"So, I'm going to go with you until you no longer do, or, another needs me more. But even then, you will have to permit me to leave."

"Wow, that's a load off my mind," I said chuckling graciously.

"Besides," he quipped, "Where else am I going to find the opportunity to get killed nearly every glowcycle!" We laughed long and hard, and my heart soared to know that the man who had become my friend was now my brother.

The glowstones were bright, and the air was warm with high humidity. I walked close to the surging water and let it splash up on my legs. It felt cool and refreshing so I stopped, slipped off my boots, sword, pack and clothes, and ran into the surf. Bril was not far behind me. We frolicked for a long time, enjoying the actions of the waves, exchanging being wet and hot for being soaked and cool. Then we dragged our clothes into the surf to give them a good washing. The water was fresh and I could smell the sand, the rocks and green life all around. If those moments could have gone on forever, I would have welcomed it. But, we had things to do, and places to go. Begrudgingly, we donned our soaked clothes, saddled ourselves with packs and weapons, and continued walking, looking, waiting for something that would take us from the island.

As we walked Bril told me about some of the things he had learned from Skelak.

"When I asked Skelak about why, or how, I was drawn to the Mists, and why I was motivated to seek my destiny, he told me it was because of my animating spirit," Bril explained. "Every being has an innate motivation to find the purpose or life that resonates with their spirits. But when a spirit is motivated toward wizardry, it is a much clearer and stronger motivation It's like you can't live until you discover that essence of your destiny. And that was why I was having all that anger and anxiousness."

"I have a question for you, and not that you have to have an answer, I'm just curious what you think," I began. "I have wondered since our experience with Uraya if I made a mistake in not asking it to allow me to try that spirit tube you used so I might regain my memories?"

"Yes, you should have asked," replied Bril.

"Yeah, I guess I already knew that," I said resignedly. "But, maybe I'll get another chance, and if it happens, I'm doing it. But, what was it like, anyway?"

"Very hard to explain. At first I felt really light, like I was floating. Then, I guess I went to sleep because I don't remember having any bodily sensations at all. No feeling of weight, or heat or cold. Just nothingness. But then I was seeing or maybe feeling, I don't know, but all kinds of scenes of these people. I didn't know them, I mean they didn't look like anyone I know, but somehow I knew they were me. Like different versions of me, and they were in strange places I'd never seen. A lot was like in another time. I saw them in all kinds of situations too, from very dangerous and scary to very peaceful and secure. But then I saw like a book and it opened and I watched myself doing things like what Skelak taught me. And it just felt so real, and reassuring, and right. It felt exactly right."

"So that was a really amazing experience for you."

"It was beyond amazing," confirmed Bril.

We walked until we came to the place where we had come ashore. Then, Bril sat down on the sand. I assumed he knew something, so I sat too. There we were for at least half a glow cycle, saying nothing, just listening to the surf and feeling the moist breeze on our skin.

I was ready to lay back and doze off, when Bril stood up suddenly and started waving his arms. I looked out across the water and saw a boat, the spray flying high above the sides as the creatures powered it toward us. It came within swimming distance and stopped. We heard a single blast of a horn and took that to mean we better get going. We charged through the water until we could no more, and then started swimming.

The ride to Tiffovan was uneventful, except for the spectacle of those huge beasts swimming in concert to get us there. On board there were a mix of beings and even some I was familiar with from Canyonlands. It was then that Brukin's words came back to me in a sort of I-told-you-so way that would have been so unlike the little languagician. When he had said that there were plenty of things here on Octa to amuse me, and he had that glimmer in his eye, I saw now that a share of that amusement lay in the diversity of life. Looking around the boat I could almost feel myself ready to burst out laughing, for the crowd was such an exuberant mix of colors, heights, widths and features. I was sure the glimmer in the little man's eyes might also have been referring to things like eekutchi and cinder strikes and wraiths, as his sense of humor strayed to the macabre. But what I was realizing at that moment, was that I was becoming a part of the place. Regardless of where I had originated, and what experiences I once had, this place, Octa, with all of its vibrance, and levels, and trials, was my place.

Back ashore, Bril and I picked our way through a bustling Tiffovan. It seemed much busier than when we had arrived many glowcycles before, and after the solitude of the island it was most oppressive. I couldn't wait to get back to the countryside, which didn't take long at all. Soon we were on the clay road we entered on and not long after we branched in the direction of the mountain where we had left the rest of our party. I was not prepared for what we found.

On the mountainside overlooking Tiffovan, where we had left Togn,

Dogn, Rarik, and Horse, we found none of them! Bril and I raced through the possibilities. Had they simply left because we had been gone so long? Were they attacked and captured, or worse? Did they fall into fighting amongst themselves and simply split up? What about Horse? Had she gone somewhere with them, or without them? Was she okay? I'd already lost her once and the possibility of doing so again was heartbreaking. The whole situation became suddenly overwhelming to me. Not knowing where they were and whether or not they were well and unhurt was terribly distressing. I worried they might be needing me, and I wasn't there for them. Then too, the aspect of not having them with us in the journey ahead made me feel simply hopeless in the face of all the potential challenges. I screamed at the top of my lungs!

That felt good and it helped clear my senses. Afterward I started considering the situation from a new perspective. The reality was that we didn't know anything. There was no evidence anybody had been hurt, or kidnapped. There was no evidence that people had fought amongst themselves. There wasn't even any evidence they had left permanently. We didn't know anything, other than four of our comrades were not where we had left them.

"Okay," I said, "enough mental speculation. What should we do?"

"I say we wait a little while," started Bril. "Let's wait and watch all around us, and see if they show up, or we get some clues about where they are. They might have just gone to get some tonc, or maybe they took Horse to some better grassy areas."

So, we each faced a different direction. Then, we just looked and listened. After awhile it was amazing how many things I started to notice. First, the area was well trampled down and the flattened grass stems looked like they had been pressed against the ground a long time. There weren't any stems standing straight up, which would have been a sign that no-one had been there for awhile. Then Bril saw something that brought a glimmer of hope.

"Look here," he said pointing to trodden grass going off in the direction of Narandier, the canyon Rarik said was the tonc source for most of the Mists. "C'mon, they can't be too far ahead."

So, off we went, following the trodden grass, and footprints in gravel where the grass gave way. I was relieved, and felt a little foolish for my earlier descent into hopelessness. I was also once again extremely thankful for Bril's confidence and composure.

The trail led us straight to the canyon, and as we entered we felt a fresh rush of sweet smelling air. The canyon walls were very close together and they towered a hundred meters above our heads. The stone was multicolored and quite porous, having plants of all descriptions growing from various sized holes and crevices. All along the walls, tonc flowed freely before collecting in a three-meter-wide stream leaving the canyon. I stopped and drank thirstily from the stream, realizing it had been along time since I'd had any sustenance. Bril followed suit and soon we were refreshed, reinvigorated and on our way.

Following the trail became difficult because of the many flat rock surfaces where no trace of passersby could be left behind. But we knew the trail had entered the canyon, so unless they had climbed up the canyon walls, they should have been in there, somewhere.

After hundreds of meters we came to a short slot canyon branching to the left. Standing right there, grazing on some short grass was Horse! She reared her head and snorted a greeting when she saw me and I ran over to her. She nuzzled my chest as I stroked her forehead, telling her I was sorry I was gone so long. After our expressions of reunion, I checked her over thoroughly. There were no new injuries or afflictions, which was a great relief. Already, my spirits were soaring and I was even more hopeful we'd find everybody else, well and in good spirits.

A few meters from where we stood there was a cave. The entrance was curved, hiding the nature of its depth and substance. Being well versed in cave exploration, we entered. Just a few meters in, beyond the curved entrance, to our surprise and horror, we found Togn!

There he was, just a shadow of the being we had left. His clothes hung off him like rags and his face was gaunt and drawn. Right beside him there was the biggest mushroom I had ever seen. It was at least two meters tall with a wide head and lots of spores beneath its thin veil. A root-like appendage went from the mushroom to Togn's hip.

Bril and I were horrified, and then remembered Rarik telling us about dangers. He had talked of something called an elemental mushroom, and then I knew that Dogn's sudden appearance was not accidental at all. Somewhere along the way, Togn must have come close to a smaller version of the mushroom that now towered over him. Once the mushroom shifted its shape to resemble a being of Togn's origins, it became Dogn so it could carry out its evil deed. I knew then why Togn had gotten fearful and paranoid. It was all part of the mushroom's plan, and once it got its tentacles into him, the feeding began.

We were seriously concerned that Togn's energy might be too low for us to sever the link between the mushroom and him. So, Bril found a small stone with a hole on its surface. He took the stone to the tonc stream, filled it and brought it back.

"Togn, Togn," I said, shaking my friend. "Wake up."

"Huh? What?" he stammered.

"Wake up and drink some of this," I instructed, cradling his head in my arm while Bril put the stone to his mouth.

Over and over we repeated the process, until Togn pushed away at the stone and opened his eyes.

He smiled broadly, "Hey, you guys, hey, it's good to see you," he said dreamily.

"Listen, Togn, we need to move you and we don't know, but it might hurt a little," I explained, wanting to alert him. We planned to cut the root and move him, but we didn't know how much he would feel when we did that. We also didn't know if more of his life force would drain from the portion of the root attached to him.

"Oh, don't worry," Togn responded, "It will be okay."

Somehow I didn't believe he really knew that. But it was clear we needed to get him disconnected from the mushroom. I wiggled my shoulders beneath his left arm and worked my right arm behind his back and under his right arm pit. Then I grasped his left wrist in my left hand. Being just a shadow of the size he used to be, he felt very light and I was confident I'd be able to move him quite easily. Bril drew his sword and on the count of three struck a decisive blow, severing the root from Togn.

After that, mad chaos ensued! I lifted Togn and took four steps away from the mushroom. As a milky white liquid drained from the root portion still attached to Togn, the mushroom twisted and turned and started stretching and straining. It contorted itself rapidly, changing form to take on the appearance of a very large Bril!

The milky fluid draining from Togn was slowing but I knew I had to get it to stop because it was now showing signs of blood coming out too. I dug in my pack, pulled out the moss rope and tied it tightly around the stub of the root. That stopped most of the flow.

In the intervening seconds, Bril had become locked in combat with his much bigger self. Well, not really him, just a being that looked like him. He had struck a couple of blows with his sword, but the larger Bril was just as aggressive as ever.

"Stay with Togn," Bril yelled, I've got this."

Bril brandished his sword in his left hand, raised his staff with his right hand and then brought the base firmly to the ground, creating a loud crackling sound. The larger Bril slammed against the cave wall, pinned by an unseen force. Bril stepped in, and with one swing of his blade, removed the head. The larger Bril slumped to the floor and as the last of a milky substance pooled beneath it, a headless mushroom slowly appeared in his place.

Bril and I let out a collective sigh of relief, and disbelief.

"Rest in peace, Dogn," Bril said with an air of finality. "I guess we should have heeded your caution," looking at me, "but I was so impressed at how much Togn liked him, that I was willing to overlook any suspicions. And where is Rarik? He should have seen this happening. After all he's the one who told us about those mushrooms. Why didn't he do something?"

"Well, " I said, checking on the bleeding from Togn's severed root, "When ever, if ever, he gets back, he better have a good explanation for this. But right now we need to do something about this root sticking out of Togn. There is less of that white stuff now, but more blood, and he's not conscious."

Bril kneeled down and regarded the situation. Finally, we decided we needed to try to cut what was left of the root from Togn, and maybe even gouge a little of it out where it connected to him. We didn't want to cause a lot of pain, but it looked like the root would be a problem if we didn't get it all unhooked from him.

We moved Togn out of the cave and right beside the tonc stream. Then we assembled some shalow root leaves nearby, ready to apply to where we made the cut. Bril took out the firebrand while I positioned myself at Togn's head, bending over and placing my forearms across his chest. Then Bril dropped a piece of firebrand on to his sword. A white hot flash rose up followed by a few seconds of flame. Immediately when the flame went out, Bril made the incision, cutting a quick circle around the root's base where it attached to Togn. Togn screamed out and lurched, but in his weakened state I was able to keep him down. The heat from the hot sword cauterized the wound. Bril immediately applied the shalow root leaves to the area. Then we rolled Togn on his side so the leaves would stay on the wound. Bril went searching for some large leaves and tree sap.

Togn slept on his side, breathing easily and seemingly dreaming. I couldn't believe how much he had deteriorated, and I realized that even if he had the strength to walk, he'd be hindered by the now-baggy pants hanging in folds from his lean frame. I felt so bad for him I wanted to cry, but held back, letting just a few tears slip between my lashes. It wouldn't do any good and would just be a selfish emotional release for myself. I needed to think of some way Bril and I could move him so we could cover some ground. But then, remembering Horse, I became hopeful that we'd be able to somehow get him up on her and figure out a way to keep him there. Of course, there was also hope that the shalow root would work a similar miracle as it had when Bril got nipped by the eekutchi.

When Bril returned he fashioned the leaves and sticky sap into a sort of an adhesive cover for the wound, placing it over top the shalow root leaves and relying on the sticky sap to hold everything in place. We moved Togn to a nearby grassy area and resolved ourselves to stay put for as long as needed. We spent the time mending our packs, collecting more shalow root plant, practicing our war craft, resting, and drinking tonc.

In three glowcycles Togn awoke. He surveyed himself in disbelief and confusion. But as I explained what had happened, and how Dogn had used him, I saw remembrance turn to anger, and not long later to shame. Shame because he hadn't seen what was happening. When I asked him about Rarik, he said he remembered that it had left once the four of them had reached the canyon. He wasn't sure when that happened. He said he was in a dream-like state most of the time in the cave, but very fearful, and that was how Dogn kept him there. He said Dogn told him he was protecting him, and so he wouldn't have to worry.

We fed Togn a constant supply of tonc for another two glowcycles and by then he was able to stand and walk a few steps. When we removed the leaves from his wound, there was a nice clean looking scar that was well healed. We had lucked out and the brood foot had worked its miracle. On a new glowcycle we were planning to leave, but that's right when Rarik showed up.

I couldn't contain my anger as I interrogated it about its decision to leave Togn. Bril threatened to end it, but us both seeing its pitiful response convinced us not to. Then Rarik actually sank deeper, begging us to finish it off. It told us it had been betraying us all along to a wraith that was working with the Tachina!

"I didn't want to and I thought I could mislead it so they wouldn't find you," Rarik whimpered. "But it was terrible. The things the wraith did to me were horrendous and I knew there would be worse if I didn't do what it wanted. I couldn't get away. But, I should have just said no and gone and killed myself. So, please do it now. Just finish me. I've always been terrible at everything so no loss to anybody," it shrank back against the rock wall, resolute, resigned.

Bril and I looked at each other in disbelief wondering how everything could have turned out so wrong while we were gone. Worse, we had no idea how close the Tachina were. It meant we'd have to try to get to the Land of the Misanthrope as quickly as possible for we knew that would throw up a new barrier to the hunters. But we said none of this out loud, instead looking at each other with an understanding and knowing. I pulled Bril aside, out of ear shot.

"It's not sorry, it just wants pity and then it'll do whatever the wraith wants. But, I wonder if we can buy ourselves a little more time?" I started. "If we tell Togn, while Rarik can overhear, that we are going on to Tiffovan and stopping there for him to rest up, but then instead, we find a passage to LoM right away. Then when Rarik tells the wraith that, we'll be well ahead of the hunters again."

"Yeah, but how do we know Rarik will tell them that," Bril reasoned.

"But it doesn't matter, right? As long as Rarik doesn't say we went to LoM right away, we've got the same result. Maybe to make it even more in our favor, we could also tell Togn that we can't go to LoM until we do something else here."

"We could say that we need to collect some more moss rope, or I know, Skelak told me about a place I should visit here, called Trinastien, a place with all kinds of wizard tools."

"Yes! Good," I said turning and heading back to where Togn was sitting.

"We're done with you, Rarik," I said. "Don't try to follow us!"

Then I spoke low to Togn telling him we were getting him to Tiffovan and that while he and I waited there, Bril would go to Trinastien to see about some wizard tools. I made sure my words weren't so low that Rarik couldn't hear them. Then, without looking back at Rarik, we helped Togn get on Horse, grabbed all our packs and marched out of the canyon.

As we moved through the countryside we looked back to make sure Rarik wasn't following, and saw no sign of it. Once at a safe distance and in a low area, Brill took out the StarStone Scepter and checked for an opening to the LoM. But, no luck, no yellow glow. We decided to backtrack toward where Uraya was. That way, we might add yet another wrinkle to our travels that could disrupt the hunters, especially if they thought we were going to Tiffovan, or assumed we wouldn't backtrack on our journey. We topped a hill and dropped into the large valley we had gone through on our way to Tiffovan. Once in a low spot, Bril tried the scepter again. This time it glowed a faint yellow. He laid the scepter on his palm and we walked in the direction it pointed.

We were traveling along the edge of the stream and when we neared one of the rock outcroppings we had stopped at before, the scepter glowed bright yellow, and in the next instant we were falling!

CHAPTER TWENTY-SEVEN

Unwelcome Land

Vortold, and the wraith known as Vasper, assailed Rarik mercilessly. They had been at it for at least one glowcycle, and now they started anew. Rarik was bleeding white profusely, and was missing all of his limbs.

"It's such a weakling, eh Vasper? Nothing but a pile of misshapen flesh and what, I don't know what else, but we're finding out, huh?" Vortold clucked and crackled the words. "Just taking it apart bit by bit. How much more can we do without killing it?"

"Not much," Vasper replied, disappointed.

"Okay, you weak blob," Vortold yelled at Rarik, "Last time. Where did they go?"

Rarik said nothing.

Meanwhile.

I grabbed Horse's reins with one hand and Bril's pack strap with the other just as our fall started. This time we fell through walls of mud interspersed with rock. Water poured from the sides of the tunnel and we bounced off the muddy, rocky walls as the tunnel twisted and turned. I focused intently, letting slow motion take over, adding some sanity to the drop. And it was a long drop.

When the fall leveled out we saw light ahead, and then in the next instant were assailed by the intense glare of the Land of the Misanthrope. We dropped gently to the ground as the mud rock tunnel twisted backward and disappeared. We were covered in wet earth, bruises, scratches and cuts. But, no broken bones and no heavy bleeding. I was especially thankful that Togn had managed to hang on to Horse using the makeshift lashing we created with the moss rope. He certainly didn't need any additional injuries.

As I surveyed the seemingly lifeless landscape I had a suspicion we were being watched. I don't know where the intuition came from, but it was strong. Within a few meters there was a tall rock spire with shade on one side. We headed for that because the glaring glowstones also generated an incredible amount of heat, much more than any of the glowstones I had encountered in the underworld. When we reached the shaded area, the wet mud that clung to us was already baked dry and hard.

We spent a long time peeling the clods of earth from our skin and tending to wounds with the shalow root. My immediate concern was water, or tonc, whichever, for it seemed the place was extremely dry and hot. That meant dehydration was imminent if we spent too long out under the glowstones when they were at full glow. So, we decided to sit and rest, waiting for a dimmer glowcycle. That also would have the added benefit of aiding Togn in his recovery.

I looked out on a vast, flat expanse of gravel-covered earth punctuated by an amazing variety of misshapen rock. There were the usual spires I had come to know well in the underworld, but there were also round rocks with holes in them, cylindrical rocks laying on their sides, and all I could describe as backbone rocks; rows, circles, half circles of flat stones sticking straight up through the ground's surface.

The glowstones appeared in every type of rock formation. There were even glowstones protruding from the ground. The glowstones up high were the brightest, and I saw some that were moving inside channels in the stone. As I watched, a moving glowstone reached a point where its intense light reflected off of what appeared to be a very large crystal embedded in the top of one of the spires. Suddenly, a bolt of hot white light shot from the crystal. It traveled to the ground striking a hole, releasing a puff of steam, and making the glassy substance around the hole momentarily like liquid.

"What do you make of that?" I asked Togn, who watched the spectacle with me.

"I've heard about these," Togn said triumphantly, as if having this piece of knowledge would help him reclaim some of his former self. "It's a crystal crown and it does that when a moving glowstone strikes it with light at just the right angle. Wherever it strikes, it turns the heavily sandy soil into glass."

"So, all we have to do to avoid that catastrophe is to watch for those holes and stay away from them?" I asked.

"Well, not so easy though," Togn responded. "The crystal crowns also move, so, you never really know where that bolt of searing light will strike. It might be a little way to the left or the right, or it might be somewhere 10 meters from those locations."

Great, I thought, moving bolts of white hot light that can strike anywhere at anytime. I was beginning to not like the LoM even more.

"Look," whispered Bril, pointing to a being walking with purpose toward us. It was a 'he' as far as I could tell from outward appearances. He looked remarkably like me or Bril with about the same proportions and features. When he got closer, we could see he had three strips of a shiny material hanging from his belt.

"Well hello, fellow humans," he said waving as he neared. "What brings you to this wonderful land?"

He was a weathered individual with stubbly beard, dirty clothes, gnarly hands filled with cuts and blood, and a few missing front teeth. On his belt, besides the strips of what now looked like reptile skin, he had a long-handled fork device and a very large knife.

"That's a long story," I replied. "How about you?"

"Hunting!" he said with a toothless smile.

"Is that what you hunt for?" Togn asked, pointing to the reptile skin.

"Sure is. Blood stalker skins with the diamond point scales. There's a big demand for these all over the underworld."

"Yes, as a matter of fact, we're supposed to get some of those for Ukino in the Mists," I volunteered, hoping maybe he'd offer to trade for something we might have.

"Well, I'll tell you what," he began. "I've been on the trail of about four of them, leastways appears to be four from the tracks. If you want to tag along and help me bring them down, I won't complain."

I knew Bril was thinking what I was by the next question he asked of the man.

"Do you know this LoM really well?" Bril asked casually.

"Oh, yes," he replied. "Although they call it Land of the Misanthrope, I can't say that being human here has hurt me. In fact, once I got past the suspicious stares, talking behind my back, and the occasional lynching crowd, I feel like I fit right in here," his laughter rang out against the spires.

"Well, since we are new here it would be helpful for us to have someone who is familiar with the place," Bril reasoned out loud.

"Oh yeah, I know it well and can help keep you out of the way of the blood ghasts, wraiths and the bleeding ruins. My name's Serik," he

196

waved at us again. We waved back, and with that unspoken gesture of trust, we prepared to go get some blood stalker diamond point scales.

We got Togn up on Horse, and set out. Almost immediately, Serik told us to stay in single file behind him and do everything he did. We fell in line and after about 30 paces, Serik dodged sharply left and started running. We did the same. Next, he swung right, still keeping up the pace and then suddenly left again. We all dutifully followed, and in the next instance we were glad we did. Out of nowhere came a bolt of white hot light, striking the ground immediately to our right and leaving a hole three meters deep with smoldering glassy sides. We all sped up, staying right on Serik's heels. After a few hundred meters, Serik slowed to a walk and announced we were clear.

Coming out of our collective stun, Bril asked Serik how he knew which way to dodge.

"Well, there's no secret to it," he said casually, "When I see one of those crystal crowns I just start dodging and running. Just happen to luck out so far."

The response left us all disappointed for we had thought he must have some kind of special power, or advanced information about the glowstones and the crystals. I finally took heart though because then I knew I was just as likely to avoid getting instantly cooked into oblivion simply by running serpentine.

Now, we walked, with Serik carefully tracking what looked like footprints followed by lines. He explained the line was the animal's tail, which dragged on the ground behind it. There were many tracks and they constantly crossed each other so it was difficult to see how many of these blood stalkers there were. Then too, with an animal having a name like 'stalker,' I wondered if in fact they might be hunting us.

Right as that thought crossed my mind, Serik stopped short and spun around, his eyes searching behind us, desperately. We were standing beside a large group of rocks, too steep and high for us to go over. But then, before I turned around, I saw what Serik was concerned about. The tracks went behind the rocks and I realized that we stalkers may have unwittingly become the stalked!

I spun around to see not four, but six creatures racing toward us, mouths open, and strips of skin standing straight up with razor like arrowheads running their length! I was most concerned about Horse and Togn who were first in line for the attack. Bril, me and Serik raced to put ourselves between them and the monsters. I yelled to Togn to get the shot stone from his pack and try to get off a round or two.

We knew that none of the spirit enchantments or weapons would work for these beings, so we had to resort to our swords and maybe some of Bril's new found powers. Togn threw his obsidian axe to me so I could fight two handed. Serik drew his long knife in one hand and the fork shaped tool in the other.

Before the beasts reached us Togn struck one with the shot stone, completely obliterating its head. Bril stamped his staff against the ground sending out a short shock wave that flipped over two of the stalkers. Now, the other three were on us, and the two that had flipped were coming back to their senses, shaking their heads as if coming back from being knocked out.

I brought the axe down on a snout causing a flood of a white fluid followed by blood, spraying into the air, covering me and Serik. Meanwhile Serik stepped toward the middle attacker, going low and then lunging upward, sinking his blade into its neck. The third beast turned wildly to its side, trying to rake its diamond point scales against Bril, as Serik rolled on the ground to keep from being stepped on. Bril stealthily moved aside and cut across the beast's tail. Then, once again, Bril stamped his staff and sent out another shock wave which disoriented one of the beasts in the now second charge.

Togn got off another shot, hitting one in the tail, while I took an attack from two of the now-wounded stalkers. I was able to get my blade into one's throat, but was caught off balance by the other, making me unable to swing the axe in its direction. It got behind me and I felt the teeth sink into my calf. As I twisted back around to bring the axe to bear, Togn got off another shot, hitting it squarely in its unprotected underside. It released my leg, spinning to attack Horse, who reared, throwing Togn to the ground while bringing her hooves together down on the beast's head.

Serik was back on his feet and in the open as one of the animals charged toward him from four meters away. Serik swung into action with his fork. It had a long shaft running its length that he flipped backward causing the fork to assume a firing position. Then he threw his arm forward sending the fork on its deadly mission. It went deep into the open mouth of the attacker. It fell, skidding toward Serik and stopping just a few centimeters from his feet.

As the battle wore on with just two wounded beasts feebly snapping and running at us, Togn got off another fatal shot, while Serik and Bril handily dispatched the other. I dropped to the ground, blood oozing from my wounded leg. Togn was back on his feet from the fall. He and Bril came to me, one digging through the packs for shalow root and the other cutting away my pant leg and fashioning the remnant in a sort of make shift wrap- around bandage.

"Well that was certainly an experience," I said. "I wonder what else this hellish place has in store for us?" When I looked up I saw an expression on Serik's face that I dreaded. He was looking out to a series of upright rocks that three beings were sneaking behind.

"It seems we're popular," Serik said. "Now we've gotten the attention of a pack of blood ghasts. Must have been drawn by the fight."

Then he explained how the creature travels in packs of three and likes to hide and ambush its prey. He said they were exceedingly smart, and could even speak languages when they needed to lure an unsuspecting victim into their hiding place.

When I asked him why the creatures there all had the word 'blood' in their names he said it was because of the environment. The lack of water and tonc made blood a substitute for hydration as well as nourishment and energy. Then he pried open the mouth of one of the blood stalkers, removed a plier-like device from his hip pocket and wrenched out a tooth. He held it up for us to see that a hole went all the way through it, creating a way for the creature to suck blood from its victims. He said that each of the 42 teeth in the stalker's mouth had those holes so they could suck in a lot of blood very quickly.

Serik's macabre show continued as he used his knife to cut a small slit in one of the skin folds of the stalker. As soon as he did that, white fluid started draining and he put his mouth to the spot to drink the fluid. When he was done he told us that the fluid was much like water and the animals had two layers of skin with the fluid between the layers. It helped to keep them cool, and hydrated. He warned us that we should all drink our fill from the dead laying around us because it might be a long time before we have any other fluids.

For a long, painstaking time we carefully drained and drank as much of the fluid as we could. It had a very bitter taste with a slimy texture. But worse, laying down beside one of the beasts and looking into its dead eyes as we drank fluid that flowed between its layers of skin, was not appetizing at all. Fortunately, Horse was smart enough to understand what was going on as I opened up a pocket near the hindquarters of one of the stalkers and created a bowl-like place where she could alternately drink and lick the fluid.

Once we satisfied our thirst, we harvested the lengths of reptile skin with the diamond point scales and cautiously stashed them in our packs, making sure some skin wrapped around the sharp scales so as to avoid cutting ourselves or our packs. Right about then I wished for a nice cool tonc or water pool where I could wash off the animal fluid, blood, and my own dirt and sweat. But, wishing and not getting only made me feel more miserable, so I put that wish out of my mind.

We had been watching where the blood ghasts had been hiding and hadn't seen them or any other movement. So, we reasoned they were just waiting to either follow us, or for some other unsuspecting prey to pass by.

So far, Serik had been a life saver and had a wealth of information about a harsh land that wasn't kind to those with human forms. When I asked him what the natives of the land looked like he said many were like orbs of light. He called them Lesania, and said they lived in the high caves and that they had the most hate for humans. Apparently, they traveled the universe, exploring and learning. Another group he called Onosauri were beings that were reptilian representations of the traditional human form. They formed communities and had a close relationship with the Lesania. They were also quite antagonistic toward humans. He said they lived in the lower caves.

As Serik spoke, Bril had taken out the contact and journal shards. Besides trying to find the Arbitans, which Serik knew nothing about, we needed to see Eana. Being one of the Superterrestrial Order, I hoped she'd have insight about the Arbitans. I needed to see Alechay for hopefully some insights about my visits from the ball creatures. And, we needed to find a messenger to get the blood stalker diamond point scales back to Ukino. Plus, we had to avoid the blood ghasts, and the Tachina, and survive!

I was growing more and more uneasy about my tattooed woman friend and what perils she might be facing if she had reached the LoM. It was all very chaotic in my mind because I wondered how she might be following the same path as me and yet we seemed to know nothing about each other.

Bril announced he had a line on either Eana or Alechay. At that point I explained to Serik about why we were in the LoM, who we were trying to locate, and a brief but vague description of our pursuers. Serik was very matter-of-fact and seemingly fearless. I hoped he would stay with us. So, when he volunteered to go along with us and serve as a guide, I was thrilled. And when Serik saw the direction the shards pointed, he was thrilled.

CHAPTER TWENTY-EIGHT

Relentless Disapointment

A long time before, in the Land of the Misanthrope, Serik had saved one of the members of the Superterrestrial Order from certain death at the teeth of blood ghasts. Back at the group's headquarters, Serik was treated like a king. He enjoyed a sumptuous variety of foods, drinks that made him exceptionally happy, and even a bit of romance, once he was cleaned up in a stone stall with flowing water. After hundreds of glowcycles, alone in the desert of LoM, it was a refreshing break, and since then, he was always on the lookout for beings in trouble, just in case they might be one of the Superterrestrial Order. Bril immediately made some connections.

"So, wait a bit," Bril started, looking at the shards. "That means that if this direction takes us to the Superterrestrial Order, then either Eana or Alechay are in the Order."

"And," I injected, "we're that much closer to finding out how to defeat the Tachina!"

The idea that we were so close to finally getting some answers to questions we had carried all these glow cycles, was both exciting and nerve wracking. Would the solution be something simple like a device, or, would we have to carry out something like seven quests to collect what we needed before we could even begin to challenge the flies? I was tired of the constant string of problems I had faced since arriving on Octa, and I was wishing that I could just find a nice quiet place somewhere other than the LoM, and just relax for 20 or so glow cycles, without the attacks of wraiths and ghasts and eekutchi, and without the feeling of always being chased.

As we set out, my leg ached from the wound, but I could feel the shalow root working. It felt like the damaged skin on my calf was tightening. There were also sharp, stinging pains that went along with the rapid healing.

By now, Togn was able to mount and dismount from Horse. All of us had been sharing amber from the nourish enchantment, which was producing a lot of food, even enough to give Horse some nibbles. But, the amber was dry, and not having water or tonc to wash it down, was uncomfortable.

Uncomfortableness it seemed was just a daily occurrence in the LoM. The glowcycles were long and at their peak the land surface became hot. The air was hot and dry and smelled like sun baked clay. The temperature extremes between full glow and minimal glow were also uncomfortable. We went from sweating to freezing, forcing us to huddle together for warmth as we rested. Then there were the shifting crystal crowns shooting white hot beams through the air and creating glass wherever they struck. We were running serpentine so much that we were adding kilometers to the length of our journey.

As we traveled around a large ring of upright stones we found an opening into its center. The area inside was sheltered by two enormous spires on one side that shed some nice shade. Since the glowcycle was at its highest, all of us but Serik started moving into the circle.

"Better hold up," shouted Serik after us.

We all stopped and turned to look at him. He stooped to pick up a stone, and then he tossed it into the center of a depression in the sand. Immediately the ground opened up revealing a pit with slick, sloping sides that ended in a point. It was like a huge funnel. Closer to the bottom of the three meter hole there were three spheres with sharp dimples all over their surfaces. The spheres were turning, meshing together.

"We call them bleeding ruins," Serik announced. "You fall down in there and the rotating orbs cut you to shreds. Your blood drains away through a tubular structure and goes on to nourish something down there. Nobody's ever come out to tell about it, so we just don't know what's down there. I've heard there are half dead beings down there, and the blood feasts help them resurrect as wraiths. They were built eons ago by native beings who either moved away, or became extinct."

"It sure is a blood thirsty place," Togn said matter-of-factly, making us all laugh at the absurd truth of it as we carefully stepped back out of the stones. Serik was such a well spring of information I wanted to know more about him.

"How long have you been in the LoM?" I asked as we started

following the shard line once again.

"I came here as a small man," he replied. "So I guess that means I've been here about 20,000 glow cycles."

"Don't you ever get tired of it, all the heat and dryness, and the dangers?" I asked.

"Well, yes, so what I do is, I go up to the Mists at a little resort tucked away in a mountain there, and spend a bunch of glow cycles getting rehydrated. Then, I come back. I guess it's kind of like home here. And, I like the solitude."

After that, we fell silent, just walking, sweating, and wishing there was a water or tonc spring. After a couple glow cycles, with restless sleep periods huddling in the cold, and no signs of other life, we were on the verge of delirium. Horse walked with her head down, her legs stumbling occasionally. Togn had to get off her and start walking on his own, and that was difficult and slowing us down. He had gained back quite a bit of his weight because we always had amber and he ate a lot of it. But, he still wasn't back to his former self. I thought the mushroom must have also taken some of his spirit and I wished for the old Togn.

My mouth and throat were parched and my lips were cracked and bleeding. Great, I thought, just what I need, yet another way to lose moisture. I would look out across the rock strewn landscape and think I saw a pond. But when I got to where I thought it should have been, there was nothing but fine gravel and sand.

Bril and Serik seemed to be equally resilient. They both still had firm steps and confidence in their posture. But, even they were showing more signs of disappointment every time we saw signs of water nearby only to discover another dry hole. Serik knew the signs to look for when searching for moisture. He even climbed up on some stones to check for shallow basins in the rock where moisture would collect from condensation. With every failure, my heart sank, and it became harder to maintain my usual optimism.

Meanwhile, the line on the shards had shrunk to about half its starting length. To me, that meant we were likely still a couple glow cycles away from relief, and if we didn't find some moisture before then, we'd probably all perish. With that thought in mind I wandered into the senselessness of it all. There I was about to die in a desert simply because I didn't think I could defend myself against a pack of flies. The absurdity made me start chuckling to myself. But then what of my brave friends who had joined my journey for reasons of their own, but also simply to help me? Would they have come this far on their own? Would Bril have gone on to greater wizardry in other lands? Would Togn have discovered a group of his own people and gone on to become one of their revered leaders?

As for myself, maybe it was just my destiny. Maybe it was always going to turn out like this, dying in a desert while running away from a foe I felt absolutely no confidence in defeating, or getting away from. And, for what? Why were they after me? What had I done to get them on my trail? The questions arising from my lack of memories, made my situation even more ridiculous. I didn't even know what I didn't know, and now I was going to die for it.

As another glow cycle came to an end, we found a small rock circle. The rocks were a couple of meters tall and directly above them was one of the biggest glow stones I'd ever seen. When we stepped into the circle of stones we could feel the heat radiating off them. All through the bright glow cycle they had collected the heat and now as the air cooled they were releasing it.

We plopped down on the sand, leaning against the warm rocks. They felt comforting, like old friends ready to help some weary travelers. I was glad we would be extra warm that night and it made the thought of dying in my sleep a little appealing. No more hot and cold. No more long glow cycles of sweat. No more dangers lurking around every corner. No more Tachina chasing me! No more everything.

My mind went back to the dream I had when I first arrived on Octa's surface. I had no body. I was just pure consciousness, floating in a void of blackness. But even in such a seemingly hopeless situation, I still felt optimistic. Somewhere in my consciousness, I knew I could just create my next reality. I knew I had complete control over the experiences I had next. But then my next mental question startled me. Why had I created this particular scenario? If I had in fact created my own existence, then why did I include an experience like this? Maybe to experience a death like this? Or, to overcome a situation like this? I fell asleep and slept dreamless.

Horse rearing up, stomping, and neighing woke us all. There at the entrance to our stone circle we saw wispy, foggy forms with a deep red tone at their centers, fading out to grayish black on the edges.

Blood wraiths!" Yelled Serik.

I don't know where our energy sprang from, but in seconds we were standing, armed, ready, and close together so we'd all get the spirit fortitude benefits of the enchantments on my pack.

The wraiths appeared initially as one with multiple heads, but now they separated. We could all feel the drain on our confidence as the wraiths applied their spells. We needed them to get close enough so we could use our mist-bender-enchanted weapons. Bril waved his staff left and right and then brought it down on the sand with two sharp strikes. Immediately a force field behind the wraiths sent them flying toward us. There were three of them and we all managed to strike at least one of them, and one we got twice. The wraiths shrank back, their confidence draining.

"Togn!" I yelled. "Try that shade stone!. It's got the life force deplete enchantment!"

Togn got the weapon from his pack, and got off two rounds as the wraiths attacked. One wraith shrank back immediately and started to wail at the edge of the stone circle. All of us got in more blows to the two that were now dodging in and out rapidly and speeding behind us to cast their spells. We formed a circle with our backs together.

Bril cast another disruptor, breaking the two attacking wraiths apart. Togn got off another round striking the largest and sending it wailing to the outer edge of the stones. Serik and I managed to hit the third wraith simultaneously, sending it wailing toward its two comrades.

Togn got off two more rounds of the shade stone, hitting the largest wraith. Then, it was over. The wraiths floated away quickly, no doubt to heal their wounds so they could attack again another time.

We all fell exhausted on the ground. At that point I wasn't even sure why we had bothered to fight them. It would have been easier and more final to just lay there and let them do whatever it was they would do. Those thoughts made me realize I needed to get out of my negativity. The glow stones were growing brighter, so I suggested in an equally bright and hopeful voice that we all start walking and find some water, or tonc, or even a blood stalker so we could drink its cooling fluid.

So, we set out once again. I forced my mind to stay in the present by counting the footsteps and paying close attention to what I was seeing, hearing, smelling and feeling. At one point I even managed to taste the air. It was tangy with a slight hint of dust. Then, a very distinctive odor struck my nostrils. In all the dry air, the smell of water was very pronounced. Horse had picked up the scent too and she started trotting out in front of us. We rounded a corner of tall spires and stopped dead in our tracks.

There just 20 meters ahead of us, at the base of a stout plateau was a large pond of water. But, all along the edges there were blood ghasts, blood stalkers, eekutchi and a few other beings I couldn't identify. Our hearts collectively sank. Really? We have to fight our way to the water? Even more disappointment.

But, Serik was undeterred.

"C'mon," he called confidently. "We just have to make a little space," as he drew his large knife in one hand and his fork weapon in the other.

We all followed his lead. If we were going to die, then what better reason than trying to get a drink. Bril cast a spell that sent four creatures three meters into the water. The spot he chose was right at the edge of the plateau so it would be easy to defend. Serik reached the opening and struck out against the closest blood ghast, making it shrink away behind some more of its ilk who had finished drinking. Horse made her way to the open spot and started drinking voraciously. Other creatures snapped and growled at us, but we brandished our weapons at them and squeezed into the space Bril had created.

Then it became surreal. There we were, kneeling and scooping hands full of water, drinking like we would never stop. Right beside us were blood stalkers, ghasts, and eekutchi totally disinterested in us as they also tried to get more than their fill. It seemed the rule was, once a being cleared a space they could drink as long as they held the space.

Creatures would come up behind us and nip at our heels so we'd spin around and wack them with our weapons, they would shrink away and then we'd go back to drinking.

The water had an acidic taste and as luck would have it, we were nearest the spot where it flowed out of the stones on the side of the plateau. I was glad for that as I watched beasts frolic along the edges, knee deep in the water. At least we were getting it before it got contaminated by all their body dirt and excretions. We took our time at the space we cleared. Each one of use sipping some, then turning to defend the spot while others took their turns. It was important not to drink too much too fast because we were so dehydrated. We also ate some amber using the water to wash it down. Eventually, we all felt full and energized, so we relinquished our space to the latest round of challengers, and set off once again.

Besides the aggravating presence of blood ghasts tracking us at a distance, we started to notice an annoying sound. It was like a high pitched whine, steady in tone, but occasionally wavering. There was something very troubling about it because I had the feeling we were being watched, or tracked, or some type of sinister act was being used on us. Bril, Togn and Serik also noticed it. Horse heard it too, and she started to droop her ears, seemingly to reduce the volume she was picking up.

Meanwhile:

Vortold sat in the shade of a tall spire in the LoM. His antennae were rigid, sticking straight up from above his bulbous eyes. Tiny hairs all along the antennae edges were shifting side to side and up to down. His proboscis hung limply across his belly, while his mandibles alternately clamped and unclamped. Nearby, his followers skulked in the shade of another spire, being careful to not move a muscle while their leader sent out his war whine in an effort to triangulate on his prey.

Suddenly, Vortold's antennae drooped. He jumped to his horse and charged off, his crew following a safe distance behind.

CHAPTER TWENTY-NINE

Respite

After another glow cycle, the red line on the shards had shrunk to show we were almost on top of our objective. We had entered a steep-walled canyon so that we were walking in shade most of the time. The air was cool and refreshing and there was a light, sweet smell to it. Every now and then we passed mysteriously stacked stones. It was as if the stones were held up by unseen forces and there were gaps between them. The stones on the bottoms of the stacks were large, while the other three or four stacked above, were gradually smaller.

As we rounded a corner, the canyon ended abruptly. A voice came on the wind.

"Rotate the top stone one half turn and the second stone down, one quarter turn."

To our right was a stack of four stones, much like all the others we had passed. Bril stepped over to the stones and followed the instructions. Directly in front of us, a doorway opened in the rock wall. It was as if the stone had suddenly melted, leaving an opening with a view into a busy hallway. Beings moved through the space, coming and going and disappearing into side rooms that lined the long promenade.

Then, a woman stepped from inside one of the side rooms and came toward us.

"Welcome," she said, eloquently, "I am Eana, the one you seek. Follow me."

Almost immediately, a man stepped from nowhere and took Horse's reins.

"Whoa," I said, What are you doing?"

Eana turned back, "She will get some hay and oats and plenty of water and be ready for you when we are done."

Eana's empathetic tone, and the welcoming smile of the man taking Horse's reins, dissolved my apprehension, so I stroked her nose and told her to go with the nice man. I'm sure I saw her wink.

We followed Eana a short distance down the hallway before turning to enter one of the rooms. Inside, the walls were covered with giant, shiny spaces that had hundreds of little, square, moving pictures on them. When I looked closer I could see pictures from Canyonlands, Firston, the Mists and LoM. It was as if they were views into places on all the levels of Octa. I could see beings passing by the vantage points, going about their daily activities. We were all transfixed, assailed by so much to see in such a small space.

"You are looking at the underworlds of Octa," Eana said. "The Superterrestrial Order oversees the planet in this way to help minimize catastrophes and maintain order. The Order has spaces like these on many planets that have asked for our assistance. But I want you to look closely at this screen over here," she pointed to a scene showing two tall spires in LoM.

In the next instant the picture changed to show beings lurking in the shade of the spires. I immediately sensed they were the Tachina that were chasing me! They were even more hideous than my brief glimpses of them had revealed. Gaunt, having a greenish cast to their bellies and abdomens with wiry hair standing out in splotches, and grotesque multifaceted eyes, not to mention being very large, I felt revulsion and fear all at the same time. They were already there, in the LoM, and that explained the strange whining sound we were hearing when out on the land. I remembered Brukin's words:

"I can tell you that the Tachina language is very distinct and you will know it by its very guttural series of clicks, squeaks and clucks. And, if you ever hear a high-pitched whine that vibrates rapidly you need to take cover because you've been triangulated by their innate tracking systems. Once locked on to you, they can paralyze you by alternating the wavelength they use. And believe me, you don't want to be their prisoner."

"There are many things you do not know," continued Eana, "and it is not my place to reveal those things to you. Just know that we will give you all the help we can, but that ultimately only you can send this vermin to its end," she looked directly at me. "What I can tell you also is that your challenges will not end with defeating the Tachina on Octa. Now," she handed two small, soft, round devices to each of us, "Place one of these in each ear whenever you are out on the land. As long as the Tachina are not too close to you, these devices will reduce the possibility they can triangulate on you."

She told me not to worry about any effect from the Tachina war whine on Horse since the Tachina were using horses themselves and would not target their audible frequencies. Then, she regarded us through narrowed eyes, and seemed lost in thought for a long time.

"It is not normal for beings who are in the spaces of the Order, to have such a strong odor and to be disheveled, injured and physically weak," she said disdainfully. Next, she pressed a round stone and a man appeared in the doorway. "This is Abercroix and he will help to alleviate all of that. Come back and see me after five glowcycles, and don't worry about the Tachina while in here. This is a structure that they can't penetrate, either physically or with their war whines."

I thought her comments made all of us feel a little embarrassed, but only a little. After what we had been through, and the lack of accommodations in the LoM, there was little we could do about our odor, clothing and dehydration. I only hoped the next couple of glow cycles would be the exact opposite of the previous two. And, I was in for a treat.

Abercroix was fastidious, attentive and knowledgeable. He first showed us to a narrow doorway, instructed us to remove our clothes and then handed to each of us a handful of a mosslike substance.

"Once you get wet inside," Abercroix motioned to the space beyond the doorway, "rub this all over and then rinse really well. I will have new clothes for you on the other side." With that, he grabbed up all our clothes and left hurriedly.

We entered a brightly lit room with water dripping copiously from the ceiling. The water was so soft and refreshing, I wanted to stand there for many glowcycles. Immediately the shalow root leaves I had bound to my calf washed off, revealing a U-shaped scar left by the bite from the blood stalker. When I rubbed the mosslike substance on my skin it produced a white, fluffy substance that immediately started changing the color of my skin. At first I was horrified, but then I realized what I was witnessing was the removal of a lot of dirt. The brown black water running off me flowed down one of many small holes in the floor.

Bril and Togn were equally amazed. Serik, however, having received an Order's hospitality before, was circumspect and efficient at using the moss and the flowing water. He was done and out the other side before the rest of us even got around to using the moss on our feet.

As we exited the room we walked through a long hallway with strong wind blowing through it. By the time we got to the end, where Abercroix stood, we were all dry. There, on a long table were piles of fresh clothes with our names posted above. Mine fit perfectly. I was already feeling like a new man. Once we were all dressed, Abercroix brought us to a private, dimly lit room. Inside were tables and chairs and on one table along the wall there were pots of food, baskets with what I knew to be bread, and all sorts of other delicacies to eat and drink.

"Please help yourselves to whatever you want," Abercroix said. "When you are full and tired, you can find some fresh moss beds in the next room." Then, he left.

For a long time we reveled in the food and drink. Taking it in slowly, and carefully enjoying the tastes, textures and aromas. We were speechless, just eating, drinking and smiling. Finally, one by one, we drifted off to the next room, where I fell into the deepest, most serene sleep I ever had on Octa.

When I awoke, the room was empty and I had an overpowering sense of peace. I wanted to lay there for a longer time just enjoying the tranquility but I sensed the others might be getting restless. Beside my new clothes a new pair of boots had replaced my old ones and they fit perfectly. I went out an open doorway at the end of an S-shaped hallway and found my friends resting pensively along the edges of a pool. The tension in the air was palpable.

"What's going on?" I asked.

There was a long silence and then Togn spoke up.

"We were just talking…we hadn't ever seen those things before, you know, the flies. They look really nasty and so we were just thinking out loud about how to defeat them."

"So, what did you come up with?"

"We didn't," replied Togn. "It just seems like an impossibility."

They all looked at me with slightly different expressions of anxiety and I knew then I had to let them know I needed to go on from there by myself.

"Okay, I understand, and look, this was always about me. Those creatures are after me. All of you are unimportant to them. I have the deepest appreciation for each of you, and I am so glad for your friendship and your support. We've been through some tough times together, times I'll always remember and treasure. But this is where we have to part ways. I can't have you endangering yourselves anymore."

"No, wait," interjected Bril. "That's not what we meant, and not an option. You wouldn't stand a chance by yourself. We were thinking maybe there is a way for us to sneak you to another level, or even somehow to another planet. It seems the Order must have all kinds of options we could explore."

"If that were the case then Eana would have said so by now. Instead she said that it was up to me, and in no uncertain terms," I said.

"What if we use the StarStone Scepter and find another level, or another way? We could just go on like this until they give up," said Togn.

"Everybody who knows anything about them says they never give up. Never. They are super beings, they can go on forever. Do you all really want to spend the rest of your lives wandering underworlds or other planets in a never ending effort to avoid being caught by them?" I paused letting my last words sink in because that was the kind of lives they'd have to live for as long as they lived.

"I'd rather be dead. But none of you have to be. You can go on and do whatever you like. You've definitely got enough skills to survive. And you Bril, just think about all the adventures you can have as a wizard! And Togn, you could be a leader for your people. You could go on to inspire them and create a resilient community, and maybe even help the Kech grow strong and populous again. So, running and avoiding is not the answer. I have to defeat them, or die. It's as simple as that."

So far, Serik had stayed out of the conversation. There had always been a sort of unspoken agreement the rest of us had with him. He stayed with us as long as it suited him. So far there was no deep friendship or long experience that was anything like what existed between me and Bril and Togn. But, now, being the older of us, he adopted a fatherly demeanor and spoke.

"There was a time in my youth when I was given the chance to do something that would have been a stepping stone to a greater personal destiny than I now have. But, it would have also meant I might die. So, I opted not to do it. Instead I wandered, and eventually made myself complacent with my current existence, which you are all very familiar with. Now, I know I cheated myself, and every moment I've waited and watched for another opportunity to become the man I should have been. To do the thing not for myself, but for someone else, or for something bigger than myself.

"I'd never seen a super being before, and yes, they are definitely scary. But if this is finally my second chance, then I'm taking it. And if I don't make it, at least I'll have the satisfaction of knowing I reached for my best self."

The silence was stunning. I was taken aback by the depth Serik expressed so simply. Here, the disheveled man who delighted in drinking blood stalker cooling fluid, and bullying his way to a drink at a pond crowded with man-eating creatures, was expressing sophisticated thoughts about life and purpose.

I immediately saw Togn's and Bril's demeanor change from pensiveness and anxiety, to confidence and resolve. They had each heard something in Serik's words that resonated with them personally. As for me, I was inspired. I felt a new sense of purpose and a new confidence arising from knowing what it was I had to do. Until then, having to defeat the Tachina was something I thought I had to do to survive. Now, defeating the Tachina was a part of the man I would become. And for the first time since arriving on the planet, I had an identity.

CHAPTER THIRTY

Revelations

As we waited for the time to see Eana again, Abercroix showed us a large courtyard complete with a nice sandy floor and lots of light, where we could practice our war craft. There were weapons of all designs and we spent a lot of time exploring their uses, and practicing our moves. Serik actually found a steel stone sword that he preferred over his large knife, although the large knife still retained a place in his belt.

Abercroix sent our backpacks to an embroidery shop where they were completely repaired and the enchantments were refreshed. That was extremely helpful since we had often neglected the packs simply because of a lack of energy or lack of interest. In the process he discovered the blood stalker diamond point scales and asked me about them. I told him who they were for, and he said he'd take care of it. Great, I thought, one less detail to handle.

After a couple of glow cycles we were led into a darkened room with the shiny screens and moving pictures. There, we received a complete lesson on the Tachina. Abercroix showed us their anatomies, their physical weaknesses, and their habits. He also taught us about their tactics, their war whines, and their history. We were amazed at the detail, and we all felt even more confident as we talked about different tactics we could use when battling them.

The time spent at the Order allowed us to get well rested and nourished. Even Togn was starting to look and act like himself again. Besides regular feedings and exercise, we enjoyed time lazing around, and in, a healing tonc pool.

So, it was with some sadness and trepidation that we greeted our last glow cycle at the Order. We met with Eana and she told us how reassured she felt about our upcoming challenges. She was impressed by how much we had trained, and with how much stronger we looked than we had when we arrived. Her final act was to ensure we had Alechay's contact shard. She told us that Alechay would have much more to tell me in particular, but she stopped short of telling me what it was about. She simply smiled assuredly, touching me lightly on the arm while telling me the information I'd receive would answer many questions.

At the exit, Horse rejoined us. She had new reins, was well brushed and very clean. Her mane was braided, she had shoes and she looked well nourished. It was a little emotional for me, seeing her well cared for after all I had been through with her. I felt like maybe I should just leave her there and if I survived, come back and get her. But when I whispered that idea into her ear she shook her head and let out a protesting type of neigh. So, it was unanimous. All of my friends were now a part of my destiny. But, I knew now that it was what they wanted, and that made my heart lighter.

We all popped the devices into our ears. The rock at the exit melted open and we stared out at the unforgiving landscape of the LoM. Then, we stepped through.

The shards showed us that Alechay was not very far away and so I took heart in knowing that perhaps I would be on the verge of getting more information that might help with my, our, future.

This part of the LoM was quite different than anything I had seen so far. There were far more rock masses and canyons. The air was also different. It had an evocative scent, reminding me of some other time, or some other place. I searched my shallow pool of memories for a time or place where I had smelled that scent before, but as often happened for me, there was no recollection.

We crossed a large open area. The glowstones were dim by now, and so the air was almost cold. The shadowed recesses of the canyons all around held hints of foreboding and we tried to avoid them. But, when following a single line pointing to a non-moving target, it was sometimes necessary to find our way around obstacles. We would follow our line into a canyon, only to discover the canyon ended in nothing other than a steep wall. Back out we would go and try the next, and the next, until finding one that allowed us to continue until we reached the next open area. We were traveling in a maze.

As a new glow cycle started we emerged from a canyon into a small open space. At the base of one of the rock walls, a liquid flowed into a shallow pool before trickling away across the flat rock floor. At first we thought the liquid was water, but after a few sips we realized it was tonc. It also had the unique quality that defined it as healing tonc - it was slightly more bitter. The idea that we'd come across a healing tonc pool right when we were all at peak health was another sign to me that the LoM really did hate beings of our kind. But, I didn't take offense, or get angry about it. I found it quite amusing. It was as if knowing my destiny, and that it might require me to die in that place, made everything else trivial. There was no grand plan to anger or insult Keln, or whoever I was. It was just the LoM, and that moment, and one of the wonders of the universe. And nobody, not even me, was privy to the answer to the question of why. It just was.

Watching Horse drink her fill of the tonc brought back memories of that time she fell off the cliff in the Canyonlands. I had forgiven the powers that be for not telling us there would be a flood. But, it was somewhat of a miracle that she survived. When I knelt at that drop off where she fell I couldn't see the bottom. Off and on, since finding her in the Mists, I had wondered how she survived. It was tempting to chalk it up to something simple like she had landed in deep water. But, the water at the bottom of a fall like that had to be like landing on stone. Instead, I was sure that Horse had come through the dark wall with her own special power, and it happened to be the same as mine. She could invoke slow motion. I hadn't seen any other evidence of it, but of all the possibilities, it seemed the most likely. It was so disappointing that she didn't speak my language because there was so much I wanted to know about her.

We continued our maze walk for the better part of half a full glow cycle. Then, we heard talking, and laughter and the noises of a crowd. Upon rounding the corner of a steep group of spires, we entered a busy street.

The beings were all reptilian-like, with very fine scales, often iridescent. They had human forms in general but their faces all had a sort of mouth and nose combination, much like the snout of many animal types.

"Onosauri," announced Serik as we huddled next to the rock wall, trying to stay inconspicuous.

"Do they hate us?" I asked.

"Oh, yes," said Serik, "Almost with a passion. But, they are not usually violent toward us unless they feel we might be staying around a while, trying to befriend them, or worse, attempting to mate with them, especially if the intended mate happens to be a daughter. Just hold your heads high, keep one hand on your weapon, and act like you are just passing through."

We all looked at the shards and saw that Alechay was somewhere straight ahead, down the long, wide, straight street. So, off we marched, confidently, in a sort of half circle with Horse taking up the rear. We avoided looking at anyone directly and pretended to be in a hurry, which we were.

As soon as individuals within groups saw we were human, they whispered quickly to their friends and then they would all turn their backs as we passed by. I couldn't understand their language, but the tones of their voices led me to believe they were expressing disgust and hatred. Occasionally I caught glimpses of some of the younger ones staring at us from discreet vantage points. I was sure they weren't born hating us, but that their adults taught them to. To the young, we were an interesting oddity that was off limits. And I could sense they didn't yet feel as strongly hateful toward us as the older ones.

"What of the other beings here?" I asked Serik quietly.

"Well, yes, like I said, the Lesania. They are light beings who appear as orbs. They float on the air and group together in high caves overlooking the landscape. They don't need food, and they rely on light for energy. Their main focus is exploring the universe and learning the finer points of creation. They are the largest group here."

"Why does everybody here have such animosity toward humans?" asked Bril.

"They mostly see us as inferior, as a sort of failed experiment that got out of the laboratory when it shouldn't have. Like a virus. And they see how humans behave across the universe by spoiling planets, always warring against each other, and generally being poor neighbors," Serik said.

Having no memory allowing me to consider the validity of the Lesania and Onosauri view, I could only relate it to myself, Bril, Serik, Togn and a few other humans I had encountered on Octa. From that perspective, I thought the beings of LoM were too critical of humans, and that assuming an entire group of beings all had the same traits, was ridiculous. So, I resolved to be an example of the opposite of what they expected. I would have little time for that, though.

We were at the end of the street and Bril announced we had reached our destination. We all stood there, turning side to side and around, scanning the stone walls and even the ground, for some signs of a doorway. Our confusion apparently caught the interest of a young Onosauri and since we were not near any of their adults, he approached rather delicately. None of our languages were understood but he seemed to know what we were looking for. He pointed to a very narrow slot in the canyon wall that we had been ignoring simply because it was so narrow. We went to the slot, examining it and the stone all around it. There was nothing peculiar about it. No distinguishing marks or even buttons like I had encountered so long ago in the device in Canyonlands.

Suddenly, a whirring noise followed by a flat sheet of stone moving beneath our feet, revealed what the young Onosauri knew. Another way to travel!

The stone rose up with us on top of it. Once it was about three meters off the ground it moved sideways and up.And up and up and up, until we were almost to the top of the canyon wall. Then, the device moved along the edge of the wall, stopping at an alcove, where it bumped against the wall with its top even with the floor of the alcove. Looking in, the alcove was deep, about three meters wide and three meters high.

We all stepped off the stone and walked in. After going about 40 meters, we entered a large room with expansive openings looking out over a labyrinth of spires and canyons. The temperature of the space was very comfortable, and there were three doorways leading into other rooms. We dropped our packs on the stone floor and just stood there admiring the views, the intricate carvings on the stone walls and the sudden appearance of a very tall, finely featured woman, exquisitely dressed in light, clinging fabric and walking toward us with enthusiastic steps.

"Finally!" She said breathlessly. "The adventurers of all adventurers have arrived."

"You must be Alechay," I said.

"And, you must be Keln," she responded, followed by, "Well, not exactly, but we'll get to that."

Already my curiosity was peaked. Someone who doubted the name given to me by Togn, might well know some things that I might want to know. She was very self assured which helped me feel comfortable that she might know what she was talking about. She stood back, assessing me, her hands raised with fingers from both hands joined and pointing upward in front of her face.

"Well, there is just so much and I'm trying to decide the best way," her voice trailed off. Then as if she needed to make a decision and just stop evaluating she said, "We need to talk alone because you have to come to grips with some information that is going to be…" she paused, choosing her words, "well, probably startling. And it would be best if you deal with that information on your own, with me, and then after you get used to it, you can share it with the others. Would that be okay with you?"

I looked at my friends, unconcerned, "Sure, I said, I've promised them I won't keep things from them so I guess no harm if I learn them first, on my own." Bril, Serik and Togn, nodded in agreement.

"And," she removed a small device from her sleeve and pressed a button, "The horse needs to go to a more fitting space, if you know what I mean."

A woman emerged from one of the doorways and I handed her Horse's reins, stroking the animal's face while reassuring her. Once again, I'm pretty sure, Horse winked at me, and then left with her escort.

"Now, the rest of you will find food, drink, entertainment, a place to get cleaned up and a place to rest, right through that doorway over there," she pointed to an overly large arch.

"I'm gonna love this," said Serik enthusiastically. "I just can't get over all the goodies these places have."

The three of them left through the arch and I could hear Serik exclaiming about his findings. Meanwhile, Alechay looped her arm through mine and guided me out through one of the large openings. We turned onto a stone pathway that wandered above the canyon floor, passing between spires and looping above the labyrinth below.

"So, I guess you've gathered a lot of information about how you got here and already know that it was through a dark wall. And, you should know that I know all about your journey here on Octa. You should also know that I know all about other journeys you've had in your lifetime. And, I know about the flies that are chasing you, and why that is happening."

My mind went into overdrive. Holy cow! Finally, someone with answers to so many questions that had been burning a hole in my skull for so long. I was speechless, and that was actually a good thing, because Alechay was about to do a serious information dump.

We stopped between two beautifully carved spires and sat on a comfortable stone bench. In front of us was a fountain, spilling tonc or water into a shallow pool. All around us there were what I knew as butterflies which took turns at the fountain and flitting about exploring the space. I was so apprehensive. I was so excited. Yet, thanks to Alechay's demeanor, I was feeling amazingly calm.

"So," Alechay paused, "where to start." She looked away from me, thinking. "Okay, first of all your real name is Cailean. Well, at least that was your name on the planet we call Earth. You were on Earth on assignment with our enforcer department, the Universal Enforcers. Remember anything so far?"

"No," I said, confused and starting to be dazed.

"To simplify, just know that you worked for the Universal Enforcers and you were a top agent. In fact, you were so good that you attracted the attention of some very bad beings. You were sent to earth in earth time 1869 to rescue a woman who was being chased by the son of Lothaire, a very evil super being. The woman had collected information about Lothaire's son that if known to any of the universal authorities, would have made him an assassination target. He was that evil. So evil that the normal rules of law would not apply, and he could be assassinated at will. Of course a whole legion of bounty hunters would have gone after him and so it would have been a death sentence had the woman's information been verified.

"Instead, you happened. There is more to this, I'm just giving you the simplified version right now. You located the woman, and in the process of transferring her to safety, you killed Lothaire's son. So, Lothaire, who never does anything himself, contracted with the Tachina, Vortold, to hit you. You and the woman were in the middle of your escape plan when Vortold and his hunters caught up to you. They can travel the universe very quickly and the two of you were hampered in your escape by the denser Earth atmosphere. Basically you couldn't reach a designated portal in time so you had to lay low and wait for another chance.

"Some of what happened next is not totally clear to us but we think it went like this. You found out that Vortold was on to you, so you sent the woman away to a safe spot to wait for you, while you held off the Tachina until we could get help to you. But, unknown to you, the woman had knowingly, or mistakenly, taken the one device you needed to make your plan work. So, with Vortold and crew approaching you decided to run for it.

"At this point the unexpected happened. A dark wall developed between Earth and Octa at about your location. The woman accidentally went through the wall, and later, so did you. The Tachina have been on your trail ever since because they want to collect on Lothaire's hit contract. Since Lothaire's son is dead, he's no longer concerned about the woman."

She stopped, letting me take it all in. I was numb. My mind was numb, my body was numb and I felt like I was falling. None of what she told me sparked any memories. Nothing she said opened the pandora's box of my brain. But, it made sense. Somewhere inside I had known all along that there was something dark and sinister about what I was going through. I knew it wasn't about me stealing something, or getting into a fight with someone. I always knew there were good explanations. I just never imagined they would be so complex and so extraordinary.

The story explained so much, like why I was so good with weapons and the ways I knew how to fight and the tactical plans I was always coming up with. More than anything it explained everything that had happened to me since I crashed through the dark wall.

"Now, according to our records you were assisted three times by seraphs of ours."

"Seraphs?" I questioned.

"Yes, they may have taken on different forms, like that of a common planetary item or possibly as an animated being like yourself?"

"The ball creatures! And the woman in Skelwora!"

Yes. Those beings are able to assume many forms and they delight in assisting others. They use supernatural powers of manifestation, healing, and clairvoyance. They exist across the universe and sometimes they are enlisted to do many different things by many different organizations. The Universal Enforcers had some seraphs tuned into your location by using the tracking chip embedded in one of your ribs. They can serve as guides to targets and also as safe havens with healing abilities. They are physiohalographic in origin but they also have powers to manipulate the physical world. Unfortunately we can't just assign one to you. We can only enlist help from those that are in your area, or in your expected path. And there are none anywhere in your anticipated journey from this point. So you will be without help from them from now on.

As I flushed the information through my mind, a glaring question arose.

"So, wait. What happened to the woman? Do you know?"

"Yes, we do," she answered. Then she reached toward my face and started tracing the tattoo over my eye with her finger.

My mind exploded with the possibilities! Was she saying the woman I met all that time ago in the founden was that woman!

She just looked at me as if seeing my thought processes, and nodded, saying, "Yes. The tattoos you share are reserved for the Universal Enforcers. She is one too. Although she is a much newer recruit than you, and she was actually recruited by you. After you rescued her, the two of you grew very close. Neither of you wanted to be separated seeing as how your assignments could take you away from her for years, so you asked if she could join the Enforcers. It was a tough decision for your handler because having two agents in a relationship was taboo. Still, they didn't want to lose you, so they gave in."

No wonder we had felt the attraction in the founden when we met. And no wonder I constantly had a desire to find her, to be with her. Somehow, just a little bit of the memory we had together, had survived the dark wall. But, what of her journey in the underworld?

"So, wait," I started, "So, she got here before me and made her way to Canyonlands, but then…"

"She actually had a simpler journey than you," Alechay filled me in. "She hooked up with a messenger to get to Firston, where she met one of your friends."

"Togn!" I exclaimed. "Togn told me he met a woman, actually helped her to learn about Canyonlands and Octa, and that she had the same tattoo as me."

Alechay nodded knowingly, "Right, and you probably don't remember, but on Earth you had a small satchel that you carried on your belt. Inside that satchel you had a tone ball, a sort of sound producing device, and your universal compass. That compass always points to the nearest place you can get help. It's kind of like a wearable safe house. When she left Earth, she had that satchel, so she used the compass to find her way through the underworlds," Alechay finished, retrieving a small leather satchel from a waist pocket and handing it to me, saying, "And here it is."

"So," I said, a realization building quickly, "She made it here?"

Alechay smiled one of her best knowing smiles and said simply, "She's right behind you."

CHAPTER THIRTY-ONE

Memory Hint - Again!

I jumped up and spun around and there she was! My heart flooded with emotion for it had been such a long arduous journey and so many glow cycles searching for answers to so many questions, that now, standing there looking into her eyes, everything seemed to be as it should be. The trials and tribulations were the stepping stones to get to this point and to find her again.

She was reticent so I reached out and she came to me and we hugged. It was a long slow hug and when we looked around, Alechay was gone.

She put her arms around my neck and whispered, "Now I know why I have missed you so much."

"You can talk?"

"Oh, yes, that. Well, I've had a couple of accidents on Octa. The first was coming through that dark wall thingy. Besides my memories, I guess I lost my voice. Something to do with an allergy to something on this planet? But, it cleared up mostly when I got to Firston, so I guess the upper levels aren't for me," she laughed.

"And the other accident?"

"Right," she said, "Moving between underworlds is...well you know...so anyway I jammed up my leg." Then she stood back and spread out her arms standing on one leg, "But, tada, and now, no walking stick. Thanks to a couple of healing tonc pools," grinning ear to ear.

"Oh, yes, those wonderful tonc pools!"

We embraced again, and this time when we pulled back, our eyes met intensely, and next, so did our lips. It was a long, slow kiss. But as we were coming out of it we both realized we didn't know each other's name.

She stepped back again, extended her hand and said, "I'm Insta. Pleased to meet you…?"

"Oh, yes, I am now…Cailean!" Our handshake turned back into an embrace and we stood there a long time, savoring how we felt against each other, warm, secure, fitting just right.

Then we wandered along the stone path, out, far from Alechay's spaces and all along a seemingly endless plateau punctuated by spires of stone.

"So, why did you leave me at the founden?" I asked.

"All I knew was that I felt a deep attraction to you but without the history to help me understand, I just chalked it up as just me feeling so alone and vulnerable. I was also worried about those flies chasing us, being in a new land, and not knowing anyone, and I was afraid to trust. Not necessarily you, but trust myself."

"Well, I'm sure glad you had the compass because if you would have had to get here the way I did…"

"What! You don't think I could have?" She chided me.

"Oh, yes, right, after all, you are a Universal Enforcer," we laughed.

We talked about our journeys through the underworlds and laughed even more about the characters we met and the differences between our experiences. We tried talking about things before Octa, but gave up because neither of us could recall anything from those times.

"It would be nice to be able to remember," she said. "If for no other reason than to glimpse how deep our relationship was before all this. And, to have some other memories that don't include wraiths and eekutchi!" she chuckled with me joining her.

"I guess it's just a fresh start, and might be good, because now we don't have any baggage we might have been carrying. Everything is fresh and new, without any of the negatives that might have existed before."

"Right, things like you forgetting my birthday," more chiding.

"Uh huh, or you reminding me that I forgot your birthday!"

We embraced again, and in a nearby sheltered cove at the edge of a pool of water, we explored our deepest intimacies on a thick bed of damp moss.

Meanwhile:

Under dark red and silver-colored glowstones Vortold surveyed the landscape. Before him lay a menacing arrangement of upright boulders. Their edges jagged and sharp, their heights, lengths and widths contorted in hideous shapes. The light in that part of the LoM was always the darkest and he knew it as a harbinger, for his speculate had foretold this as the likeliest place for him to finally meet his prey. This semicircular stand of stones guarded the funnel-shaped entrance to the Novadisk, a portal to the grand universal highway. Behind him sat the Seve Slot, a narrow canyon that once passed through, offered no way to go back. Gale force winds raced up through a narrow crack in the ground right at the base of the Seve Slot, further ensuring nothing could reenter.

Dust whipped up behind him as Vortold popped the second eyeball from Amorro's head and downed it with a slurping gulp. Then he tossed the head so it landed at the base of the very center boulder. He wanted his prey to feel intimidated, and hopefully angry, so they'd make mistakes.

"They'll be coming here," Vortold said to the hovering blood wraith. "It's their last chance to prolong the fate they know I'm bringing to them. We'll be in the circle. Once they reach here, there's no going back so they'll have no choice but to try to go through us. And that won't turn out well for them," he laughed. "When it's over, if you perform well, I'll let you have all the blood. I just want the eyeballs."

Meanwhile:

Serik, Bril and Togn took turns in a sand floor arena brandishing their weapons against a mechanical hoodvark that was proving to be superior at anticipating and blocking their moves. Nearby, a stone table stood piled with foods none of them had been familiar with before entering the room. There were round, juicy fruit, crispy breads and something Serik couldn't get enough of - a puffy pastry with white cream inside. Besides plentiful tonc, there was a beverage having a fizzy character that tickled Togn's large nose whenever he put a stone cupful to his mouth.

"I could stay here the rest of my life," enthused Serik.

Even Togn, who had been not quite himself lately, was unusually jolly and optimistic. He swung his axe again at the hoodvark and this time managed a glancing blow. His smile split his now fatter face and he challenged Bril to do as well. Instead of using his sword, Bril stamped his staff on the stone floor, sending an arc wave at the foe. But, it missed. Togn broke out laughing.

"I guess there are some things a Kech can do that a wizard cannot!" he quipped.

Bril just smiled, a wide, knowing smile of confidence and flipped a salute at his friend. The two of them had developed a strong, easy bond like the bonds between long time friends who have weathered many challenges together. They knew each others' abilities and each trusted the other to know when those abilities were stretched to their fullest. They were in their prime with the seasoned glow of accomplished adventurers.

Alechay, me and Insta walked into the arena just as Serik was beginning to try throwing Togn's axe at the hoodvark.

"You!" Togn exclaimed moving toward Insta.

"Hi again, Togn," Insta said warmly.

"But, you're talking."

"Yes, it seems I was a little bit allergic to Octa. But it's better now."

Bril and Serik moved in while the introductions happened and I couldn't help but think how lucky I was to have ended up in their company. Over the course of a leisurely interlude, and copious amounts of enticing foods, Alechay and I, with some help from Insta, filled everybody in on the backstory.There were murmurs of surprise at many places in the story because Serik, Bril and Togn had little understanding about much beyond Octa's underworld. Even the information about the Tachina I had previously shared with them had not opened their minds fully to the concepts of a universe laden with many life forms, let alone groups like the Universal Enforcers and the super beings they battled.

At the end of the glowcycle we rested. I had immense dreams that were fluid and filled with turmoil. There were no clear events and the beings were scattered and misshapen, but there was a clear feeling to it all - danger. I awoke to Insta caressing my face, comforting me from my dark torment. But then, I fell back to sleep in her arms and rested comfortably.

Early in the next glow cycle Alechay joined us in the arena where she confided in us about what lay ahead. She told us that there was only one place where I could meet the Tachina if I wanted to deal with them once and for all. She told of the Seve Slot, a narrow canyon that ended in a drop off that went deep into the remaining underworlds of Octa. After the Seve Slot was the Novadisk and beyond that the entrance to the portal leading to the universal highway. That highway, she explained was a series of interconnected portals that opened to millions of other worlds.

Then, she produced a device she called a portalink which was the same size and shape as my steelstone sword handle. At the top was a round, clear disk. She explained the disk functioned as a sensor that was able to ascertain the life force of the being holding it. Once the device knew the being's life force it automatically determined which portals opened to worlds that supported the holder's life force. Those portals then appeared as options which the holder could scroll through. The names were codified to the holder's language and experience so everything was relevant.

"Now," Alechay began seriously, "If you go through the Seve, you cannot return. Not only is the wall you must climb to get out covered in very sharp crystals that would instantly shred your hands and feet, but there is also a dred wind of amazing force flowing up from below and curling toward the Novadisk. Your only option once you go through the Seve is to continue through the Novadisk and take the Universal Highway. Basically, you'll leave Octa for whatever destination you select on the portalink, and, anybody with you who has the same life force type will go too."

There was a moment of stunned silence. I could see Togn and Bril seriously weighing the words. Serik though, seemed nonchalant, as if he had always expected to be cast off into the universe through a portal guarded by a dangerous array of death traps. But, I knew all three now had to reconsider their earlier insistence on accompanying me.

For Insta, I already knew the answer. We had previously faced the Tachina, and we had also previously been faced with being separated while I pursued my role in the Enforcers. She had then decided to join the Enforcers and accept everything that went with it. We were a team, and although we had no memory of how we worked together, I was confident we'd figure it out. And, she had already told me as much since our reunion. Our two fates were sealed. Now it was a matter of who else would join us.

The first to speak was Serik.

"As I've said before. I'm in this to the end, whatever that might be. I've only been with you three," gesturing to me, Bril and Togn, "for a short time. But in that time I've found an uncommon camaraderie that I know was meant to be. Whatever I've done before this was just training for this one event. You can count me in to the end."

Togn started at the same moment as Bril, but then stopped motioning for Bril to go ahead.

"When you agreed to take me to find my destiny," motioning to me, "I wasn't sure you were the right choice. Being new to Octa and not knowing anything, I was almost sure I'd probably never make it to the Mists. But then, you saved me, and again, and again," nervous laugh. "But you also let me learn, and you let me lead, and you listened to me. And," laughing, "you sat there on that boring island for an eternity of glow cycles while I trained to become a wizard! So, I've never been more sure that I am where I'm supposed to be. Besides, who's going to keep Togn away from elemental mushrooms!"

Togn, Bril and Me laughed heartily.

"Wait, elemental mushrooms," shouted Insta. "What's that story?"

"We'll fill you in someday when we're all sitting around in a cave," said Bril.

As the laughing subsided a palpable silence fell with people looking down at their feet or into a corner of the arena. Togn stood up.

"Most of my short life I've lived alone. You probably don't know this but the family that you stayed with in Firston, Insta, wasn't really my family. They were dear friends who offered me a place whenever I needed it. You see, after my family died I was always a wanderer, always wandering between Firston and Canyonlands trying to figure out who I was and what I should be spending my time doing. When I saw you there on the edge of the canyon," motioning to me, "crying over your lost horse, I saw something I might be able to help with. I saw an opportunity to help someone when they needed help. It turned out I liked you, and Bril, and so you became like my new family. All the adventures just made me feel closer to you along the way so that now, you're the kind of family that means the most to me. Not one based on blood and birth, but based on friendship, concern, and caring. I'm not worried about the Seve Slot or the highway thing because I know as long as I'm with you, everything is as it should be. And, that's saying a lot coming from someone who isn't always the bravest of beings," he chuckled, "So, I'm in."

With that, all our fates were entwined. Little did we know what that would lead to.

CHAPTER THIRTY-TWO

The Making of a Team

We started a new glow cycle preparing for what we all knew would be a horrendous battle in a place with little protection. Since we were assuming we'd prevail in that battle, we also needed to be prepared to continue on through the Novadisk to the Universal Highway and the planets beyond, for there was no coming back. Fortunately, we were getting a lot of help. Two armorers prepared special reinforced jackets for us, the long kind that went down to our ankles. They were interlaced with lightweight softstone which was heat sealed on the insides so that when the jackets were closed, our critical organs were better protected from projectiles and melee weapons. The attached hoods functioned the same and offered excellent protection for everything but our faces. The armorers also sharpened and made repairs to our weapons and provided us with belts to hold multiple canisters of shot and shade stone along with clusters of faze darts.

Meanwhile an enchantress mended our packs with special threads that could survive universal travel and boosted all of the pack enchantments so they would be more effective in the conditions we'd encounter. Insta received her own pack with all the enchantments we had and everybody's pack got upgraded to include the singular enchantments that had been on my main pack since the beginning. We would no longer need to be holding on to a particular pack, or be near it for the enchantments to work.

As all of that was going on, we spent our time in the arena practicing with our weapons, trying out others' weapons and considering tactics that might be effective against our foes. I received special training in using the tone ball since I had no memory of using it. We all received training to help us get a deeper understanding of the skills and abilities of both the Tachina and blood wraiths, which we were sure would be helping the flies.

So, on what we assumed would be our final meeting with Alechay during the next glow cycle, we were all feeling very confident. Togn was back to his old self with more muscle than fat. Bril was extra confident and increasingly skilled in wizardry. Serik was displaying his usual cool, calm, take-at-as-it-comes attitude, and Insta was intently focused on learning all she could about the enemy, the weapons, and all of us. She was at a disadvantage since she didn't have any history with us and how we approached battle. Bril, me and Togn, and to a lesser degree Serik, knew what we could expect from the others and how each other approached the process of staying alive in a fight. Insta however, would be going in blind to those nuances, except for whatever she could glean by observing us as we practiced our war craft. So, she watched intently and I would catch her smiling to herself when she spotted something that helped her understand each of our ways and methods. She was very astute and now I understood, perhaps for the second time, why she had been accepted into the Enforcers.

As we gathered around, Alechay became serious.

"I've watched all of you closely and I can honestly say that in all my time working with the enforcers I've never seen a more committed and skilled group. You make me feel proud. Two of you need to reaffirm your oaths of commitment and three of you need to take yours for the first time. You can't go further unless you do. So, in a way, this is your way out if any of you have any doubts about continuing to face the Tachina. If you take the oaths, you will share in the next assignment with Cailean and Insta."

"Wait," said Bril quizzically. "Cailean?"

"Yes, it seems that's my real name, from before Togn named me Keln. But you can continue to call me Keln if you like."

"It IS easier to pronounce!" laughed Togn.

With that, and with nobody bowing out, Alechay administered the oath to all of us, followed by a group hug and lots of cheering. We were officially a team, but we already knew that. After all we'd been through there would not have been any other outcome. And I basked for just a moment in my good fortune to be a part of it. When Alechay started telling us about the next assignment, I already knew what it was about.

Our task, should we survive the upcoming battle, was to capture, or kill, Loathaire and dismantle the organization he was building. It meant many more battles against the Tachina and no doubt other super beings he was enlisting in his cause to control as many planets as he could. It was all a giant game to him and one that entailed the enslavement and genocide of multiple civilizations. It would be a planet hopping expedition involving unimaginable dangers. Yet, here, my friends and team, showed no signs of concern. They were resolute and accepting of whatever they might face in accomplishing the goal.

Up until this point I had been assuming that Horse was also part of the package. Alechay explained there was no prohibition against me using a horse in my duties and while there was no way to have her take an oath, there was no reason she couldn't be part of the team. As an oxygen-breathing animal, she fit the same life force characteristics as the rest of us and so would travel just as well with the portalink. She did warn me however that we might encounter terrain when first landing on some planets, that could limit her movement because of being a quadra-ped. There could also be an issue with food, since she required a different diet than we did. When I thought more deeply about her going with us, planet hopping, I started to wonder if including her would be the right decision. I wished so much that I could ask her. That she could choose. And, although she had fared well so far, there would be untold dangers that might affect her more seriously than us. I also weighed her usefulness. In that regard she was stellar. Not only had she saved my life a few times, but others' as well. And if not for her, we would have been hard pressed to carry Togn on the journey in the weakened state he had been in after his stint with the elemental mushroom. After a while, I knew the decision I should make, but I wanted to put it to the others.

So, I gathered them together and asked.

"You know, there is one team member missing right now. And my question to you is, should we take Horse?"

"What!" Togn, shouted. "We hadn't better leave her behind!"

"Oh, yes," said Bril. "She has to come."

Serik just grinned, giving a thumbs up, and Insta hugged me with a hearty YES hug. The final piece had fallen into place.

As the glowstones dimmed, we enjoyed food and drink and the camaraderie that only those whose destinies are locked together ever experience. As I looked around the room, watching their expressions of humor, surprise and thoughtfulness, I had to hold back the tears when thinking of any one of them not making it. It was far less painful to imagine myself dead on that battleground.

CHAPTER THIRTY-THREE

Showdown at the Novadisk

We met the new glowcycle with uneasy determination. Alechay accompanied us to the exit, reminding us that the Tachina were not far away and to be sure to use our ear devices. A solid stone wall melted before us and once again we faced the relentless heat and bright light of the LoM. It was somewhat of a shock after the cool, dim interior we had been staying in.

Before us was an open expanse with spires and canyons in the distance. Alechay had given us a contact shard for the Novadisk. It seemed that even places could be added to those helpful little pieces of smart stones.

So, we set off, each of us in our own little world of mentally practicing war craft moves, imagining the possible attacks we'd face and using every mental and heartfelt strategy we could to bolster our confidence and envision victory.

The world had changed drastically for me since finding out my history and learning all the answers to so many questions that had haunted me for what seemed like a lifetime. The idea that I even had yet more history that I might never know made me continue to feel unsure about who I was.

Who was I before joining the enforcers? How and why did I join? Did I have others in my past with whom I might still have meaningful connections? Were there even answers to all the new questions I found arising? I had gone from being a total blank, to being a partial blank, and that seemed even more unsettling.

The glow cycle wore on until we finally reached the spires and canyons we had been aiming for. The Novadisk shard pointed in no uncertain terms to the canyon on our left and so we entered. The walls were very steep and made of pock-marked sandstone that appeared ready to crumble with the slightest vibration. We spotted eekutchi moving within the holes and caves but fortunately none seemed interested in us. The last thing we needed was an energy depleting event before we even reached the Novadisk. So, we stayed at the ready and moved as stealthily as we could.

The canyon continued to grow narrower until we were finally in single file but still had our shoulders touching the walls every few steps so that we were constantly turning side to side to make our way through. Although we were glad for the extra protection the battle dusters would offer us, right then, in the confined space and heat, they were terribly uncomfortable. But, having been tested by discomfort many times, we were battle hardened to it, which allowed us to consider the current discomfort as just a necessary annoyance.

Finally a light appeared ahead and above, and before long we were standing on a narrow ledge, side by side with Horse behind, looking at the Novadisk. The rough, misshapen stones in a convoluted semicircle stood as sentries guarding the door to the universe. Between them and us was a boulder-strewn landscape that we assumed would become our battle hell. Closest to us was a deep chasm falling to depths unknown. Rising up from it was a horrendous wind filled with the stench of the planet's guts. The wind rose above our heads and then arched inward quickly toward the Novadisk, and then back toward the chasm, leaving a shallow gash in the ground where it struck.

Then we heard it!

A high-pitched, vibrating whine told us our foe was nearby. We scrambled to check our ear device fit while peering back behind us and overhead to see if we could spot the Tachina. We watched and waited some more. When we felt we had waited long enough to see them if they were behind or above, we realized they were ahead of us. To my horror I surmised they had the preferred ground, safely guarded by the Novadisk boulders, while we, were exposed until we reached cover behind the smaller boulders between us and the Novadisk.

As the Tachinas' first bolts started landing we leapt, hand in hand over the edge hoping our forward momentum would carry us over the narrow chasm and beyond the wind. Our hope paid off in one instance. We all cleared the chasm easily. But then the wind hit us, sending us flying upward only to be crashed down a moment later and assailed by the backdraft which tried to pull us into the chasm. I anchored my sword into the ground and held on, getting my resolve. I saw the others using whatever they had to anchor themselves as well. With a good feeling for the speed and strength of the wind, I waited until I felt the telltale sign of a surge coming. Then, I dug in my toes and as soon as I sensed the surge ending, I pushed my body forward with all my might and broke free.

As the others followed my lead I whistled for Horse to jump. For a second I thought I saw fear in her eyes and my heart sank at the thought she'd not jump. But then, undoubtedly realizing she had no other choice, she took two strides and stretched out her legs. The next instant she was grounded and actually landed clear of the descending wind. There was one boulder tall enough to get her behind so I grabbed her reins and bolted for it. More crossbow bolts followed us, but we made it without getting hit.

By now, everybody had cleared the wind and were safely stashed behind rocks. Bril immediately started throwing random force field shocks in the Tachina's direction which totally disturbed the crossbow bolts in mid air, causing them to fly up and outward. That gave the rest of some some moments to recompose ourselves and start thinking tactically again.

We knew we'd be at a stalemate with each party well protected. That meant it would become a siege with each side waiting for the other to make a mistake or eventually die. Of course the Tachina, having direct access to the Universal Highway, might be able to not only come and go but also to bolster their defenses and supplies. They could conceivably last forever.

As I looked toward the center stone I saw something I didn't want to see. Although there were no eyes, the Tachina had left enough of Amorro's face in tact for me to know it was her. When I looked over at Togn I could see he had seen also. I'd never seen Togn mad but in that instant I knew I was witnessing his body no longer under his mind's control. He flailed away with his axe against the rock, crying and screaming. Insta and Bril constrained him so he wouldn't run toward the danger. In the melee one of his ear devices fell out and the Tachina war whine got to him. He dropped down and sat shaking, looking blankly at nothing.

It was then that the wraiths descended, three of them, all focused on Insta and Bril. I knew there was room for cover for another person where Insta and Bril were so I motioned to suggest Serik move to them. Right after another rain of bolts, he did. By then Bril and Insta were in mortal combat with the wraiths. Their enchantments and Bril's ward stone were holding off the wraiths' attempts at spirit control, but their swords even with the mist bender enchantment were not doing much damage. Serik joined the melee with his fork and sword and immediately injured one of the wraiths. Then I remembered.

I dropped my pack and pulled out the shot stone and loaded it with shade stones. Then, I took aim and fired at the wraith farthest away from my comrades. Within seconds it shrank back from the battle and started to cower. Serik struck another blow, Insta sliced at the second wraith and Bril finally had enough distance and time to send a force field at one of the injured wraiths, which shattered and disbursed as black dust in the wind.

Meanwhile, Serik frantically searched for Togn's ear device and found it jammed between Togn and the rock. As he fitted the device to Togn's ear I got off another round, striking the most aggressive wraith. But it only deterred it a little. It was still fighting at most of its strength. Then Bril conjured an enderether, a wispy spirit being that feeds on wraiths' accumulated stash of fear and uncertainty. Immediately the stronger wraith shrank back from battle just as Insta dealt a decisive blow to another. But in the next instant, Serik saw she was exposed and he dove, knocking her off her feet as multiple bolts pierced the air where she had just been standing. But, his save was disastrous.

A bolt pierced his neck sending arterial blood gushing. Insta also got hit in the shoulder. Bril, the lone defender, sent more shock waves at the remaining two wraiths. I got off another round of shot stone and this time the strike was decisive. The victim shrank away and then puffed out.

I reasoned it might be time for me to use the tone ball because we couldn't keep fighting wraiths. I also knew my friends needed a lot of help where they were, so I wedged Horse's reins in a crack in the rock, rubbed her nose and told her to stay, and then after a bolt volley, I raced to the others.

Serik was in a bad way and I could tell he didn't have long. My heart grew so heavy I wanted to burst. He was so excited about his role as an enforcer and he was just getting started at what he had called "getting on with the best part of my life." And to have it cut so short. I was angry at the randomness of the universe. I was angry about chaos and angry about beings like the Tachina. But mostly, I was angry at myself for letting him and the others come. At that moment I felt like a total failure.

"It was an honor," Serik gasped breathless to Insta and me. Then he let go of my hand and the life drained from his eyes.

As Serik died, Togn had rejoined the battle against the wraiths with Bril, and the two of them finished out the lone holdout. There was an eerie silence that came over the field. All I could discern was a faint whine from the Tachina.

"Farewell my friend," I said to Serik. As I was regaining my composure and my battle mind, the unthinkable happened.

The Tachina charged!

Racing like unhinged entities their mounts gaunt, sweating faces dripping foam and blood. There were still five. Four of them rode with arms alternatively cradling and firing crossbows while Vortold swung a long sword with six blood grooves staggered along its three foot length. The flies charging was indeed a sight to see, and I knew then why so many simply gave up. Fighting against any other enemy that moment might have been filled with concentration and focus. But seeing what they had done to Amorro had transferred that into focused rage. But rage can have its beneficial and not so beneficial effects. In my rage I had dropped my tone ball and was having a hard time finding it. The tone ball was our last chance at defense and ultimately victory for it alone could not only cancel out the Tachina War Whine, but it could also reduce their will.

The five were bearing down on us. Togn got off three rounds of shot stone while Insta fired all the faze darts she had. Bril let lose a mighty shock wave sending two Tachina reeling. Meanwhile I was desperately searching the ground, digging along the base of the rock, trying to find the tone ball. Suddenly, a glint, a metal object, and I had it in my hand.

I had practiced the tone ball settings many times and could do them from memory without looking at the device. I moved the dials causing a tone that canceled out the Tachina War Whine. Now, they were on us. Vortold's face appeared over me, a hideous contortion of man and insect. His horse dripped foam on my head and I saw the blade flying through the air. I rolled. Then I was behind him so I summoned all the remaining strength I had, found my feet and brought my sword across his back.

Meanwhile Bril, Togn and Insta stood back-to-back battling the two other Tachina that were still on the attack. Vortold was flung forward over the head of his mount as it stopped short. He rolled across the ground just as I dialed in another code on the tone ball. That one disoriented Tachina, and it had an immediate effect on the three Bril, Togn and Insta were battling. Suddenly they shrank away, looked confused and then started to cower.

I had Vortold in my sights with a shot stone and let it go. It tore through his shoulder sending a spray of blood across the stone. I could see the tone was also working on him, but not nearly as much as it was on the others. Bril and Insta were getting the upper hand on one, while Togn was finishing off the other.

I knew it was then or never. I knew Vortold was in a weakened state and I had to move in for the kill. I took three steps and our swords met. The strength still behind his blow was incredible and I feared my steelstone sword would shatter. But it held, and I got in another blow, feigning before striking one across his shoulder. He was swinging wildly around, rapidly hatcheting the air, the massive blade hell bent on flesh and blood. I couldn't keep up with the speed of his attack.

But suddenly I saw my opening and took it. His blade danced across my battle duster. But my blade found its home deep in his chest, and I knew he was done. He fell hard, his proboscis gyrating from side to side and his huge bulbous eyes losing their light one lens at a time. Fearing his super being powers, and the potential for regeneration, I stepped in and with one swipe removed his ugly head from his body.

Bril, Togn and Insta dropped to the ground simultaneously, letting out sighs and cheers! All the other Tachina were already headless.

I inspected my wound to find it was just flesh deep. The relief was tremendous. I had been running from him for so long, I had lost track of what it felt like to not be running. And it felt good. I could see the relief in my friends' faces. It just felt so good to be free of that constant worry, that we just sat there, grinning, laughing and catching our breath for a long time.

We had triumphed, although at a great cost. I looked over at Serik and knew there had to be a more fitting end for such a gallant old guy. So, once we had fully regained our collective breaths, we stood around him and remembered the portion of his life we had known. Then, we moved his body to the edge of the down blasting air at the chasm and rolled him into it. The air swept him into the void. There were no dry eyes in our little band of adventurers.

Later, we went arm in arm into the Novadisk, and on to our next adventure.

www.ingramcontent.com/pod-product-compliance
Lightning Source LLC
Chambersburg PA
CBHW022010170626
46808CB00001B/349